A MESSAGE FROM CHICKEN HOUSE

I *love* old clothes, especially family items. They are a bit magic, aren't they? Full of memories and feelings! But in James Nicol's new world, clothes can *actually* be magic. Meet the Danellis – they're spell tailors, which means they sew spells into clothes for a living. But everything's about to change. If they're to survive, they'll have to figure out how to protect their gorgeous cosy business from exploitative new clothing factories – full of bad magic and evil intent! Then, our young hero Hen discovers a way to stitch memories into clothes – a rare skill that might just turn everything around . . . or ruin everything for good! Funny, warm and thrilling, this is a book that you'll wear out from rereading.

BARRY CUNNINGHAM
Publisher
Chicken House

JAMES NICOL

THE SPELL TAILORS

Chicken House

2 PALMER STREET, FROME,
SOMERSET BA11 1DS

Text © James Nicol 2022
Illustration © Jenny Zemanek 2022

First published in Great Britain in 2022
Chicken House
2 Palmer Street
Frome, Somerset BA11 1DS
United Kingdom
www.chickenhousebooks.com

Chicken House/Scholastic Ireland, 89E Lagan Road, Dublin Industrial Estate,
Glasnevin, Dublin D11 HP5F, Republic of Ireland

James Nicol has asserted his right under the Copyright, Designs and
Patents Act 1988 to be identified as the author of this work.

Cover and interior design by Steve Wells
Cover and interior illustrations by Jenny Zemanek
Typeset by Dorchester Typesetting Group Ltd
Printed and bound in Great Britain by CPI Group (UK) Ltd, Croydon, CR0 4YY

FSC
www.fsc.org
MIX
Paper from
responsible sources
FSC® C171272

1 3 5 7 9 10 8 6 4 2

British Library Cataloguing in Publication data available.

PB ISBN 978-1-913322-86-1
eISBN 978-1-913696-85-6

For Kate Shaw – who helped pin out the pattern
for this story – with my love and thanks.

Also by James Nicol

The Apprentice Witch
A Witch Alone
A Witch Come True

L. E. DANELLI & CO.

GENTLEMEN'S & LADIES' SPELL TAILORS & OUTFITTERS

-EST. 1776-

4 BEACHAM TERRACE, SPARROW DOWN,
EAST MILLINGHAM, INGLE

BY APPOINTMENT TO
Her Majesty the Queen of the Giants,
His Excellency the Emperor of Ustavar,
The Duke & Duchess of Fangle

COSTUMES FROM 4 GUINEAS

We wish to call to your attention the following advantages
of having your garments made to measure by an experienced
firm of spell tailors. You are guaranteed a perfect, comfortable
fit with the most uncommon fabrics and spells that have been
in the family for hundreds of years, and that distinguished
appearance that can only be obtained from having clothes built
and spelled to individual requirements.

THE VERY FINEST SPELLED CLOTHES, SHOES, HATS & GLOVES

CHAPTER ONE

SPELL-STITCHING

'Stitching a spell is tricky,' Nana said, laying out the jacket on the large pine workbench. The jacket was dark green velvet, like a midnight forest, with a high collar, wide sleeves, and three gleaming jet buttons to hold it closed just above the waist. 'But it's also the easiest thing in the world.'

Hen smoothed out the material. Velvet always made the hairs on the back of his neck stand on end ... or maybe it was nerves. 'Are you sure?'

Nana seemed entirely unbothered. 'Of course. You know what you're doing now, love. This'll be your fourth garment, yes?'

He nodded and swallowed. 'But this is just for practice, like before, right?' Hen asked, peering closer.

'It's an order for Mrs Place. A gift for her daughter, I believe.'

Hen looked up at Nana and then back at the jacket. 'But . . . a real order for an actual customer . . .'

'And?'

'Well, what if I . . .'

He paused.

'What if you muck it up?' Nana asked.

Hen nodded. He knew that if a spell stitch went wrong, unpicking it and starting over rarely helped. Hen had seen garments vanish, totally unravel themselves, and even burst into flames once – there was still a small scorch mark on the wall just behind him.

'My boy, if you get it wrong, you get it wrong.' Nana shrugged. 'You'll learn from your mistakes, hopefully. Besides, you'll need to practise more if you want to enter a garment for the Guild Fair.' Nana's eyes twinkled.

'How did you know about that?'

She chuckled. 'I saw the flyer pinned up in your bedroom.'

'Can I then, please?'

'Well, your mum and dad will have to agree. You can write to them later. But now, tell me, what do we need to do first?' Nana asked.

Hen took a deep breath, set aside the practice square he had been working on and glanced across the basement workroom. The floor was covered in large creamy flagstones, the wood-panelled walls painted a soft green. Light flooded in from the high windows that looked across the back garden. The deep window ledges were empty but for one that held a small clay figurine of Hestia, the goddess or patron saint of tailors and dressmakers. She held a skein of yarn in one clay hand and in the other a needle that pointed up at the sky. Many believed Hestia had been the one to stitch the universes into creation. She had sewn every star and leaf, every seashell and pebble, spun every soul. She watched over the workroom always.

The little clay statue had been in the Danelli family since they first travelled from the Scillian Islands, far to the east to Ingle, and established the shop here in Sparrow Down.

'It's always lucky to make an offering to Hestia before starting a new spell stitch,' Hen said, glancing at Nana, who nodded and then bowed her head, her thin lips fluttering in silent prayer. Hen copied, praying for good luck, for his threads not to break and his stitches to be strong and true.

'And next?' Nana asked. 'Because praying will only get you so far. Hestia won't do the work for you, love.' She *always* said that.

'Um, make sure you have everything you need?' Hen offered.

'Yes . . . but there is one more thing to do before you gather up your bits and pieces, remember?' Nana smiled, her eyes twinkling with laughter. She inclined her head towards the corner of the workroom. A thick wooden beam stuck out of the walls and from it hung the family's shleep, Marjorie. Of course! How had he forgotten?

'Feed Marjorie!' Hen called, reaching for a bunch of carrots from the special shleep treat basket they kept under the workbench.

Marjorie's body was covered in soft, fast-growing, voluminous white fleece that looked like a high summer cloud and which provided the Danelli family with a continuous supply of strong yarn. She was a little larger than a dog and her dark, marble-like eyes blinked at Hen as he approached, her wide mouth – which always seemed to be smiling –

smiled even more. In the wild, shleep spent the majority of their time hanging from rocky outcroppings or old twisted trees on the rough, windswept moors. And whilst Marjorie had freedom to roam anywhere around the workroom or apartment, she was happiest on her beam where she slept (and snored!) for about twenty-three and a half hours a day!

Hen hung the carrots next to her and reached up to scratch behind the horns that curled around at the side of her head. Her large damp nostrils sniffed towards the treat and she made the soft *huh, huh, huh* sound that Nana always said was Marjorie laughing!

On his way back to the workbench, Hen gathered everything he would need for the task ahead.

'Good strong thread,' he called, hurrying to collect a reel of cotton from the sideboard at the far end of the workroom, near the stairs that led back up to the shop. Danelli stitches were usually sewn with white or black thread – this had been the way for ever. Sometimes, on very rare occasions, Hen knew golden thread had been used – but that was often too costly, even for the fanciest Danelli customer.

'The needles,' Hen said, reaching for a small set of

drawers that held all sorts of different shapes and sizes of needles. They were kept tucked in a small wallet of soft folded felt. Each needle pierced through the felt, held securely in place. There were brass, bronze and copper needles, alongside gold, pewter, silver, and even ones made from tin. Each needle helped to form a particular type of spell stitch. Hen opened the wallet and laid it beside the jacket. He knew these needles were many years old, a family treasure.

'And scissors,' he said, at last, reaching for a small pair of scissors to trim stray threads.

Hen took a deep breath as he sat down and looked at the workbench before him.

'Very good,' said Nana. 'Now, there's just one more thing.'

As Nana moved across the workroom, a metallic jingling filled the air, like dozens of small bells. The sound came from the collection of keys – for the shop, apartment and various cabinets and cupboards in both – that always hung at Nana's waist, held tight to her belt with a large silver clip. The jingling was such a familiar sound to Hen, like her laughter or her voice singing along to the workroom radio.

At the far end of the room, Nana selected a large brass key and used it to open the storage cupboard.

Then, she pulled out the box.

It was unremarkable in design, plain except for a small 'D' for Danelli on the lid. But what the box held was quite possibly the most remarkable and magical thing in Hen's world. Nana brought the box over to the workbench and placed it carefully beside Hen and his assembled tools. Then, from the keys, she selected the smallest of all – as unassuming as the box it unlocked. Hen heard the click of the lock and then Nana was lifting the lid. She reached carefully inside and lifted out a book made entirely of fabric.

This was the greatest of their family heirlooms – more precious, even, than the statue of Hestia on the window ledge. More valuable than the golden thread or the silver needles.

Like any garment being stored in the workroom, it was wrapped in several layers of pristine white tissue paper, which Nana peeled away. Her wrinkled hands passed the floppy cloth book to Hen. It was wider than it was tall and thicker than a loaf of bread. The book had been handed down through the many generations of the Danelli family.

The stitches inside the cloth book were not like the sturdy, regular stitches that held a garment together. They were not even like the beautiful embroidery resembling flowers or leaves or birds or whatever the fashion was at the time that sometimes adorned collars or cuffs.

These stitches held the remnants of ancient spells. *Spell stitches.*

Spell stitches could infuse a garment with strange properties, from a summer dress or shirt to keep you cool on a hot day, to a glow stitch that made a garment shimmer and shine like the moon or a starlit night. These wonders and more resided in the Danelli family spell stitches. These were the secrets they brought to their garments – secrets that had secured their business for nearly 400 years.

Hen opened the book, turning the cloth pages carefully. The stitches looked like ripples in water, circles within circles. Tilt your head just so and they looked a little like a spider's web. More stitches connected the circles, like the spokes of a wheel.

'Why are these important?' Nana pointed at the connecting stitches with a long knitting needle.

'The spacing of those is what makes the spell stitches unique. They determine what sort of spell stitch it is and what magic will fill the garment.'

'Where should your spell stitch be located on the garment?'

'Um, well, that depends on what stitch you use and what type of garment it is. A cooling or warming spell stitch is generally added twice, to the front and back, one slightly smaller than the other but both should be large-ish.'

'And how will you know when the spell is set?'

'The stitches will all but disappear. You might see a slight shimmer if you know where to look and what to look for,' Hen said proudly.

Nana beamed at him. 'Today, you are going to stitch a protection spell into the green jacket. It's for travelling.'

Hen knew there were several different types of protection spell stitches in the book. Occasionally new stitches were created or changed as old magic faded or shifted. Every generation or so, a Danelli would devise a new spell stitch. Nana loved to experiment, but she had yet to add her own stitch to the book. 'I'd like to do it before my thread runs out!' she would laugh. But she was secretive and would never reveal what it was she was working on.

Hen needed to pick just the right protective spell stitch for a travelling garment. He flipped past the love spell that had been stitched into the wedding dress for the Queen of the Giants and past a flying spell that now only really worked in shoes – you wouldn't fly, but it helped the wearer appear much more elegant on the dance floor. There were fire spells used for toasty warm pyjamas or nightdresses, cooling spells for summer clothes and light spells that helped repel dirt and kept a garment cleaner for longer.

Then he came to the protection spells. The first was one he was fairly certain Nana only used in clothes for expectant mothers or newborn babies. The second had a small black cross stitched into the corner to show it no longer worked. No one really knew why the spell stitches would just stop working, sometimes, after hundreds of years.

Hen was sure that the third protection spell stitch was the correct one for travelling clothes. The stitch kept the wearer a perfect temperature, no matter the climate, repelled dirt and would even act as a life jacket if you fell overboard at sea or into a river. Danelli ancestors had once stitched this spell into the jackets of a whole Scillian battalion.

Hen lifted the spell stitch book to show Nana, just to double-check.

She smiled and said, 'Good. Now, crack on and I'll go make us some tea. Lottie bought scones today I do believe!'

Nana turned and hurried out of the workroom, humming to herself as she went, leaving Hen quite alone, staring hard at the green velvet jacket.

He took a deep breath, lifted the garment in one hand, the threaded needle in the other, and started to sew the outer circle of the spell stitch.

Hen's tea and scone sat untouched on the workbench as he finished off the spell stitch. Nana had gone to sit near the fireplace, had pulled out her ever-present ball of red wool and needles and was busy knitting yet another one of her scarves. She knitted at least two every week and always gave them away to customers, friends or family. Hen had a collection of six.

She glanced up, caught Hen looking and asked, 'How are you getting along?'

Hen blushed. 'Oh, finished . . . I think!'

'Let's have a look.' Nana walked over to the workbench, huffed on her silver glasses, buffed them with the hem of her jacket and plonked them back on her nose before leaning over Hen and peering closely at his work.

Her lips pursed, her forehead creased. Hen had no idea what she was thinking.

He counted in his head.

One.

Two.

Three.

'Not bad, my boy, not bad at all.' Nana beamed.

'Really?'

There was a commotion at the top of the work-room stairs, the sound of the door banging against the wall and something falling, followed by several words Nana had told Hen never to use.

Lottie – Nana's faithful, if rather scatty, assistant – came rushing down the stairs, all arms and legs and flapping apron. She was a few years older than Hen, skinny, tall and rather fidgety. She helped out in the shop and with sewing tasks, as well as helping Nana around the house sometimes. She spectacularly missed the last two steps, landing in the workroom with a flurry of more bad words.

'*Lottie!*' Nana said gently but warningly. 'Steady on or you'll break your neck.'

'Sorry, Mrs D,' she said, a little breathless. 'But you'd best come up to the shop at once.'

Nana smiled. 'Have you jammed the till again? You just need to give it a whack with the hammer under the desk.'

Lottie shook her head and blushed.

'No! It's . . . it's Mr Bertrand.'

'On the telephone?'

Lottie pointed up at the ceiling and pulled a face.

'Upstairs?' Nana asked, clearly even more puzzled.

Lottie nodded mutely and puffed her straggly fringe out of her eyes.

Uncle Bertie rarely visited the shop these days unless it was for what Nana liked to call a 'meddling visit', and he wasn't due for one of those for about six months at least.

So what on earth was he doing here today?

CHAPTER TWO

FAMILY VISITORS

Hen hurried up the stairs behind Lottie, Nana followed them a little more slowly. An afternoon of his uncle was all Hen needed. Uncle Bertie ran two spell tailor shops in Hampston but visited them here in Sparrow Down a few times a year to 'keep an eye on things', as he liked to say. It always seemed to Hen that he liked to turn up, get everyone in a flap and boss them all about for an afternoon before retreating to Hampston.

'Bertie will take over the business one day as eldest,' Nana had explained. 'Your mum and dad aren't interested in running the shop, more's the pity and

Bertie has a good head for figures, I'll give him that.'

Even though Nana was still the owner of Danelli's, in the last couple of years she had let Uncle Bertie take charge more so that she could spend her time just sewing. 'That's what I really love, Hen,' she would say happily. But he still more or less left them to their own devices. 'Your uncle couldn't wait to get away. He thought Sparrow Down was too tiny a place for his talents – too unimportant. He always wanted to be serving the very finest customers in Hampston.' And at this Nana would always thrust her nose into the air and do a funny walk which always had Hen in gales of laughter.

Hen emerged from the workroom steps into the large back hallway. Two doors led off on one side into the fitting rooms, and another staircase rose up to the two floors that formed the apartment where Hen and Nana lived. Ahead of Hen, an archway led into the shop itself. The heavy green privacy curtain was pulled back and Hen could see Uncle Bertie waiting in the shop, silhouetted against the large window. He was running a finger over one of the glass display cases. Hen prayed to Hestia that Lottie had dusted that morning!

A tram trundled past outside on Beacham Terrace

as Hen hurried through, past Lottie, calling as brightly as he could muster, 'Hello, Uncle Bert—' but then he stopped in his tracks.

Uncle Bertie wasn't alone.

Aunt Lucia and Connie, Hen's slightly younger cousin, were with him . . . on a Wednesday afternoon.

And they were surrounded by suitcases and travelling trunks. Were they off on holiday?

'Ah, Henryton! There you are, *at last*. Goodness, my boy, whatever are you wearing today?'

Uncle Bertie was the only person who insisted on using Hen's full name most of the time. It was quite annoying. He was staring at Hen's waistcoat. Hen brightened. 'Do you like it? I made it out of an old jacket that was going to be thrown away. Look.' He turned around, showing Uncle Bertie the back. 'The patchwork panels are three different types of red corduroy.'

'So I see!' Uncle Bertie didn't sound impressed.

'Well, I think it's delightful, Hen,' Aunt Lucia said with a sniff and a sad sort of smile.

She looked rather pale (which just seemed to make her even more beautiful). Her eyes were red-rimmed, and she held a lace hanky close to her mouth. Had she been crying? Hen hated seeing grown-ups cry. He recalled once finding his mum in floods of tears, not long after his other grandmother had died. It had felt so strange, a bit like the world had turned upside down.

'Thanks, Aunt Lucia. Hi, Connie.'

Connie didn't respond at all, but then they barely knew one another. They'd maybe spent about two hours in each other's company in their whole lives.

Hen couldn't help looking at the solid brown suit-cases again, stacked alongside the counter.

'Have you . . . come for a visit?' he asked carefully. Though why would they, when Hampston was only an hour away by car and they had a huge house there in the leafy suburb of Richwood?

A lot of shuffling of feet and half-mumbled replies followed as Nana came into the shop. Her eagle eyes swept the room quickly. Lottie hovered by the curtained archway, keeping her distance.

'Hen, love, why don't you take Aunt Lucia and Connie upstairs and make us all some fresh tea?' Nana said gently but firmly. It was not a suggestion.

'Let's go pop the kettle on, then,' Hen said reluctantly, leading Connie and Aunt Lucia through the archway to the back hall and stairs.

The walls of the staircase were filled with paintings and photographs of all the important Danellis, going back and back and back. Nana called it 'the gallery'. At the very top of the stairs was Domenico Danelli, the first spell tailor, the son of a sorcerer who had transformed his father's beautiful spells into magical stitches. Domenico, being a shrewd man, had quickly seen their potential, and established the first spell tailor shop. That was nearly 400 years ago. It was one of the first family stories Hen had ever been told. Most other spell tailors had bought, begged or even stolen their spell stitches. Danelli's were unique.

The gallery was where all Danellis aspired to be. It was how you knew you had done well, or achieved something amazing. Hen, too, longed to have his picture on the wall. When he was little, he'd often created self-portraits with crayons and paints and added them to the gallery, much to his parents' and Nana's delight and amusement.

He showed Aunt Lucia and Connie into the sitting room and then hurried back to the kitchen along the landing to make tea. While the kettle boiled, he leant over the bannister to see if he could hear anything from downstairs. Nana and Uncle

Bertie must have been talking incredibly quietly, though, because Hen could usually hear most of what was going on in the shop from here, all he could make out now was low murmuring.

A cough startled him and he spun around.

Connie was right behind him. She held her hat in her hands, her bobbed hair shiny as a conker. 'My mum would like a glass of water, please,' she said very politely, but like she was asking a waiter in a cafe, not her cousin.

Hen felt himself blush. 'Oh, OK,' he said and hurried back to the kitchen where the kettle had just begun to whistle.

Five minutes later, Nana, Lottie and Uncle Bertie joined them upstairs. Hen pictured the shop sign flipped to 'CLOSED' . . . Danelli's closed in the middle of the afternoon! Which meant, whatever was happening, it was important. The sitting room was quiet but for the sounds from Beacham Terrace – a gentle background song of chattering shoppers, trundling trams and the occasional clip-clop sound of a passing horse and cart.

Everyone held their teacups but no one was drinking . . . or talking. In fact, everyone appeared to be trying incredibly hard not to even look at each other, until Nana eventually said, in as bright a voice as she could muster, 'Um, Bertie and I feel that, as business hasn't been quite so good of late, that we . . . er, well, we all need to focus on trying to sort that out.'

Had things been so bad? Hen wondered. It was always a little quieter in the shop in the late winter and early spring, but Nana and Lottie had been busy working on the spring and summer collection and that was nearly ready. Things would pick up soon, they usually did.

'Those blasted Pepper factories seem to be popping up all over, undercutting us at every turn,' Uncle Bertie added.

Hen had seen a few adverts for 'Tiberius Pepper's Affordable Fashions' in the local paper. *Affordable, as if!* Mass-produced spelled garments weren't that much cheaper than handmade ones. Danelli's had always tried to create all kinds of garments, and reasonably priced too. Their customers were farmers and factory workers, lords and ladies. Nana always said they prided themselves on making clothes for anyone and everyone.

'So,' Nana picked up, 'we're going to . . . *consolidate*.' She smiled at Hen.

'Everyone's going to be working here?' Hen asked, his mind fizzing.

'Yes!' Uncle Bertie said, as though it was a splendid idea indeed.

'But what about your shops?' Hen asked.

Uncle Bertie blushed a little and pulled at his starched collar. 'The leases have already been signed over to new businesses,' he said quickly, glancing out of the window.

'There was that outbreak of spell-brats . . .' Connie said quietly but fell silent when Uncle Bertie glared at her.

'Just to be clear though . . . we're all going to be working *and* living here . . . *together*?' Hen thought of the stacked suitcases downstairs.

Uncle Bertie puffed himself up. 'Absolutely, Henryton. Like one big happy family! Won't that be jolly? It is a family business, after all.' Uncle Bertie's eyes slid towards poor Lottie, perched on a wonky stool near the sitting room door, fidgeting like she had spell-brats in her knickers.

Hen wasn't sure what he thought about having them all here.

Uncle Bertie could be a bit of a blithering windbag, but he was mostly OK. Aunt Lucia was always nice and baked the best biscuits, and Connie seemed harmless enough, he guessed. And anyway, she went to some fancy school in Hampston so he probably wouldn't see much of her.

Perhaps it might be fun having them all here for a bit? He missed his mum and dad, the black shleeps of the family who had no interest in clothes or designing or sewing. They were both scientists and spent most of their time travelling all over doing research. With just Hen and Nana on their own it did sometimes feel a little lonely. And it wasn't as though the apartment didn't have enough space for everyone. Nana had told him that all of Beacham Terrace had once been large, grand houses – full of attentive servants and fancy furniture. Now they had mostly been converted into flats, offices or shops with living space above, just like Danelli's – but the rooms on the upper floors were still quite fine, if a little faded these days.

'I'm rather tired,' Aunt Lucia said in a tiny voice. 'Might I lie down?'

'Of course, dear Lucia,' Nana said, getting to her feet. 'Use Betsy and Hector's room while I make up the spare beds.'

'Henryton,' said Uncle Bertie, 'why don't you go

fetch the luggage up? I'm sure you can manage, big strong lad like you. And . . . um, Lucy can help you.' He squinted across the room.

'It's Lottie,' Hen said as Lottie turned puce and whimpered. She always seemed nervous around Uncle Bertie, and Hen couldn't blame her.

Uncle Bertie beamed as everyone started to move, the tea un-drunk and cooling in abandoned cups. 'I'll just have a look at . . . everything downstairs, shall I? Make sure everything is in order and what-not.' He rocked back and forth on his heels.

Hen grabbed Lottie's hand as he passed through the door and back out on to the landing.

'Come on . . . *Lucy*!' he said with a grin.

Hen and Lottie made two trips each with various bits of luggage before Lottie had to sit down breath-less, quivering and rather pale.

'You go back to the shop, I can manage the rest,' Hen offered.

He fetched the remaining cases and bags as quietly as he could up two flights of stairs – sixty steps! – to the upper floor, aware that Aunt Lucia was lying on his parents' bed with a damp flannel over her face and the curtains drawn. Hen staggered along the landing towards the first of the two spare bedrooms, where Connie would sleep. It normally only had boxes stashed in it and neither of the two beds had been made up for as long as he could recall, the mattresses bare. The other spare room, which he guessed would be Aunt Lucia and Uncle Bertie's, had a larger bed and a hulking old wardrobe that Hen recalled hiding in on his last birthday, during a game of sardines.

But as he went into the first bedroom, footsteps echoing on the bare floorboards, he was surprised to find Connie there already, framed in the dusty window, staring out over the back of Beacham Terrace. It was a nice view across the little yards and gardens that backed on to the houses and shops. A pile of sheets and a blanket waited at the foot of the bed.

'Not as nice as your bedroom at home,' Hen said.

He'd glimpsed Connie's bedroom through a partly open door once on a visit to their house in Richwood. It had been stuffed with toys and books. Compared to that, Hen thought this must seem quite a comedown, really. Poor Connie.

'Do you need anything? Extra blankets? Another pillow?'

Connie didn't say anything, she just kept staring out of the window.

'Connie?'

Still no reply.

'Oh yes, thank you dear cousin, that would be so kind of you,' Hen replied to himself, trying to sound like Connie but extra snooty.

When she still didn't say anything, he turned around and headed for the door. *What was the point?*

'He lost it all.' Connie spoke so quietly that at first Hen wasn't sure she had spoken at all. He paused by the door.

'What? Who?' Hen asked, turning back to her.

'My dad,' Connie explained, keeping her voice low. 'The shops, the house in Richwood – we can't afford to live there now. It's all gone.'

Hen glanced back at the door, worried that Connie was sharing secrets she shouldn't be, and a grown-up might overhear. But he was curious to know more. 'What do you mean? This isn't permanent, is it?' Hen felt his stomach squeeze nervously. 'Nana said it was just to . . . um . . . consolidate the business?'

'That's just one of those grown-up words that doesn't really mean anything,' Connie said bitterly. 'Get used to it. Things haven't been great for a while,

Hen. Dad closed the Thornton Arcade shop at the end of last year and Carlyle Row closed last week after the spell-brats finished off most of the stock. There were already lots of debts, that's why he sold the house.'

'Sold the house?' Hen gaped. He couldn't believe what he was hearing. Uncle Bertie had said they'd be living and working here together . . . but he hadn't said it would be for ever!

Connie finally turned and faced him. 'I know this is just a massive inconvenience to you, Hen, but trust me, I'm not exactly mad about the idea of living here either, thanks. So let's do each other a big favour and leave each other alone, OK?' And with that, she turned back to the window. Only the slight moving of her shoulders gave away that she was crying.

CHAPTER THREE

[Not] Business as Usual

'Things aren't all that bad,' Nana said later as she was wishing Hen goodnight. 'Connie's heard something and got a little over-excited by the sounds of things.'

She stood by his bedroom door, her knitting needles moving so fast they were almost a blur as she started yet another red scarf. But Hen could tell she was keeping something from him. She looked tired and her face was creased with worry, which wasn't like Nana at all.

Hen had written to his mum and dad to tell them everything that had happened. He always did this when he was worried or upset. He knew they would reply straight away, even if the postal service was slow. Thankfully, just writing the letter made him feel a little better. And yet, worry still coiled in his stomach. He shook his head.

'But Connie said Uncle Bertie had to sell their house. That sounds pretty bad to me, Nana. Will we have to sell here, too?' Beacham Terrace was the only home Hen had ever known.

'No,' Nana said, as though it were a daft suggestion. 'Things have been unfortunate for your uncle in the last year – lots of bad luck. Right now, we need to support each other. Bertie will take over the business entirely one day, Hen, so we thought this was for the best. Listen, your uncle and I have everything under control. Don't you worry about a thing, OK?' She glanced down at her knitting and tutted. 'Bother. I was sure I'd got it that time...'

If Nana thought everything was OK then it must be, right? But she hadn't actually said what Connie had told him was wrong. He didn't feel all that reassured.

'Goodnight, Nana,' he said, and burrowed down under his blankets and quilt.

'Goodnight, little Hen.' She stepped across the

room, her keys singing their bright jingling song. She planted a gentle kiss on Hen's forehead. 'Sleep tight. Don't let the spell-brats bite.'

Hen slept late the next morning and rushed to get dressed and ready for his regular morning tasks – daily deliveries and errands around town. Hurrying downstairs, he nipped into the kitchen and grabbed an apple for breakfast. Then popped it back and grabbed a raisin and oatmeal biscuit instead.

In the shop he would usually find Lottie busy sweeping and tidying, getting ready for the day ahead, but this morning there was no sign of her. Instead, he found Uncle Bertie poring over the appointment diary – a huge, green, leather-bound book that recorded all the customers coming for fittings or measurements or to select new outfits or collect items. Nana stood beside him, looking thoroughly annoyed, and Aunt Lucia and Connie were fidgeting anxiously near the door.

'Perhaps we should move these two appointments to a bit later?' Uncle Bertie said, reaching for the pen.

'Don't you dare, Bertie,' Nana growled and slapped his hand. Nana was always in charge of the appointment book. It was filled with her beautiful, careful writing and nobody else dared to touch it, usually.

'But if this lady could come later today—'

'Mrs Cutter can't do afternoon appointments because of her parrot,' Nana explained.

'Well, then—'

'No, Bertie. Mr Palooza likes to call for his fittings before lunch at the tea rooms.'

'But it would just make—'

'I know my customers, Bertrand,' Nana said, dragging the appointment diary out of his reach. 'Leave well alone!'

Uncle Bertie, noticing Hen, sighed, adjusted the measuring tape that hung about his neck and then rather dramatically checked his pocket watch.

'Well, now we are all here.' He glanced pointedly at Hen. 'We have quite a lot to do today. There are – unfortunately – three fittings booked in before lunchtime, which Mother and I shall see to.' Nana clutched the diary tight to her chest.

'Lucia, you can see to the workroom this morning, please, and Henryton, you're on deliveries and this list of errands.' He thrust a long, curling list at Hen and gestured to the stack of parcels Hen had got ready himself the day before.

'Thanks, Uncle Bertie,' Hen said as graciously as he could. At least he would be out of the way for a while.

'And Constance will go with you.'

'WHAT?' Hen and Connie blurted together.

Hen had thought she would be off to her fancy school, back to Hampston, and most assuredly out of his way. But then he realized how silly that was, given the revelations from yesterday. Fancy schools cost money, after all.

'Do I have to?' Connie asked, not even looking at Hen.

Uncle Bertie gave Aunt Lucia a stern look.

'Darling,' Aunt Lucia said in her most soothing voice, 'we discussed this. You need to help with the business and as a trainee you'll have to do things like running errands and making deliveries.'

'Just until you get the hang of things, of course,' Uncle Bertie added.

Connie glared at her father, who had already turned back to fiddling with his tape measure. Aunt Lucia fussed and made more soothing sounds and quietly promised various treats if Connie behaved. Eventually, realizing she wouldn't win, Connie sighed, grabbed half the parcels and said, 'Let's go then, Hen.'

'Oh wait, here, my loves!' Nana said, hurrying forwards to wrap two new red scarves around their necks. 'Fresh this morning,' she said, with an air of disappointment. *Another one to add to my collection*, thought Hen.

As they headed out of the door, Aunt Lucia called, 'You'll look after her, won't you, Hen?' She sounded rather traumatized. 'It isn't too dangerous out there, is it?' Aunt Lucia asked Nana.

'If you ignore all the thieves and murderers,' Nana replied, winking at Hen.

'What?'

'Mother, is that your idea of a joke?' Uncle Bertie asked.

Nana smiled. 'Oh, I'm deadly serious.' She met Uncle Bertie's steely gaze.

'Well, perhaps I should go with them?' Aunt Lucia stepped towards the door.

'Oh, Mum, we'll be fine,' Connie said quickly.

She grabbed Hen by the scarf and dragged him out of the shop. Aunt Lucia followed but stopped and watched from the top of the steps as they walked down Beacham Terrace. 'Don't talk to any strangers,' she shouted, her voice trembling. 'And be careful when you cross the street. Watch out for the trams!

Oh, Hestia protect them!'

'Is she always like this?' Hen asked, avoiding the amused glances from passers-by.

'Not usually this bad.'

'Oh, Connie!' Aunt Lucia called. She made the 'e' go on far longer than was necessary.

They both stopped and turned.

'Dearest, you did remember to put clean knickers on, didn't you, yes?'

Hen snorted with laughter as Connie went a horrible purple colour.

'MOTHER!' Connie blurted and then turned away muttering. 'Hestia's needles! I'm tempted to throw myself under a tram! What are you laughing at, anyway?' She stormed off along the street towards the chapel that stood on the corner of the marketplace. 'Let's go!'

'Actually, we need to go this way first,' Hen said, pointing in the opposite direction. 'We have a delivery for Mrs Ele and she lives in the park.'

'Is she . . . *homeless*?' Connie asked, coming to a dead stop.

She really was clueless. 'No, Connie, she's not homeless. She runs the tea shop in the park.'

'Oh,' Connie mumbled quietly. 'Well, how was I

supposed to know?' Then she pretended to study the names on the packages she was carrying.

They turned and crossed the street during a brief lull in the traffic. Connie paused to gaze into Widget's Toy Shop, the window filled with all manner of dolls and toys and games.

'I usually get something from Widget's for my birthday,' Hen said proudly, and waved at Mr and Mrs Widget through the window. They both peered out, eyes huge behind magnifying spectacles, their faces already dotted with bright spots of paint. 'Everything is handmade by Mr and Mrs Widget,' Hen explained.

'Toy shops are for little kids,' Connie said dismissively, and wandered off. A truck was turning into Apple Yard at the back of Widget's, and the driver called out brightly and tooted the horn.

'Mornin', Hen.' A greasy face grinned out of the driver's window as the truck trundled on to the cobbles.

'Who's that?' Connie asked, her nose wrinkled a little.

'That's Mrs Henderson, my friend Simon's mum. She's the best mechanic in Sparrow Down. She's great at fixing sewing machines too!'

Connie said nothing, but raised her eyebrows.

She's such a snob! Hen thought to himself. It was going to be a long morning!

At the next house, a man was up a ladder fixing a wooden sign in place just above the door.

FOR SALE BY AUCTION
Contact Babu & Hara Auctioneers, for particulars
Sparrow Down 7851

The house had been empty for a year or more now, since the Aldridges had moved away. And it wasn't the only one in Sparrow Down. As Hen glanced along Beacham Terrace, past the park gates where the road then became Park Street, he could see at least three other 'FOR SALE' boards up on various buildings. He tried not to think about it too much. It wasn't that unusual to see houses for sale, though it seemed just recently people only ever moved away.

Shaking the thought off, Hen led Connie through the tall, gleaming black gates of the park. A shiny gold crest was emblazoned on each gate, depicting two sparrows in flight.

'This is Jubilee park,' Hen said with a flourish, hoping it might cheer Connie up a little. 'There's a pond down there, some swings and a good slide. And music on the bandstand on Sundays, when it's warmer.'

'It looks quite small,' Connie said. 'The park in Richwood is about ten times as big as this.'

He had been quite excited to show Connie around Sparrow Down, but now he saw it through her eyes, it didn't seem quite so sparkly. He felt a bit fed up.

'And I suppose the gates were solid gold and operated by unicorns,' Hen muttered – but not too quietly.

Connie sniffed and they carried on in silence again.

Mrs Ele's Tea Shop was not far from the gate, nestled under the trees with seats and tables out the front where a few people sat drinking coffee. A small dog yapped excitedly at Connie and Hen as they walked closer and a tiny but fast woman dashed out of the tea shop, already in full flow as she emerged. 'Darling, sit yourself down, I'll whip you up some warm milk in a flash and I've just baked— Oh, but who have we got here?' Mrs Ele beamed and slowed as she spotted Connie beside Hen. 'What a beauty!' Hen noticed his cousin blush.

'Erm, Mrs Ele, this is my cousin Connie, she's –' he suddenly didn't quite know what to say – 'staying with us.'

Mrs Ele smiled her wide smile that could light up a windowless cellar. 'Well, of course I can see now she is clearly a Danelli. Those eyes – only Danelli's have eyes that sort of blue, oh and those lips. Gorgeous, gorgeous, gorgeous! Sit yourselves down, my darlings. Sit, sit!' She ushered them both into seats and hurried off into the tea shop again. As the door swung open, she shouted, 'Hercules, two warm milks and some shortbread – quickly!'

'We should be getting on, shouldn't we?' Connie asked, looking about herself. 'Not stopping for a snack already.'

'It's fine, Connie. Besides, it would be rude not to take up the offer and Mrs Ele's shortbread is the best. Trust me.'

Mrs Ele burst through the door again – she clearly only had one speed and it was fast! She served fresh coffee to the other customers, settled in some new ones, and then she brought the warmed milk and shortbread to Hen and Connie. Once she had unloaded the tray and wiped her hands, Hen handed her the parcel.

'Here you go, Mrs Ele,' he said, smiling.

She jumped up and down and clapped her hands together. 'Oh wonderful, wonderful!' She hurriedly ripped the brown paper open.

Mrs Ele held up the new dress and Hen heard admiring murmurs from the other customers. He felt a flush of pride. The dress was dark, dusky pink and the front folded into itself, creating a tuck and knot of material rather like a large blooming flower.

'It's a spell tailor outfit, I bet,' someone nearby whispered.

'Danelli's, you can be sure of it.'

Holding the dress against her body, Mrs Ele twirled for her appreciative audience, who clapped and cheered. 'I am going to look so, so beautiful at my cousin's wedding. Thank you. Your grand-mother, she is the very best.'

She twirled around again and then, as she quickly but carefully folded the dress up, she said quietly, 'And I don't believe a word of what people are saying about spelled garments making folks ill. I say to them, "Not Danelli's! Never Danelli's!" Clothes spelled with care and love, never make you ill! No doubt it's these things made with less care and atten-tion in factories, by machines. My mother always said, the saints preserve her, "You buy cheap, you buy twice!"'

She dashed away again, leaving Hen and Connie staring at each other.

'What did she mean?' Connie asked. 'About spelled clothes making people ill?'

Hen shrugged. 'Probably just gossip. It's not the first time I've heard it – but it always seems to be somebody's neighbour's mother-in-law's cousin, you know?'

Connie snorted, a half-smile twitching her mouth – but she quickly pouted when she noticed him watching, saying rather crossly, 'Well, hadn't we better get on? If we have to stop for tea and cake with every delivery, we'll never get home.'

Hen took a deep breath.

He knew she must still be feeling angry and hurt with everything that had happened, but why did it feel like it was all his fault?

After milk and shortbread at Mrs Ele's, Hen and Connie dropped off another couple of garments on the far side of the park, then delivered some invoices. Afterwards, they headed back into town, calling in at Henderson's Garage and Workshop to check on the repairs to Nana's favourite sewing machine.

'Should be done by the end of the week,' Mrs Henderson called, her voice echoing from under the bonnet of a large red motorcar. Hen would've liked to introduce Connie to Simon and his mum, but she refused to venture inside the workshop.

'It was so . . . greasy,' Connie said snootily, wiping imagined dirt from her skirt and jumper.

Next, they posted Hen's letter to his mum and dad, returned Hen and Nana's library books, and had a quick chat with Mrs Mori the librarian. Whenever they were out of earshot of anyone else, Connie would start grumbling. 'What's any of this got to do with the business anyway?' she said. 'Aren't I supposed to be learning something?'

Hen bit his tongue.

They nipped around the corner to Mr Amin the butcher to pick up a chicken for dinner and were crossing to the greengrocer to collect their vegetable order when Connie asked, 'Must you stop to chat to everyone?'

Hen had had just about enough. 'It's rude not to say hello around here. I don't know what it was like in snooty Richwood but—'

'Richwood isn't snooty,' Connie said.

'Well, maybe it's just the people who live there, then,' Hen said before he had time to stop himself.

Hen went inside to fetch the order and Connie didn't follow. When he emerged a minute or two later, she had wandered off. Hen spotted her down Bishops Lane, outside Jelani's. The shop had been boarded up since it closed last summer. Connie was peering up at the building. 'Was this a spell tailor's too?' she asked quietly, their quarrel apparently forgotten – at least for now.

Hen nodded. 'Mr and Mrs Jelani's. They were good friends with Nana. It closed last summer.'

'What happened?' Connie asked, her voice small.

'They kept having spell-brat infestations too,' Hen explained, thinking back to the evenings he and Nana had spent trying to help get the problem under control. The shop had been crawling with the insects, their thin little bodies scuttling for dark corners when you switched on a light. The Jelani workroom had been filled with ruined garments by the time they'd shut down. 'They'd get rid of them, only to have them come back. Eventually they had to close. They moved away not long after.'

He remembered watching Nana hug her friends and wave them off as their moving truck trundled along Bishops Lane. When Nana had turned back, Hen had seen her eyes were watery with tears.

'That's so sad,' Connie said. It felt like the first *real* thing she'd said all day.

CHAPTER FOUR

INVENTORY

They had barely got through the Danelli's shop door when Aunt Lucia dashed over to inspect Connie, turning her this way and that, no doubt making sure that she hadn't lost an arm or leg at some point during the morning. Satisfied Connie was indeed still in one piece, Aunt Lucia sighed, gave them both a tight hug, whispered a quick prayer of thanks to Hestia and went back to the counter.

Hen noticed that things already looked a little different in the shop. There was now a large table in the middle of the shop floor piled with scarves and gloves. Several more mannequins had been brought in, and were standing about all half dressed and half constructed. Uncle Bertie was in the middle, battling with an outstretched wooden mannequin arm.

'Where's Lottie?' Hen asked. 'Is she ill?'

'Who? Oh, yes.' Uncle Bertie looked flustered. 'Well, now that we're consolidating, we simply don't require her services any longer.'

'You ... *fired* her?' Hen asked, outraged.

'It was best all round—'

'Not for Lottie! She needed to work to help her family! She's been here for years!'

Uncle Bertie returned his attention to the mannequin. 'We are a business, not a charity. We can't take in every waif and stray.'

And yet we took you all in, Hen thought, fuming.

'Anyway,' Uncle Bertie said, brushing Lottie away as if she were no more than a scrap on the workroom floor. 'I thought the shop could do with a little facelift.' Uncle Bertie gestured around the room. 'What do you think?'

Hen wasn't entirely sure. He wondered what Nana would make of it – Uncle Bertie should be more concerned about her reaction!

'Well, I think it looks much smarter.' Uncle Bertie filled the uncomfortable silence. 'This is how it's done in Hampston, you know.' Uncle Bertie sniffed. 'Now, this afternoon, Constance, you will assist your grandmother in the workroom and, Henryton, I will require your help carrying out the inventory.'

'There's one in the workroom, Uncle Bertie,' Hen said, recalling how his parents had helped Nana complete it on their last visit just before the New Year celebrations almost three months ago.

'Ah, yes. I have that one.' Uncle Bertie tapped his clipboard. 'But I wanted to do one for the whole building.'

'The apartment too?' Hen asked uncertainly.

'Yes.' Uncle Bertie fiddled with the tape measure around his neck and then turned quickly to refold a perfectly folded scarf on the large table.

'Why?' Connie asked.

Uncle Bertie gaped for a second like a fish out of water and then said quickly, 'Insurance purposes. Anyway, isn't it your lunchtime? Chop chop! Off you go.' He ushered them through the curtain.

Hen glanced over at Connie as they climbed the stairs. She was frowning.

'This is how it started before,' she whispered,

glancing back down the stairs.

'How what started?'

'The shop closing. The house being sold. Every-thing.' Connie's voice was tight.

Hen swallowed, his throat oddly dry. Nana had said there was nothing to worry about – but what if she was just trying to protect him from the truth?

After wolfing down his lunch, Hen visited Nana in the workroom to bring her a sandwich and to ask about Lottie. Uncle Bertie had said she was too busy to eat upstairs. Sure enough, Hen found her hunched over the sketches for the summer collec-tion, which she had finished at the end of last year. But now she was redrawing skirts and blouses and jackets as though her life depended on it.

'Something wrong with the collection, Nana?' Hen asked carefully.

'Your uncle and I thought it best if I looked at it again.'

'But you'd already started sewing, hadn't you?'

Nana blinked up at Hen through her spectacles and said sadly, 'Yes. But, well, business isn't great so we really need to make sure this collection is the very best it can be. But you don't need to worry, Hen.'

Hen felt funny. *You don't need to worry*, she'd said – but what if Nana wasn't telling the whole truth? 'Then why did you let Uncle Bertie sack Lottie?'

'Oh, Hen . . .' she sighed. 'I feel terrible. When it was just you and me, we needed all the help we could get. But with everyone here now, we were going to struggle to find Lottie work to do. And she's always such a nervous wreck around your uncle . . . Honestly, I think she was a little bit relieved.'

'But it's Lottie,' Hen said. 'She's practically family.' He paused. 'And why is all of this only happening now – after Uncle Bertie arrived? You never said the business was in trouble before.'

Nana reached out and squeezed his shoulder. 'Your uncle's business and ours, they're linked. We're all Danelli Spell Tailors, you see? So when his shop failed, ours suffered too. But Hen, we're going to be all right. We're all working hard to make things right – as a family. Do you see? It might be difficult, but everything will be all right, love. OK?'

Hen nodded slowly.

'Henryton, are you down there?' Uncle Bertie's voice echoed down the workroom steps.

Nana smiled sadly at him. 'Don't keep Bertie waiting, love. And thanks for the sandwich.'

Uncle Bertie was waiting at the top of the stairs, clipboard in hand. He checked his pocket watch as Hen hurried up the last few steps and made a rather unimpressed sound.

'I was just chatting to Nana,' Hen said. 'I do usually have an hour for lunch before I start work in the afternoon.'

But Uncle Bertie wasn't listening and handed Hen the clipboard. 'I trust you have satisfactory handwriting, Henryton?'

'Nana always says it's nice,' Hen said, peering at the sheets on the clipboard, which included the existing inventory for the workroom.

Uncle Bertie pulled a face and said, 'Well, luckily I've made a copy of each sheet so you can write it all up again extra neatly.' He said this as though it were a great treat – but Hen couldn't help feeling he was being punished, though he wasn't sure what for exactly.

'Let's begin, shall we?'

They started right there in the hallway. Uncle Bertie charged about calling out every object, piece of furniture, picture – even the light switches and doorknobs – for Hen to scribble down. After a couple of minutes, Hen was already struggling to keep up and had to ask Uncle Bertie to stop and repeat himself.

'Unsigned painting of river,' Uncle Bertie said carefully, 'small painted table, brass lamp with mauve shade, blue-and-white vase . . .' He glanced over at Hen. 'Keeping up, Henryton?'

Hen nodded. His fingers ached from gripping the pen and the sheet already looked rather chaotic.

When Uncle Bertie was satisfied he had seen everything in the downstairs hall, he went across to Hen and inspected the clipboard. 'Oh dear, oh heavens.' Uncle Bertie tutted. 'Is this the best you could do, Henryton?'

'I'm sorry—'

'It looks as though you've written this during an earthquake, blindfolded . . . is *that* even a word?' He turned the clipboard and pointed to two words that Hen was fairly sure read 'large rug'.

'Perhaps Connie would be a better person for the job?' Hen suggested. 'I bet she has lovely handwriting.'

But Uncle Bertie wasn't listening; he was already heading for the staircase. 'Come along!'

Hen gulped, looking at the hundreds of pictures and portraits on the walls, all the Danelli ancestors.

With sinking dread, he asked, 'We're not going to have to list every single one of those, are we, Uncle Bertie?'

'Don't be silly, Henryton, of course not. We would never sell the family portraits.'

Sell? He'd said this inventory was to do with insurance . . . Connie hadn't believed him, and now Hen definitely didn't either. Worry churned his sandwich-filled stomach.

They reached the first floor and started in the kitchen, listing every pot and pan, even the exact number of knives, forks and spoons. Cushions were counted and catalogued in the sitting room and then every dish and plate in the dining room. The afternoon dragged on, Hen's writing growing worse as his hand cramped up.

As they emerged back on to the landing, Hen sighed with relief. They were done, surely? He screwed the cap back on Uncle Bertie's pen and stared down at his ink-stained fingers.

Uncle Bertie coughed rather pointedly.

Hen glanced up. 'Did I miss something?' he asked, glancing around.

Uncle Bertie pulled out a small key, dark with age, which he poked into the wooden panelling that lined the walls. A slim door popped open, revealing a narrow staircase vanishing upwards into a slice of darkness.

The attics!

Hen groaned.

He hated the attics. He'd only been up there once or twice, usually to fetch things with his mum or dad – like decorations or luggage. It was full of Hen's least favourite things: dark, dust and spiders.

'We don't really have to go up there, do we?' Hen asked, his hands already sweaty with nerves.

'Of course we do! Who knows what treasures might be tucked away up there?' Uncle Bertie grinned and gestured to the doorway. 'After you.'

Great, Hen thought and stepped into the tight space. The stairs were so narrow that Hen could only just fit his whole foot on them – he had no idea how Uncle Bertie was going to manage! After a few steps, his eyes had almost adjusted to the gloom. It wasn't all that dark; there was muted light coming from above. Up and up Hen climbed, strands of dusty webs tickling at his face. He heard Uncle Bertie lose his footing once or twice behind him, uttering curses as he stumbled against the stairs or wall.

When Hen finally reached the top, he found that

a tall dresser – with half of its drawers missing – had blocked the doorway into the attics proper. Someone had obviously tried to move it and lost the battle, most likely Hen's dad!

'Brilliant,' Hen muttered. He found a foothold in one of the empty drawer spaces and started to climb over it.

Just as he reached the top, the dresser wobbled, creaked and pitched forward, sending Hen sliding down into a pile of dirty sheets. He sat up, coughing, and untangled himself as dust plumed everywhere.

'What a tip!' he coughed.

The ceiling arched low and rather cave-like, but dusty light flooded in through a row of windows that looked down over Beacham Terrace, the sounds of the street far-off and muted. The windows were hung with more cobwebs and Hen tried not to think too much about the spiders that had spun them. As he glanced about, he realized every inch of the attics was stuffed with the wreckage of a hundred lives. Hen spotted old chairs, dressmakers' dummies, baskets of letters and photographs, a dressing table with a cracked mirror, bookcases with missing or broken shelves and, in one corner, a collection of lamps that looked like a rather strange garden.

Against the back wall were what Hen guessed were hatstands, more dressers and wardrobes, all mostly covered in sheets so they looked rather like spectres having a meeting.

Fabulous, Hen: now you're thinking about spectres, too!

'Henryton!' Uncle Bertie was calling from the other side of the furniture barricade. 'Are you all right?'

'Yes,' Hen said. 'I'm fine.'

Together they tried to shift the dresser away from the door. Hen could hear Uncle Bertie grunting and groaning as he heaved. Eventually they managed to make a narrow gap between the wall and the wardrobe that Uncle Bertie just about squeezed himself into. After a tense moment, he sort of popped out of the gap like a cork from a bottle. He stood in the attic, panting, hands on knees, his dust-streaked face dark red and cobwebs fluttering in his hair.

After taking several deep, gulping breaths, Uncle Bertie pulled his jacket and tape measure straight, looked around the attic and groaned.

'I know,' Hen said. 'It could take months to sort through it all.' The thought made him thoroughly miserable.

'Well, let's have a look around and see if there's anything worth adding to the list straight off, shall we?' He didn't sound enthusiastic.

At first, Uncle Bertie held up a few bits and pieces, mostly broken old toys or paintings that had been damaged or were falling out of their frames. But then he stopped showing things to Hen and grew quieter as he searched. Hen wondered if perhaps one of the old-style mannequins might do for the shop – that might cheer Uncle Bertie up. He moved through the stacks of stuff to try to get a better look, but was quickly distracted by a bundle of rich-looking fabric hidden in the shadows at the back of the attic.

Uncle Bertie wasn't paying attention, so Hen moved in for a closer look.

It was a pile of old garments, some unfinished. Hen guessed they must be over fifty years old from the unfashionable styles, but the fabric, though a little dusty, was all perfect. Hen lifted up a long skirt and his mind was suddenly alive with three different designs he could use the fabric for. He wondered why the garments were here, forgotten and never worn.

As he folded the skirt and placed it back in the

pile, his eyes fell on a large wardrobe to his left. It was slightly out of reach. Suddenly, the air seemed to fizz and crackle as though some charge filled every atom between him and the wardrobe, like when you hold two magnets close and they pull towards each other.

Hen was stretching towards the wardrobe over the crush of chests and boxes when Uncle Bertie snapped, 'Henryton, I don't think you're listening to a thing I'm saying!'

Hen turned around quickly. Uncle Bertie was right – Hen hadn't even realized he had been speaking. 'Sorry, Uncle Bertie—'

'Oh, what's the point anyway?' Uncle Bertie interrupted. 'It's all just a load of useless old junk.'

'How about these?' Hen gestured to the pile of old garments he'd just discovered. 'I think I could rework them?'

'No, Henryton.' He sounded utterly dejected, and threw aside whatever it was he had been holding and headed for the stairs.

CHAPTER FIVE

Repairs

Hurrying down to the workroom the next day after lunch, Hen noticed there had been more changes. The store cupboards and racks had been moved and the walls were now quite bare.

'Where are the sketches?' he asked Nana, who was bent over a length of silky yellow fabric. Sketches of vintage Danelli designs had always covered the workroom walls.

'Your uncle thought they were distracting, so he's packed them away,' Nana said through pin-gripping teeth.

Hen offered Marjorie a fresh carrot. She purred

gently as he scratched her behind her horns.

That was when Hen noticed the radio wasn't playing, which was most unusual.

He looked across at the old dresser where the radio usually sat. It was gone.

He glanced around. There was no sign of it in the workroom.

'Nana, where's the radio?' Hen asked.

'Oh,' Nana said. 'Your uncle's taken that away too.'

'What? Why?' Hen asked.

Nana raised her silvery eyebrows and pointed up to a new sign, the only thing that now adorned the walls.

<u>WORKROOM RULES</u>

1. SHIFTS LAST FROM 8.30 A.M. UNTIL 12 NOON
AND FROM 12.30 P.M. UNTIL 6 P.M. – TARDINESS
IS UNACCEPTABLE

2. A CLEAN WORKPLACE IS AN
EFFICIENT WORKPLACE

2A. NO FOOD OR DRINKS TO BE CONSUMED IN
THE WORKROOM OR SHOP AREAS

3. ORDER CREATES ORDER. CHAOS CREATES CHAOS

4. CHATTERING SHOULD BE KEPT TO A MINIMUM
OR SHOULD BE WORK RELATED

5. ALL MATERIALS MUST BE LOGGED IN THE
RELEVANT RESOURCE LEDGER (YES, EVEN PINS!)

6. SHLEEP MUST BE CONFINED TO THE
BASEMENT AREA AND ARE NOT PERMITTED
IN THE SHOP OR APARTMENT

7. NO radio

The last one seemed to have been added later,
by hand.

'What's that all about?' Hen asked.

'Let's just give it a try, shall we?' Nana replied,
patting Hen's hand gently. 'We have to share the
workroom now and not everyone wants to listen to
the radio, love.'

Did Uncle Bertie really think this would help to
get the business back on track? Hen wasn't so sure.

He glanced over at the dresser where they stored
unfinished garments – a set of large, wide drawers.
He had stashed something in there last week and he
rather hoped Uncle Bertie hadn't found it – he
would not approve. Hen was about to go and check,
when suddenly a small wooden crate sailed through

the air and landed at his feet, splitting in two. Hen dodged several more objects that flew out of the old store cupboard.

'Ah, Henryton.' Uncle Bertie emerged from inside the cupboard.

'Do you need any help, Uncle Bertie?' Hen asked.

'No, no. It's all under control. I'm going to turn this into my office.' Uncle Bertie smiled proudly.

'Your office?' Hen asked.

'Yes.'

'But that's a cupboard, Uncle Bertie,' he said uncertainly.

Uncle Bertie's eyes narrowed. 'Do you need a task, Henryton?'

'Hen, dear,' Nana called. 'Can you help me pin this pattern? The fabric's not cooperating.'

Hen picked his way over the piles of discarded junk from the cupboard to help Nana, shaking his head.

Later, when Uncle Bertie had finished shoving a small desk and chair into the cupboard, Hen finally opened the bottom drawer, his drawer, of the storage dresser. It was mostly filled with practice pieces, all made from muslin or rough cotton offcuts. There were also squares that he had practised spell stitches on, over and over again. He shoved all that aside and reached to the very back of the drawer.

Where was the jacket? He'd promised Mrs Clump it would be ready by the weekend!

'Ahem!'

Hen startled and turned. Uncle Bertie was standing at the far end of the worktable. And there, in front of him, was Hen's package for Mrs Clump – the tissue paper all unfolded, exposing the dark purple woollen jacket.

'Looking for this?' Uncle Bertie asked.

'Twist it!' Hen mumbled quickly.

'Well?' Uncle Bertie's voice was measured and calm, which only made Hen feel even more nervous. Nana and his mum were always super calm just before they exploded.

'I'm . . . fixing it,' Hen said quietly, not meeting his uncle's eyes.

'But it isn't one of our garments . . . is it?'

Hen shook his head. 'No, Uncle Bertie.'

'And do we do general repairs, Henryton, on garments we have not designed and constructed?'

'I . . .' Hen fell silent and studied the whorls and knots of wood in the workbench. 'No,' he said in the smallest of small voices. 'It was a favour,' he explained. 'For Mrs Clump, the baker.'

Nana spoke, then. 'Oh, Bertie. It's just a little patch on a jacket. Can't Hen just—'

Uncle Bertie's eyes flickered sharply to Nana. Then he sighed and sank into the seat next to Hen. 'Don't you see? We can't afford to be doing work for free. And if we *repair* things nobody will ever buy any new clothes, and that's our business, Henryton, selling *new* clothes! You do understand, don't you?'

'Well, yes but . . .' Hen thought fast. 'You see it wasn't for free, really. Mrs Clump always gives us extra bread—'

'Bread won't pay off debts,' Uncle Bertie said.

Hen squared his shoulders. He wasn't about to let go of this so easily. 'Then this can be the last one I do for bread – but why shouldn't we repair things for people and reuse old things nobody wants to wear any more? We could make some money from doing that, surely?'

'Hen does have a talent for fixing and altering things, Bertie,' Nana offered.

Uncle Bertie dropped the jacket on to the work-table and then stood in one slow movement, as though carrying the weight of the world. 'And be like any run-of-the-mill seamstress in some grubby little shop? Is that what we want to aspire to? We are Danellis! Our reputation must be upheld at all costs! No more repairs,' Uncle Bertie said quietly but firmly, and walked off across the workroom to his little cupboard-office.

CHAPTER SIX

SPELL-BRATS

Hen knew it was wrong to go against Uncle Bertie but he was determined not to let Mrs Clump down. After dinner, he crept to the workroom and smuggled the jacket out under his jumper, along with needles and thread – which he *didn't* log in Uncle Bertie's precious book! – and took it all back to his bedroom.

'I've put up with all of Uncle Bertie's silly changes,' he grumbled as he stowed the jacket under his bed. 'But this is one step too far! Nana was always fine with it. Why does he have to be such a stick in the mud?'

Hen had always felt strongly that it was a waste to throw away perfectly good clothes just because the fashion had changed or they needed a small mend. And he knew the jacket was a favourite of Mrs Clump's. He couldn't contemplate not finishing the repair.

The next day, Hen skipped lunch and went straight to his room to continue the repair. He was just trimming off the extra thread from a line of stitching when he heard a loud bell ringing. The Sparrow Down fire engine, perhaps?

Hen returned to his work.

The bell stopped.

But seconds later it started again – and Hen realized it was *inside* the house. Drawn to the staircase, he peered over the bannister.

'Hello?' Hen called. 'Is everything OK?'

He heard hasty footsteps on the stairs and Uncle Bertie appeared on the landing below, red-faced and panting. 'Henryton ... didn't you ... hear ... the ... the bell?' he wheezed.

'That was you?'

'Yes, yes! Hurry downstairs at once!' Uncle Bertie seemed rather agitated. Hen followed him downstairs.

Everyone was assembled in the back hallway. Uncle Bertie clutched his trusty clipboard in one hand, whipped out his pocket watch with the other, muttered to himself and then scribbled something down.

'Bertie, dear, is this really . . .' Aunt Lucia started to ask but after a sharp look from Uncle Bertie, she fell quiet.

'Henryton, that was . . . well, frankly, a pitiful response time. Two minutes and thirty-nine seconds! I dread to think where that would leave us in a real-life situation.'

Hen looked at Nana and Connie, hoping one of them might be able to explain what situation he was talking about, but they both looked equally confused.

'Constance, good job, twenty-two seconds!'

Connie smiled, but stopped when she noticed Hen watching.

'Lucia, dearest. Adequate for now, but perhaps speed things up next time?'

'I had to close the shop, Bertie – we had customers.'

'Yes, yes. And Mother . . .'

Nana scowled at him.

'Well, a little more effort next time would be appreciated,' he said quickly without looking at her. Uncle Bertie made a few more notes on his clipboard and then shouted, 'Spell-brats!'

Everyone jumped.

'Who can tell me something about spell-brats?' Uncle Bertie asked. Connie's hand went straight into the air, of course. 'Ah, Constance?'

'Spell-brats are one of the most dangerous pests for spelled garments,' she said.

Hen knew that. Everyone knew that. That was the easy bit!

'And why is that . . . Henryton?' Uncle Bertie pointed his pencil straight at Hen.

He sighed and started to explain. 'Because they're attracted to the magic in the spell stitches and they—'

'Well, no, that's not exactly correct,' Uncle Bertie cut in before Hen could finish. 'They *feed* off the magic in the spell stitches, Henryton. I rather thought you would have known that, my boy.'

Hen felt his cheeks burn. 'But that's what I was about to say!' he said.

Spell-brats were bad news for spell tailors, along with the hissing weevil and great purple moth. They had been around as long as there had been spelled garments. He thought about Mr and Mrs Jelani again – and hadn't Connie said a spell-brat infestation had helped finish off Uncle Bertie's shops, too?

Uncle Bertie ignored him and unfurled a small poster that read:

KNOW YOUR PESTS IN THE WORKPLACE

It was covered in pictures of spell-brats, hissing weevils and great purple moths, as well as their eggs, chrysalises and various development stages too. All labelled in great detail.

'And what's the best method for deterring spell-brats?' Uncle Bertie asked next.

Hen put his hand straight into the air before Connie even had a chance to and smiled across at Nana. They had discovered a foolproof way to keep spell-brats out of the shop.

'Yes, Henryton?' Uncle Bertie sounded rather disappointed.

'Dried shleep dung and lavender oil,' Hen said proudly.

Nana gave him a thumbs up across the hallway.

Connie snorted with laughter and Aunt Lucia pulled a face.

'I beg your pardon?' Uncle Bertie said, stepping closer to Hen. 'What did you just say?'

'Dried shleep dung and lavender oil,' Hen repeated, wondering if Uncle Bertie hadn't heard him properly.

'Oh, Hestia preserve us,' Uncle Bertie said, glancing up at the ceiling and clutching his clipboard to his chest.

'But it really does work,' Hen said.

'Yes, Bertie,' said Nana, 'Hen's right. Dried shleep dung mixed with lavender oil repels spell-brats. We make little bundles of them wrapped in hessian and all tied up with ribbon.'

'Oh, so that's what they are,' Connie said, sounding more intrigued than disgusted.

Uncle Bertie's mouth was gaping, a bit like a freshly caught mackerel, and eventually he said, 'Well, I've heard it all now! You can't have dried shleep poopy around garments. What would our customers say if they found out?'

Nana silently mouthed, *Poopy?* at Hen, who smothered a laugh.

Nana said, 'I imagine they'd be quite pleased to know that it was keeping away spell-brats, Bertrand, dear.'

'Well, I'm sorry, but we cannot continue like this. Henryton, you will please remove all of the . . . homemade cure. We will be ordering some of the new spell-brat traps to deal with any future situations.'

'No,' Nana said firmly.

'Mother?'

'Bertrand, you will leave the spell-brat remedy in place. I am not arguing with you about this. If you want to order traps, too, that's your decision – but aren't we trying to keep costs down?'

They stared hard at each other for a few seconds before Uncle Bertie huffed and changed the subject.

'Well now, back to the real purpose of the drill.' Uncle Bertie reached for a large brass bell. 'If any spell-brats are spotted anywhere in the shop, work-room or house, then you are to come straight to the bell and ring it thus—'

Uncle Bertie set about ringing the bell again, shaking it vigorously for about twenty seconds and then thankfully stopping, before starting up again almost straight away. Hen was sure he had burst an eardrum at some point. Even when Uncle Bertie held the bell still and quiet, Hen could still feel the ringing in his head.

Eventually, Uncle Bertie continued his explanation. 'If you hear the bell you are all to assemble here immediately – no matter what other task you are performing. I shall then supervise a thorough search of the building, starting with the location of the initial sighting. All spelled garments are to be secured at once. Constance and Henryton, that will be your job. There will be two large metal trunks in the workroom for that purpose. Mother, Lucia, you will assist with searching out the spell-brats and . . . eradicating them!' At this Uncle Bertie stamped his foot on to the tiles and made a very definite grinding motion with his shoe.

'Does everyone understand?' Uncle Bertie asked, looking from Hen to Connie, to Nana and then finally to Aunt Lucia who was busy inspecting a fidgeting Connie – no doubt to be sure she hadn't already been infested with spell-brats.

Everyone nodded.

'One last thing. Please be on the lookout for—' Uncle Bertie suddenly brandished a small crocheted spell-brat, slightly larger than the real thing and rather more jolly looking too, Hen thought. 'I have hidden several of these dummies throughout the house. Whoever finds one and rings the bell will initiate our first spell-brat drill. So be on alert at all times. Your diligence could be the very thing to save us all!'

Uncle Bertie smiled and tucked the crocheted spell-brat back into his waistcoat pocket. Then he clapped his hands and called, 'Dismissed!'

Hen kept a lookout for crocheted spell-brat dummies on his way up the stairs, wondering where Uncle Bertie might have hidden them. He was both relieved and annoyed not to have found one by the time he got back to his bedroom.

He flopped on to his bed and had just picked up Mrs Clump's nearly fixed jacket when, from downstairs, he heard the clamouring call of the bell and groaned loudly.

No doubt Connie had found the first one – she was insufferable!

CHAPTER SEVEN

BAD NEWS

Once Hen had fixed Mrs Clump's beloved jacket – thank goodness! – life settled into a new rhythm for a few weeks, as everyone adjusted to living and working together. Hen didn't like Uncle Bertie's new rules but whenever he spoke to Nana about it she would smile and say, 'You catch more flies with honey than with vinegar, Hen. Besides, needs must.'

He wasn't entirely sure what any of that actually meant.

And his parents' letters had been full of nothing but positive, encouraging words on the subject: 'chin up old boy' and 'things can't be that bad!'. So he was trying his best, he really was!

One wet Saturday, as the chapel bells were sounding out midday, Hen and Connie were hurrying back home after a busy morning of errands. As usual, their conversations had been brief, polite and businesslike. Hen was slowly getting used to her being there and tried to chat, but she never chatted back and tended to keep any answers as short as possible. Hen had decided she'd make a great spy! And the few times he had asked her to join him in a game, she always had something important or urgent to do in her bedroom or had forgotten something downstairs.

They were passing Fancy's Department Store when Connie stopped dead, upsetting a few passers-by who swerved around her. She tugged on Hen's jacket and pointed into the shop window where a large poster was being unfurled:

COMING SOON TO FANCY'S –
SPELLED GARMENTS FROM
TIBERIUS PEPPER

A photograph of Tiberius Pepper was underneath. Despite his smile, he appeared to glare out of the poster at Hen and Connie, half his face hidden behind his huge beard. 'So that's him, is it?' Hen asked. 'I always assumed he was just a made-up person – it doesn't sound like a real name at all. But there he is. And look at that beard – reminds me of Great-great-uncle Guido's!'

Hen had always been rather afraid of the painting of Uncle Guido in the staircase gallery, but he kept that part to himself!

So now Fancy's was selling spelled garments? *And* from Tiberius Pepper?

'Oh, knots!' Hen moaned.

'That's what happened back home,' Connie said, her voice trembling. 'Suddenly everyone seemed to be selling Pepper garments and everyone else wanted to buy them. They're a bit cheaper than traditional tailored clothes – and off-the-rail so you don't have to wait. People went mad for them. Dad's shops went downhill pretty fast and that was even before the spell-brats.'

Hen blinked at her. She hadn't said so much to him in ages. 'Don't worry,' he said, gently. 'Your dad and Nana have got everything in hand, right?'

'I bet they don't even know about this,' Connie said flatly. 'They're so preoccupied with fixing things that don't need to be fixed . . .'

Hen blinked again in surprise. She *agreed* with him? 'Well . . . should we tell them?'

Connie sighed. 'Honestly, Hen, I don't think they'd listen.'

'Besides,' Hen said, 'a small collection in a department store is hardly competition for us, is it?'

But Connie didn't reply.

They trudged silently back to Danelli's and were climbing the short flight of steps to the entrance when a very tall woman emerged from the shop. She was swathed in dark velvet from neck to ankle and her hat, perched on top of her head, was a twist of stiff material with a little net veil. It was a striking outfit, Hen thought – not to his taste but it certainly made an impact! Hen and Connie stepped aside on to the pavement to let her pass.

'Thank you so much, Mr Danelli, a true . . . delight,' she said, glancing up again at the shop. 'Such a pleasure to meet you at last, and see your lovely *little* store.' She smiled a smile that was all teeth and no joy back at Uncle Bertie, who stood in the doorway seeming totally entranced.

Uncle Bertie held a huge woven basket in his hands, overflowing with fruit, flowers, cakes, biscuits and paper twists filled with sweets. It wasn't unusual for grateful customers to leave gifts, but Hen had never seen anything so extravagant before.

'This is very generous, Mrs Thackerey,' Uncle Bertie said from behind the huge basket.

'Oh, but it's our complete pleasure, Mr Danelli,' Mrs Thackerey said, her voice as sweet and smooth as treacle.

'I will need time to consider everything,' Uncle Bertie added more gravely. 'I do need to make sure that this would be right for— Ah!' He jumped slightly when he noticed Hen and Connie waiting beside the door.

'Oh, of course,' Mrs Thackerey replied as though she didn't really care one way or the other. 'Take all the time you need. Ah, these must be your dear children?' She leant forward and pinched Connie's cheek with her bony fingers.

Hen felt oddly protective of his cousin and had to stop himself from slapping Mrs Thackerey's hand away. He hadn't been sure at first, but now he knew there was something about this woman he just didn't like.

'My daughter, Constance,' Uncle Bertie beamed.

Connie half smiled and rubbed at her cheek,

which had gone red after the pinch.

'Oh . . . and my nephew, Henryton,' Uncle Bertie said, as though Hen were an afterthought.

'Delightful,' Mrs Thackerey said, already fixing her attention on the street. She paused to fasten a button on her coat and snap open her umbrella. Then she cast one last look at Uncle Bertie and sailed down the steps and into her waiting motorcar. 'I look forward to speaking to you again soon, Mr Danelli!' she called through the open window.

The car pulled away into the traffic. Hen saw a single gloved hand raised in farewell as Uncle Bertie called, 'Of course, Mrs Thackerey. Good morning, Mrs Thackerey!'

'Ahem!' Hen coughed. 'It's afternoon now, Uncle Bertie.'

'What? Is it?' Uncle Bertie ambled absent-mindedly into the shop, setting the basket on the counter. He was clearly preoccupied and blushing.

'Who was that?' Hen asked, following him inside. 'A new customer? What's with the huge gift basket?'

'Not a customer . . . an . . . admirer,' Uncle Bertie said eventually.

Something didn't feel right to Hen, though he couldn't put his finger on it exactly. He glanced over at Connie. She looked just as worried as he felt.

At dinnertime, Aunt Lucia was singing happily to herself in Scillian, a language which Hen only knew little bits of, even though Scillia was where Nana was from, originally. He stopped and listened for a few moments. Aunt Lucia had a lovely voice.

'You know she was a famous singer before she met Dad?' Connie said, appearing at his side. 'Isn't she good?'

'She really is,' Hen agreed, shooting her a small smile.

'Ah, all done down there, my dears?' Aunt Lucia said, hurrying towards them from the kitchen door and patting them both on the head and face as if checking for injuries. 'Hen, you look tired. An early night for you, I think. And Constance, did you manage to go to the toilet yet? I know you get a little bound up when you're upset about things.'

'Oh, Mother,' Connie groaned.

Aunt Lucia smiled sweetly. 'You can set the table, if you like.' She moved gracefully as she lifted a bubbling pot from the stove and brought it to the vast white sink, which had a colander sitting at the bottom. With one quick move Aunt Lucia poured out the boiling water, instantly shrouding herself in clouds of steam.

Hen and Connie went through into the dining room. Hen fished out the cutlery while Connie grabbed dishes and they started to work their way around the table. The usual polite silence settled between them and Hen felt rather disappointed. He wasn't sure, exactly, but today Connie had seemed a little less aloof – and a little more like an ally. He liked to pretend that he didn't care one bit how things were with Connie, but he did.

At the head of the table, the spot that Uncle Bertie had claimed for himself the very first evening they had arrived, Saturday's edition of the *Hampston Courant* waited to be unfolded. The newspaper was Uncle Bertie's very favourite and he always read it after dinner with a cup of coffee, in total peace and quiet. As Hen went to move the paper so that he could set out a knife, fork and spoon for Uncle Bertie, he glanced at the front cover.

'Oh!'

Hen dropped the cutlery, which jangled on to the table. Connie jumped.

'What's the matter?' she asked.

Hen pointed down at the headlines.

'"Gloria Garden to film new moving picture on location at Hightop Moor"?'

'No.'

'"Shleep rustlers strike again on Craggy Head"?'

'No, Connie – the main headline!' Hen jabbed his finger at the newspaper.

TIBERIUS PEPPER TO OPEN NEW FACTORY IN BRACKWOOD

'Oh, Hen, no!'

Connie started to quickly read the article, keeping her voice low. '"The *Hampston Courant* has recently learnt that fashion factory owner Tiberius Pepper is opening a new purpose-built factory in Brackwood—"'

'That's only half an hour away,' Hen interjected, his heart racing.

'"Mr Pepper, who already owns three clothing factories, is believed to be opening his new premises to focus on his . . . expanding range of spelled clothing."' Connie's voice faltered before she continued. '"Tiberius Pepper confirmed his plans, saying, 'There is clearly a huge demand for my stylish yet affordable products. Just look at my sales figures and the queues at every store stocking my clothes. People want cheaper, more convenient clothes. Nobody uses old-fashioned spell tailors any more.'''

Connie peered over the top of the newspaper at Hen, her mouth a perfect circle of shock.

'This is bad,' said Hen, thinking back to the poster in Fancy's window that morning, his mind racing. 'Way worse than a few dresses in a department store. If they're opening another factory, that must mean they're really scaling up—'

He stopped suddenly as he heard Aunt Lucia, Nana and Uncle Bertie on the landing.

'Oh, quick, hide it!' Connie thrust the newspaper back at Hen. 'My dad'll have a fit!'

But Hen thrust the paper back at Connie. 'No, you hide it!'

'Hen!' Connie shoved the paper back at him; it was getting more and more crumpled as a result. 'Just stash it somewhere, anywhere, quickly! Please.'

She looked thoroughly distraught, and in that moment, Hen felt nothing but pity for her. He took the paper.

'It smells delicious, Lucia!' Nana called brightly as she arrived in the dining room doorway. Hen glimpsed Uncle Bertie behind her and quickly shoved the crumpled newspaper on to his chair and plonked down on top of it.

'Steady on there, Henryton, old chap,' Uncle Bertie warned as the chair wobbled, threatening to tip over. 'Got spell-brats in your pants?'

Before he could reply, Aunt Lucia entered carrying a big dish of steaming pasta which she placed in the middle of the table. The aroma of the herby, garlicky, rich tomato sauce filled the room. Connie leant forwards, her hand stretched towards the serving spoon, but stopped as Uncle Bertie warned, 'We shall still say our graces, Constance, thank you. We are not animals!' Connie coloured. Hen had never seen Uncle Bertie tell her off before.

They all bowed their heads.

'Watch over our household and our work, gentle Hestia,' everyone murmured. 'May all our stitches stay strong and the threads of our lives be long and always twist back together.'

A few more seconds of quiet thought followed, interrupted only by the loud gurgling rumble of Hen's stomach. And then Aunt Lucia was dishing out servings and the dining room filled with gentle chatter and even some laughter. As they ate, Hen cast his mind back over the past month and a bit, since Uncle Bertie, Aunt Lucia and Connie had arrived. The time had flown by *and* taken about a hundred years, somehow. How different this was from him and Nana eating by themselves in the kitchen!

After the last spots of sauce were mopped up with warm bread, Hen and Connie set about clearing the table. As Hen set the dirty plates on the kitchen counter, he realized he had forgotten entirely about the newspaper! He hurried back, but Uncle Bertie was already staring at the crumpled remains of the *Hampston Courant* on Hen's seat. 'Were you sitting on my newspaper, Henryton?' Uncle Bertie asked, puzzled.

'Um...' Hen looked quickly at Connie for help of any kind; after all, she'd got him into this tangle!

'It was delivered like that,' Connie fibbed, taking Hen entirely by surprise.

'What?' Uncle Bertie sounded far from convinced.

'It was. It was all smooshed up like that when it was delivered.' Connie smiled quickly at Hen, her eyes wider than wide.

'Oh yes, just like that,' Hen agreed.

'Well, that's utterly disgraceful. But why were you sitting on it?'

Hen clammed up. 'Um...'

'Hen was trying to, er . . . flatten it out!' Connie supplied – there was no stopping her now!

'By sitting on it?' Aunt Lucia asked with a little giggle.

'Yes,' Connie said.

'Well, that's most peculiar, I must say.' Uncle Bertie sighed. 'Anyway, you can let me have it back now, Henryton. Thank you.'

'Who's for pudding?' Aunt Lucia asked, getting to her feet.

'I'll have mine later,' Uncle Bertie said and held out his hand for the newspaper.

Hen glanced at Connie, who shook her head slightly, eyes pleading.

Uncle Bertie leant forwards to lift the paper from the seat, but Hen was faster, snatching it up.

'Henryton, the newspaper, please,' Uncle Bertie said crossly.

Terror snatched at Hen from all angles. He couldn't think what to say but he really didn't want to let Connie down, so he held the paper mutely.

Uncle Bertie took hold of the paper and tugged.

Hen held tight and tugged back.

'Henryton, is this some sort of game?' Uncle Bertie asked. 'It's rather tiresome. Will you please give me the newspaper!'

Aunt Lucia and Nana were watching this rather bizarre tug of war across the dining table with increasing puzzlement.

Hen knew he couldn't win; he was just delaying the inevitable. He glanced at Connie, who shrugged helplessly – she knew it was hopeless too.

With a sigh, Hen let go. Uncle Bertie staggered back a little. Sheets of newspaper fluttered to the floor and Uncle Bertie huffed and puffed as he gathered them up and tried to straighten them out. 'What on earth has got into you this time? I'll have to write to your parents—'

Uncle Bertie fell silent.

He had seen the headline.

Connie's face paled. 'Dad—'

Uncle Bertie held up his hand, silencing her.

'Bertie, dear, what is it?' Aunt Lucia stepped forward.

Uncle Bertie glanced around at them all and then back at Hen before hurrying out of the room.

CHAPTER EIGHT

THE UNHAPPY CUSTOMER

Uncle Bertie locked himself in his little cupboard-office in the workroom for the rest of the evening. Hen heard him talking quietly on the telephone when he went down to feed Marjorie. And later, as Hen was drifting off to sleep, he heard Uncle Bertie climbing the stairs, every one of his footsteps heavy and slow and tired. This was followed by a hushed conversation just outside Hen's bedroom door between Uncle Bertie and Aunt Lucia, and then everything went quiet.

Connie and Hen met the next morning on the landing outside the bathroom, both wrapped in their dressing gowns. Connie looked as though she hadn't slept well.

Hen was just about to slip into the bathroom when Connie grabbed his hand and said quickly, 'It was really really kind of you to do that last night and get yourself into trouble with my dad.' Connie had two bright red blotches on her cheeks and her eyes were watery.

'Oh, it's OK, Connie—' Hen started.

'No, it's not. I've been horrible and this can't have been easy for you at all. Us all just landing here and taking over like this. I promise I'll try to be better.' She reached out her hand. 'Friends?'

'Friends,' Hen said, shaking her hand. 'Now, can I go? I really need the loo!'

Later, Hen was helping mind the shop when a lady bustled in, brandishing a Danelli-branded box and looking rather angry. 'Who. Was. Responsible. For . . . this . . . this absurd garment?'

Hen couldn't recall the lady's name, though he did recognize the dress she pulled unceremoniously out of the box, waving it in front of Uncle Bertie's face over the counter. It had been the second garment Nana had let him complete the spell stitch on.

Hen felt cold and hot all at once.

'I am so terribly sorry that you're not satisfied with your purchase, Mrs Crab. Of course we would be only too happy to—'

'All I wanted was one of the famous Danelli dresses,' Mrs Crab said, her voice tremulous and nasal. '*Get one*, all my friends told me. *Worth every penny! You'll look a thousand guineas!* I'll be a laughing stock, more likely.' She threw – actually *threw*! – the dress straight at Uncle Bertie and it smacked him in the face and then slid silkily down on to the counter.

Uncle Bertie was quite purple at this point. 'If I could just ascertain what the defect is, Mrs Crab . . . an issue with the cut, perhaps, too long? Too short? Too tight, maybe?'

Mrs Crab flashed Uncle Bertie a dangerous look that made him go from puce to pale in a second. 'And what exactly does *that* mean, Mr Danelli?'

Aunt Lucia stepped forwards quickly, like a calm breeze on a scorching hot day. 'I think my husband just wants to know what's wrong, Mrs Crab. Then it can be fixed – at no extra charge, of course.'

Hen watched her examine the stitches quickly. 'A standard spell stitch to . . . flatter your figure,' she whispered. 'All the stitches seem to be in order and correct.' But then she squinted and peered uncertainly at the dress. It was just for a second and then she beamed up at Mrs Crab again. 'Excuse me for just one moment,' she said, then rang the silver bell to summon Nana upstairs from the workroom.

What had she seen? Hen wondered, starting to panic as they waited for Nana to arrive, Aunt Lucia pouring Mrs Crab a soothing cup of tea from the pot on the side. Nobody could stay mad at Aunt Lucia for long.

Nana reached the shop floor a few moments later – Connie following close behind. Uncle Bertie quickly relayed the story in hushed tones. Then, Nana lifted the defective dress up, a puzzled expression on her face. She cast a quick worried look straight at Hen.

Oh knots! he thought. *What on earth have I done now?*

'But there is certainly something wrong with it, Mrs Danelli,' Mrs Crab was telling Aunt Lucia. 'It's the singing, you see. I cannot bear the singing, it drove me quite to distraction and brought on one of my tension migraines.' Mrs Crab clasped the bridge of her nose between her gloved right thumb and forefinger.

'Oh dear,' Aunt Lucia said gently.

'And that's not the half of it,' Mrs Crab said. 'It got far worse.'

'How so?' Uncle Bertie asked.

Mrs Crab checked there were no other customers around and quietly said, 'Last week at the chapel service . . . *I* started singing.'

Uncle Bertie looked at Aunt Lucia then back at Mrs Crab. 'Singing? Singing a hymn?'

'Not a hymn,' Mrs Crab said darkly.

'What was it, then?' Connie suddenly burst into the conversation, her voice full of mischief.

'Constance!' Uncle Bertie and Aunt Lucia said quickly, silencing her.

'Well, that's the very worst part of this whole thing. It was . . .' Mrs Crab took a deep breath. 'It was "Honey, Get Me Some Pie". I, er . . . gather it's quite popular on the radio.' She sniffed and looked away.

Aunt Lucia, Uncle Bertie and Nana exchanged bemused glances.

Hen knew the song – it was on the radio all the time. He and Nana would often sing along to it or dance around the workroom with Lottie.

Honey, I don't need me no love!
Don't promise me the moon, stars or sky.
Honey, don't want me no jewels nor silver nor gold,
Those things just gonna make me sigh.
I know what I want, I know what I need,
Honey, get me some pie.
Get it or I'm surely, surely gonna die!

Connie was stifling her giggles into her bunched-up apron behind the counter.

But Hen felt quite cold. He had stitched the spell, so whatever had gone wrong – and by Hestia it had gone wrong with bells on! – it was his doing. He could already imagine Uncle Bertie's reaction. He wouldn't be allowed near another spelled garment until he was about thirty-seven!

'Mr Danelli, something must have gone wrong with your spells.'

Uncle Bertie straightened to his full height and fiddled with the measuring tape around his neck. 'Danelli spell stitches are the finest in the whole of Ingle, Mrs Crab. My mother would have personally stitched this garment, spell included, and she sewed the wedding dress for the Queen of the Giants—'

'Yes, I know, Mr Danelli – even though, if you'll excuse me, that was all quite some time ago. And I'm sure none of them had to put up with the singing!'

Nana glanced across the shop to where Hen had been standing this whole time.

'Perhaps there was something wrong with the last shipment of fabric, Bertie?' Aunt Lucia suggested quietly.

Uncle Bertie seemed to consider this for a moment. 'Well, we've not had other garments returned like this. I don't think it was the fabric. Where was that thread from? Holbein's? Snackett's?'

Hen had a sinking feeling. Actually, it was more of a 'being swallowed up by the whole world' sort of feeling. 'Mother?' Uncle Bertie asked again. 'The thread?'

Hen knew Nana would cover for him, somehow. But he couldn't let her – he couldn't bear it.

'It was me, Uncle Bertie,' Hen said into the silent shop. He couldn't look at Mrs Crab, though, and he tried not to look Uncle Bertie in the eye. 'I stitched Mrs Crab's dress. I must've messed it up, somehow.'

'Oh!' Mrs Crab gave a little gasp. 'You let apprentices work on finished garments, do you? I'm quite sure that's not how things work at DuMarnier's in Feddleston.'

DuMarnier's had long been seen as a rival to

Danelli's, though Nana and Madam DuMarnier were actually very good friends.

Uncle Bertie was glaring at Hen and breathing fast – in angry little snorts, like a bull. But he quickly composed himself as he turned back to Mrs Crab. 'Leave this with me, Mrs Crab. I will get this all sorted for you as soon as possible, or you are welcome to a full refund if you would rather.'

Mrs Crab sniffed. 'I suppose I should let you try to correct whatever this error is, but I can't wait for days on end, Mr Danelli. I want it back by the end of the week.'

Uncle Bertie nodded his head solemnly at the unnecessary deadline. 'Of course. That's very gener-ous of you, Mrs Crab.'

Mrs Crab sniffed, swept the room with a disap-proving gaze and then hurried out of the shop. Hen could hear her barking at a passer-by outside. 'Get out of my way, *imbecile*!'

Everyone stood quiet for a moment, listening to the hustle and bustle of Beacham Terrace through the door, which Mrs Crab had left wide open.

'Hen, the door,' Nana said quietly.

Hen pushed the door shut, grateful for the brief chill of the afternoon air on his hot face.

Uncle Bertie breathed out slowly and turned away from Hen, towards the curtained archway. 'We will discuss this later, Henryton. But there will be consequences, you understand?' He vanished through the curtain before Hen could reply. Aunt Lucia followed him with quick footsteps, casting Hen a sympathetic glance – and after a moment's hesitation, Connie hurried after her father, too.

'What did I do wrong?' Hen asked Nana quietly.

He stepped towards the counter, peering carefully at the dress, which Nana was holding gently. It looked like any Danelli-style dress: the cut, the shape of the collar, the pleats. All trademark Danelli work.

And then Nana reached forwards, took his left hand and placed it gently on to the folded material. It was cool and silky under his fingers.

And after a few seconds he heard it.

'Honey, I don't need me no love!
Don't promise me the moon, stars or sky . . .'

It was as though the radio were playing in the next room – nearby, but out of sight. Except, the frequency wasn't great and the song was stuttering out in snippets and fragments, as though snatched by the wind.

But Hen knew the radio wasn't playing in the next

room – or anywhere in the house. Besides, when he lifted his fingers from the dress, the song stopped.

'What is that?' Hen asked eventually.

Nana hesitated. 'I'm not sure,' she said. She stepped back to the counter and placed the dress carefully into its box.

Her voice trembled as she spoke. She was lying, Hen was sure of it. The cold wave of fear crashed against him again.

'Nana?'

She turned – forced a smile on to her pale, drawn face. 'Oh, you've just muddled the spell threads, that's all, love.' She peered at him through her silver spectacles.

Hen was quite sure he hadn't. He remembered checking several times before he began – and Nana had checked afterwards, too. 'No, I don't think I did.'

'Look, it's nearly time to close anyway. I can sort things here, you run on up and help Lucia get dinner started. We can discuss it tomorrow when Bertie has calmed down a bit, OK love?'

The dress boxed away, Nana reached up and tucked it on a high shelf.

Out of sight.

But not out of mind . . .

CHAPTER NINE

Other Duties

The next day, Hen, Uncle Bertie and Nana sat in the workroom over three steaming mugs of tea. 'Now, Henryton,' Uncle Bertie began gently, 'as head of the household—'

Head of the household? Hen gulped. He really meant business!

Nana patted Hen's hand. 'Bertie,' she said, a warning edge to her voice. 'Remember what we talked about?'

Uncle Bertie cleared his throat. 'Ah, well . . . it falls to me to be the one to deal with any . . . problems. And we certainly seem to have experienced some problems recently, don't we?'

'Yes,' Hen said miserably, picturing Mrs Crab's angry expression as she'd chucked her dress at Uncle Bertie.

'We're not angry, Henryton. But I want to understand what happened with Mrs Crab's dress. Have you been practising your spell stitches properly?' Uncle Bertie asked.

'Yes, of course.'

'And you haven't been ... experimenting?'

'No,' Hen said. 'I only use the stitches from the book. Nana knows that.' He looked at Nana. Why wasn't she standing up for him?

'Then how do you suppose the error occurred?'

'I swear on Hestia's needles, I don't know how that happened to Mrs Crab's dress.'

There was a pause, and then Uncle Bertie said kindly, 'I don't believe you do.'

'Then tell me!' Hen said, exasperated. 'I won't get better if I don't know what I did wrong!'

Nana seemed to be on the verge of saying something but Uncle Bertie got there first. 'The main point is, Henryton ... Mother and I have spoken and we think it best if you perhaps take a break from stitching for a while.' Uncle Bertie beamed, as though this were a wonderful idea and would be lots of fun.

Hen felt like the world was caving in.

'Nana?' He looked at her pleadingly.

She smiled so kindly that it hurt all the more when she said, 'I have to agree with Bertie on this, love. I think it's for the best, just for now at least.'

If he couldn't stitch, what was he supposed to do? He wouldn't be allowed to help with the new collection, he wouldn't even be able to practise. And worst of all . . . 'What about the guild contest?'

'We'll have to see about that,' Nana said carefully.

Hen knew grown-ups always said 'We'll see' when they didn't want to say 'no' outright!

The workroom shuddered with silence. Hen was pretty sure he was about to cry. 'But I want to help,' he said. 'With everything that's going on . . .'

'Oh, and you will, my boy,' Uncle Bertie said. 'See, the broom is just over there.' He pointed across the workroom. 'You'll start by sweeping up in here. Then, you will please sort the button trays. How anyone can find anything in them is beyond me!'

'All afternoon?' Hen asked with a sniff.

'A clean workplace—' Uncle Bertie began, pointing to the workroom rules up on the wall.

'—is an efficient workplace,' Hen finished with as much enthusiasm as he could muster.

Which wasn't much at all really.

After dinner, Hen returned to the workroom to finish sorting the buttons. There was something calming about the job; at least if his mind was focused on sorting, he didn't think about everything else. About what an utter tangle his life seemed to be in at that moment!

He heard the clock in the hall strike nine and Nana called down, 'Hen, love, it's getting late. You should be getting ready for bed.'

He didn't reply. He didn't want to talk to Nana just then – he was feeling really sore about how she'd sided with Uncle Bertie, banning him from any stitching. *Let her worry about me!* Secretly, he wanted her to come down and check on him, and when she didn't he felt more abandoned than ever. Eventually, he stood up, put away the tidy buttons and gave Marjorie a scratch behind her horns and a fresh carrot.

'Goodnight, Marjorie.'

The shleep blinked her huge dark eyes sleepily at him and gave a deep purr of satisfaction before she started to munch.

As Hen stood at the bottom of the stairs leading up into the family apartment, he looked up at his Danelli ancestors staring back at him from their paintings and photographs. 'I don't suppose any of you spent the day sweeping up and sorting buttons,' Hen mumbled to them.

He guessed that was probably why they had ended up in the family gallery, after all; by not being troublemakers. As he started to climb the stairs, his mind flicked back to Mrs Crab's dress.

Perhaps he should take a quick look?

Perhaps then he might know what he had done wrong?

If nobody wanted to tell him, he would have to find an answer himself!

He slipped through the green curtain and into the shop, which was all in darkness, though one of the gas lamps on Beacham Terrace cast just enough light to see by.

Hen quietly moved the stool behind the counter to the shelves where Nana had stashed the box containing Mrs Crab's dress. Carefully, quietly, he clambered on to the stool, reached for the white box and placed it on the counter. He lifted off the lid.

There it was, neatly folded. Hen glanced quickly at the curtained doorway and then over to the window of the shop.

He carefully lifted the dress up, holding it to the flickering light from outside.

The spell stitch Hen remembered rested in the middle of the garment's back panel. An elegant stitch for concealing and flattering, straight from the family book. And yet . . .

He squinted.

There was something here he didn't recall – something different, extra.

Near-invisible stitching blossomed from the main spell circle, pluming out across the fabric, twisting and curving in different directions. The effect was rather like a cloud or a strange flower. In some parts the stitching was little more than a single line and in others it was dense, stitches sewn and over-sewn again and again.

It felt so familiar to Hen . . . but he had no memory of doing it. How was that possible?

It was mesmerizing. Hen felt himself reaching out.

He let his hand rest lightly on the extra stitches and heard the song again.

But it was more than that. Hen felt a gentle laugh

bubble up inside him. He felt light and happy . . . which was amazing, given the day he'd had!

'Hen?' It was Nana calling again from upstairs.

Startled, he snatched his hand from the dress. The singing stopped immediately, but he still felt the joy, the lightness. He could even feel the warmth from the workroom fire and the gentle smell of Nana's favourite hand cream!

What was going on?

Quickly and carefully, Hen put the dress back into the box and the box back on to the shelf, shaking the whole time.

CHAPTER TEN

The Attics

A few days later, Hen and Connie walked along Beacham Terrace after the morning's errands. Connie was suggesting ways for Hen to get back on her dad's good side – and into the workroom on something other than sweeping duty.

'Maybe ... bake him a cake?' Connie said.

'Really?' Hen asked.

Connie shrugged. 'I don't know. My dad has never been mad at me for more than a day before, and he's certainly never made me sort button trays!'

Hen smiled and shook his head. Connie had been

true to her word; they were friends, now, and it felt good to have someone on his side. He hadn't told her about the odd stitches on the dress, though – honestly, he wasn't quite sure what to say, or what it all meant.

'Actually I did have an idea, Connie,' Hen said. 'I've been thinking about it for a while.'

'Oh?'

Hen slowed his pace, delaying their return to the shop. 'The Ingle Tailors' Guild Fair is coming up next month. There's a contest for young spell tailors and it's going to be at the Cloth Hall in Hampston this year.'

'And ... you want to enter?'

'Well I thought perhaps we could, together. Something we design and stitch, and everything.' Hen suddenly felt nervous. He studied his shoes. 'It's always more fun working with someone. And ...' *And perhaps Nana and Uncle Bertie were more likely to let him enter if Connie was involved!* he thought. But he said, 'And if we win, that might show Uncle Bertie and Nana that I can stitch, after all.'

Connie had stopped and was looking at him.

It was a bad idea. A stupid idea – he should never have suggested it!

But then Connie reached out, grabbed his hand and smiled.

'Well, it's really sweet of you to ask me, Hen. Especially after everything . . . but I'm not sure my dad will go for it.' She smiled.

'Well, maybe we could chat to Nana and your mum first? They might help us out.'

'Yes, OK, why not,' Connie said a little reluctantly. 'Leave it with me.'

As they drew closer to the shop, Hen saw Rosie Metcalfe, whose parents ran the Dragonfly pub. She was waiting on the steps and looked rather agitated. She held a small parcel wrapped up in brown paper.

'Oh, no,' Hen mumbled, a sinking feeling forming in his stomach.

'Hi, Hen,' Rosie smiled. 'How're you doing?'

'Hi, Rosie, this is my cousin, Connie. Is everything OK?'

'Yes, well, no, actually. I was just wondering if . . . well, do you think you might be able to fix something for me? Tommy Burman from the chemist said you were the man to ask. I'll sneak you a free lunch next time you stop by?'

Hen's heart sank. 'Oh, Rosie, I'm sorry but—'

'Oh, but you have to help. It's my sister's favourite blouse and she doesn't know I borrowed it and she will go bananas if she finds out I had it and . . . ripped it.'

'I'm not really supposed—'

Rosie thrust the blouse into Hen's arms. 'Say yes, Hen, go on! Just say, "Yes, Rosie, I'd be delighted to fix this for you."'

'*What* is this?'

The shop door had swung open behind Rosie and Uncle Bertie loomed in the doorway, glowering down at Hen, who now held the torn blouse in his hands.

'Hen was just offering to fix this for me,' Rosie said brightly, with not a clue as to the damage she was doing.

Hen looked up at his uncle.

'It wasn't like that, Dad, honestly.' Connie tried to help.

'Inside, Constance, please . . . now!'

Connie sighed, gave Hen a desperate look and shoved rather angrily past her dad.

Uncle Bertie took a deep breath and looked from Hen and the damaged blouse to Rosie and back again.

Hen braced himself for Uncle Bertie's scolding. But he just turned and slowly went back inside without a word. He left the door wide open and Hen could see him watching from the counter.

'I'm really sorry, Rosie, but I can't fix this.' Hen passed the blouse back, turned and hurried inside.

He had to explain. He had to make Uncle Bertie see this wasn't his fault. 'I'm very disappointed, Henryton,' Uncle Bertie said as soon as Hen stepped through the door.

Connie and Aunt Lucia were behind the counter, watching. Nana must have been down in the workroom.

'I thought I had made it quite clear that, as of now, we, and specifically *you,* no longer repair clothes.'

'I know, Uncle Bertie, I was just—'

'No. No more explaining. No more excuses. I'm sorry it's come to this, but well . . . you will not set foot in the workroom or shop until further notice.'

'But I—'

'Is that clear?'

'Bertie!' Aunt Lucia said.

But Uncle Bertie wasn't listening. 'You will be going up to sort through the accumulated junk in the attics for the inventory.'

Hen couldn't believe it. 'For how long?' he asked.

'As long as it takes,' said Uncle Bertie.

Hen paled. *Sorting through all that junk? I'll be stuck up there for months most likely. Years, even.*

'Once the work is complete, we will reassess the situation.'

Hen's head buzzed like it was filled with bees. He could feel himself shaking with anger and frustration. This was so unfair! He'd said no to the wretched repair! He wanted to argue but he couldn't find the words. So in the end he just blurted, 'I suppose you'd prefer it if I lived up there too? Then it'd be like I didn't even exist!' And at once he felt tears sting his eyes and rush down his cheeks. He didn't want to cry, but he couldn't stop now.

Uncle Bertie just stared at him with a face full of disappointment.

Connie hurried to Hen's side. 'Dad, Hen didn't agree to mend that girl's blouse. This isn't fair!'

Uncle Bertie turned on Connie. 'Constance, go and have your lunch and then help your grand-mother in the workroom with the collection samples. I don't wish to hear any more about it.'

'But—'

'NO!' Uncle Bertie said, his voice booming around the shop. It made Connie jump, made the glass in the display cases jingle. 'Everything he's done is damaging what little reputation we have, don't you all see? We are a reputable spell tailor's. One of the finest in all of Ingle. We don't stitch silly mistakes into our dresses. And we are certainly not some tuppenny-ha'penny old seamstress fixing tears in a back room!'

Connie scowled at her father and stormed through the curtain and upstairs.

Hen felt a little emboldened by her sticking up for him and asked sharply, 'Can I have some lunch? Or am I banned from that now too?'

'Take it up to the attics,' Uncle Bertie said, and Hen knew from the look on his face that now was not the time to argue.

Uncle Bertie handed Hen the key.

'Fine,' Hen said. 'I'd rather be up there anyway . . . away from you!'

And he raced away, tears streaming down his face once again.

Hen squeezed past the rickety chest of drawers and into the attics. He wiped away his tears with his sleeve and dumped the wretched clipboard on the floor. The attics were as awful as he remembered: there was barely enough space to stand. Everywhere seemed quite stuffed with . . . stuff. It sat in huge heaving piles and quivering stacks or lay in long drifts everywhere. More stuff than he'd ever have time to sort through, let alone log on Uncle Bertie's stupid inventory.

Hen groaned. If he was doomed to spend time here, he had to let in some more light.

A cloud of dust wafted into the air as he fought his way over to the three arched windows looking down over bustling Beacham Terrace. Dead and dried-out insects were caught in the net of dusty cobwebs that straggled across the grimy window-panes. He found an old broom with a wonky handle and an almost bald brush, and used it as best he could to sweep away the cobwebs. A startled spider hurried across the window ledge. Hen jumped and was about to bash it with the broom but he hesitated. The spider rushed away to the top corner of the window, well out of reach. Hen shuddered. 'OK, well, you stay up there out of my way and . . . I won't broom you, OK?'

Next, he took a tattered old dust sheet that was

thrown over a pile of boxes and cleaned some of the grime from the windows. The spring light grew stronger and tiny dust specks danced in a beam of sunlight, which landed on the pile of old garments Hen had spotted before.

'So much waste,' Hen muttered. 'These could be used! *Should* be!'

Despite the dust and cobwebs, he started sorting through the junk, his curiosity piqued. Among the furniture, chests and boxes he'd noticed last time, he spotted wardrobes, crates and baskets full of more old and abandoned garments. He opened a chest and pulled out two long dresses no one had worn for a hundred years or more – then, a stiff collared jacket. A nearby suitcase contained a pile of strange hats and shoes with tarnished old buckles.

Hen couldn't see any reason why he shouldn't sort through the old garments first. He dragged two large, wonky tables into the light of the windows, creating a makeshift workbench. That done, Hen started to sort through the piles of clothes, dragging anything that looked beyond repair to one side, and starting new piles on the workbench of things he thought could be reused somehow. Hen held each and every piece up to the light, heartened as his imagination fired with new ideas, new shapes, new styles! There was enough fabric here to make ten or more new collections of outfits! His mind whirred with ideas...

Then he remembered Uncle Bertie.

He wouldn't want to keep any of it. If he found out about all of this stuff, it would just be thrown away.

It made Hen feel so sad to think about it all just going in the bin.

He worked tirelessly, occasionally hearing the chapel bell which sounded the hours throughout the day. When the light started to fade, Hen realized it must be late afternoon. He had no way of lighting the attic so he would have to finish up – he was surprised at how disappointed he felt. As he turned back from the windows he was amazed by how much he had already achieved and also how much like a workroom the attic now looked, with the makeshift workbench and all the sewing tools he'd found in an old dresser. And a plentiful supply of fabric! He could make a start on his and Connie's competition entry easily...

Did he dare?

No. It was a silly idea – he was already in enough trouble. And he should probably hide away what he'd found just in case Uncle Bertie decided to poke around again.

Hen was searching for somewhere to stash what he'd sorted when his eyes fell on the cupboard he'd noticed last time. He felt, again, the strange crackling tension. What was in there? He picked his way over to the cupboard and pulled the doors open . . . but all he found inside was an old biscuit tin. As Hen lifted it out to make space for his fabric collection, the lid of the biscuit tin popped loose and clattered to the floor. Inside was nestled a piece of creamy silk.

Hen popped the tin back down and reached for the silk to see what it was. Perhaps this was another old garment he could reuse somehow?

As he touched the silk, a quivering tremble raced through him and it felt like the air in the attic had been swapped. A warm, soft breeze tickled his neck. When he breathed in, he smelt not the dusty attic but the sunshiney, summery scent of lemons and unmistakably sea air.

He turned, expecting to see that the windows had somehow blown open. But they were closed and the dust sheets near the window were as still as ever. The warm breeze was only blowing in Hen's immediate vicinity . . . but how could that be? Even as he watched, the light around him changed too, brighter and warmer. And even the floorboards where he crouched looked different. Then he heard someone muttering quietly as though whispering a secret to themselves. And from outside he was sure the velvety cooing of the resident pigeons had been replaced by the wheeling cry of seabirds.

Hen turned and peered around the attic, which now seemed to ripple with a soft light. And just a few feet away from him, close enough to touch, sat a girl, head bent carefully over a long piece of fabric. She pulled a needle and thread quickly and expertly through it, one foot gently tapping against the honey-coloured floorboards at her feet as though keeping time to a piece of music.

He felt sure he was looking at a spectre, and therefore that he should probably be scared, should scream out for someone to come . . .

But Hen had the most overwhelming sensation that he was safe here, that there was nothing at all to fear. That, in fact, he was in the safest place in the world.

He was overcome with the very certain feeling that he was home.

Then the girl looked straight at him.

'Hello,' she said.

CHAPTER ELEVEN

SPECTRES?

'Pins and needles!' Hen jumped, dropping the spelled fabric.

There was one more gentle ripple of warm, lemony air as the piece of silk slid to the floor, but then the breeze stopped, and the musty smell of the attics returned. The soft light, honey-coloured floorboards and the girl, so focused on her work, had vanished.

The warm, safe feeling began to dissipate as Hen tried to work out what had just happened.

Shock ran through his body. Suddenly, he didn't want to be in the attics alone any longer.

He hurried to the stairs. He was in such a rush to get out that he slipped on the steps and ended up at the bottom much quicker than he'd expected.

'Twist it!' Hen muttered to himself as he tumbled on to the landing.

'Santa Hestia!' It was Aunt Lucia. She hurried towards him. 'Oh, Hen, are you OK?' She helped him to his feet and began to check him over. 'Look at you, all covered in dust and cobwebs, my poor darling. Are you hurt?' She hugged him tight. 'Have you been up there all this time?'

Hen opened his mouth but nothing came out. What should he say to her?

What *could* he say to her?

Well, actually, Aunt Lucia, I saw a spectre sewing upstairs in the attic and could hear seagulls and smell lemons.

As soon as he got wind of it, Uncle Bertie would have him carted off to the Underbridge Sanatorium before you could say doolally-flip!

'I'm fine . . . I just . . . slipped on the stairs,' Hen said.

'Poor love. Why don't I run you a nice warm bubble bath before dinner and you'll be all fresh, yes?'

Aunt Lucia was already bustling off along the landing towards the bathroom, humming to herself. Hen caught sight of himself in the mirror on the wall, his dark hair and face grey with dust and cobwebs dangling from his clothes. No wonder Aunt Lucia had suggested a bath. *He* looked like a spectre!

He couldn't believe the attics were haunted! He had just seen an actual, real spectre up there . . . hadn't he?

So why wasn't he more frightened?

The sensation that he had travelled somewhere – somewhere *safe* – lingered. It was too confusing – it was giving him a headache!

He could hear the water gushing out of the taps into the bath as Aunt Lucia bustled out of the bathroom with a fresh towel.

'Dinner won't be ready for a while yet, so have a nice long soak. You look like you need it,' she said.

Aunt Lucia went off downstairs and Hen made his way along the landing to the bathroom. As the door closed behind him, he gave a long, shuddering sigh.

The following afternoon, back in the attic, Hen moved carefully towards the piece of fabric from the biscuit tin as though it were a wild animal that might attack him if startled. It lay just where he had dropped it, on the floor beside the makeshift workbench.

Even at a distance, he could feel it: the gentle but powerful hum of the magic at work on the fabric; the vibration of the spells stitched into it was like a regular spell stitch and yet . . . not.

He jumped clear out of his skin when a sudden noise sounded nearby – but it was just a lone pigeon flapping past the windows.

He leant closer to the fabric, looking for the spell but not daring to touch it. There *was* something about the near-invisible stitching that spread out across the panel, something *familiar*.

Yes, there was no doubt in his mind: it reminded him strongly of the odd stitching on Mrs Crab's dress. Except, these threads were even more elaborate. The curious stitches bloomed out across the fabric like flowers or fireworks. There was no spell stitch he knew that looked like it. There was no order to this spell stitch. It was wild and beautiful!

Hen reached for the piece of silk.

What was he doing?

He held it in his hands and stared at the unusual

stitches for a while, taking slow, deep breaths. Then he let his fingertips brush ever so lightly against them.

The thread was smooth and oddly warm, like the first rays of spring sunshine. He quickly dropped the material back down on to the floor.

He was suddenly pretty sure of two things.

One, it wasn't a spectre he had seen in the attic yesterday, and two, the strange stitching on the fabric panel and the stitching he had done to Mrs Crab's dress were somehow, impossibly, the same.

But he didn't know what to do next. Should he tell Nana and Uncle Bertie about it? He probably should. Or was it possible they already knew? They'd both been rather odd about what they thought his 'mistake' might have been. Perhaps he should investigate a bit more first, by himself, and then decide whether to tell anyone?

And there was only one way he was going to find out more.

'Hestia protect me,' he muttered, and breathed out slowly as he reached again for the piece of silk and those strange, beautiful stitches.

Because it had fallen among a drift of dust, it now also carried a collection of dead, dried insects and tangles of cobwebs. He spotted two large husks, brittle and see-through, like empty butterfly cocoons but larger. He made a mental note to bring up some of Nana's spell-brat remedy – just to be on the safe side – though these husks were probably from decades ago. He swept all the debris and dust to one side with his shoe and shook the panel of fabric out, the light dancing across the delicate stitching of the peculiar spell.

He realized that this was what he had been planning to do all along. He had just been trying to convince himself that he was thinking it through.

He held the swirling stitches in both his hands. This time, he wouldn't let go.

Hen felt that strange sensation of the room changing, the light altering, brightening. He felt the air get warmer and soon he could smell the scent of lemons and the tang of the sea, hear the gulls crying out. Hen held the stitches more tightly and the scene continued to not only unfold before him like an opening blanket but surround him, wrap him up and draw him in until . . .

. . . until his attic was no more!

Hen was now somewhere else, somewhere quite different. A row of cobweb-free windows flooded the space with light and the view outside . . . Well, it wasn't the rooftops of Sparrow Down. He saw sloping hills, covered in lush trees and dotted here and there with small white buildings with orange-tiled roofs.

The room he was standing in was a bedroom, tucked under the eaves of a different house. Here, the whitewashed ceiling sloped along the pitch of the roof, meeting the whitewashed wall. A cosy bed waited in the far corner. Beside it was a small cupboard with books stacked on top and a small oil lamp beside them. A warm, brightly coloured rug covered the floor nearby.

This was not a room where junk was dumped. This was a room that was cleaned and looked after and cared for. A room where someone lived.

Hen turned around, his eyes widening as he noticed how, behind him, a swirling circle of golden light had appeared. The circle seemed to be made of hundreds and thousands of threads. Instinctively, he thought it might be an opening of some sort . . . He peered closer. Somewhere between the swirling golden threads he could glimpse the safety of his attic.

The back of Hen's neck prickled. He turned around.

A girl, the same girl he had seen the day before, sat on the edge of the bed. She was leaning over a flowing tumble of fabric, absorbed in the task of sewing, chewing her lip in concentration.

She was perhaps a year or two older than Hen and wore a long dress of light creamy fabric that skimmed her ankles. Her pale hair was tied with twisting ribbons that fluttered over her shoulders and down her back.

She fixed him with large blue eyes.

'Oh, Hestia protect me. Look, I'm sorry,' Hen spluttered. 'I'm not sure how I ended up here...' He trailed off and laughed nervously.

'Hello,' the girl said. She smiled warmly, as though she had been expecting him. She let the sewing rest in her lap as she turned her full attention to Hen.

Hen swallowed. Why wasn't she surprised to find a strange boy in her bedroom? She surely hadn't been expecting him?

'My name is Milly,' the girl said.

'Hi. Um, I'm, Hen,' Hen said, reaching out a slightly shaking hand. But then he realized too late that the girl hadn't actually finished talking. 'Oh, I'm so sorry,' he said, blushing.

But she carried on as if she hadn't heard him.

'This is my memory of home. You are very welcome here and free to explore.' She gestured to the door and the hallway beyond, flooded with brilliant light.

'This is a memory?' Hen asked. His mind raced. No wonder she wasn't hearing or responding. She was a memory of a person, but not a person herself. Hen's pulse quickened as he realized what he was experiencing – a different type of spell stitch! A new one . . . or actually, a forgotten one!

He glanced down the corridor again. He was keen to explore and find out what else might be contained in the memory . . . but then he turned his attention back to the gateway of stitches. He didn't fancy venturing further before he knew how to return home. 'Is that the way out?' he tried.

Milly's eyes were fixed somewhere in the distance – but this time, she sort-of answered his question. 'If you stray beyond the edge of the memory you will return to this place. You will come to no harm here. To leave, simply return to the aperture.' She indicated the strange swirling golden circle.

The light in the room flickered slightly and suddenly Milly was leaning over her sewing again. Hen frowned. She looked up and repeated her greeting, as if noticing him for the first time. 'Hello. My name is Milly. This is my memory of home. You are very welcome here and free to explore.'

Hen stared at the aperture as Milly continued her speech – her words, inflections and motions exactly as they had been before.

He glanced over his shoulder regretfully at the corridor bathed in light. He so wanted to venture deeper into the memory – but he was scared. He'd never experienced magic like this before. Besides, he was already in enough trouble as it was! For once, he would do the responsible thing: return home and tell Nana and Uncle Bertie everything.

Hen stepped through the swirl of golden threads and back into the attic, where he found his fingers had lifted away from the elaborate stitches. Otherwise, everything was as it had been when he'd left. He stood for a few moments, catching his breath – he felt as if he'd just sprinted up the attic stairs. A warm waft of air lingered, as did the feeling of safety, togetherness and home. Hen felt quite wonderful – and a little dizzy with excitement!

He gazed down at the spell threads, holding the cloth carefully in his hands. 'They hold a memory!' he said aloud to the quiet attic. And if the stitches held a memory, and his stitches on Mrs Crab's dress were the same type . . .

'Oh!' Hen cried. Suddenly it made sense: Mrs Crab's dress contained his memory of sewing while listening to the radio! The stitching had been simple, compared to this – perhaps that's why only the song had been fully captured?

Hope fluttered in his chest. What if these memory stitches could help Danelli's somehow? If he discovered how to use them properly? He was pretty sure the factory garments of Tiberius Pepper wouldn't have anything like memories!

And maybe, just maybe, Uncle Bertie would stop being so cross with Hen once he showed him what he'd unearthed . . .

He clutched the material excitedly. Hen felt sure this could change everything.

He raced downstairs, eventually finding Nana and Uncle Bertie in the workroom with Connie. Although he had quickly planned what to say, his excitement got the better of him and he blurted, 'I know I'm not supposed to be down here, but did you know you can stitch memories into clothes? I think that's what I did with Mrs Crab's dress!'

Connie glanced up from her pattern pinning,

alert. Nana locked eyes with Hen and shook her head slightly, as if in warning. She looked as though the wind had been taken out of her sails, even reaching for the edge of the table for support. Hen had never seen her look so old. His elation crumbled.

'What's going on?' he said, weakly. Glancing from Nana to Uncle Bertie to Connie in confusion.

Then, Hen realized that there was another person in the workroom, a lady. Smartly dressed, she had a small hat perched on her neatly curled grey hair. Uncle Bertie would never bring a customer into the workroom, Hen was sure. So who was she?

'We're just in the middle of something, Henryton.' Uncle Bertie said it so politely that Hen knew full well he was going to be in a heap of trouble again later. Then he turned back to the lady and asked, 'You're quite certain, Councillor Bir?'

The lady twisted her lips and sighed. 'I'm afraid so, Mr Danelli. I saw the papers this morning myself. I came as soon as I could . . . I felt certain you would wish to be informed at once.'

Hen moved around the workbench towards Connie as the grown-ups continued talking. 'What's happening?' he whispered.

Connie glanced quickly at the grown-ups and

then edged a little closer to Hen but carried on pinning out the pattern. 'That lady is from the town council in Brackwood. She says Tiberius Pepper isn't building a new factory at all, he's setting one up in an old mill. He could be operational in a few days, she thinks.'

'Oh, knots!' Hen murmured.

Connie nodded in agreement. 'Double knots!' Then she leant closer. 'Anyway, what were you saying about memories when you came in?'

'Oh, I . . .' he fluffed, feeling his face turn bright red. He wasn't sure about sharing his discovery with Connie, not just yet. He really should tell Uncle Bertie and Nana first. 'I'll tell you later,' he said eventually.

Connie turned back to her work. 'Can you hold that bit of the pattern straight for me?'

Hen smiled and reached out to hold the pattern still.

The grown-ups' conversation was coming to an end.

'It was very kind of you to come, Councillor Bir, thank you so much,' Uncle Bertie said sadly.

Councillor Bir sighed. 'I'm sorry to be the bearer of such grievous news for you all. But I knew you'd want to know, Mr Danelli.'

'Business is business,' Uncle Bertie said, forcing a smile. 'We're not done for just yet, Councillor.'

'Glad to hear it, Mr Danelli,' she said softly, though she didn't sound convinced. 'I'll see myself out.' She smiled across at Hen and Connie as she walked back towards the stairs, and Uncle Bertie sank straight into the nearest chair and brought one hand to his forehead as though he had a bad headache.

Hen stood up and walked over to Nana. The timing felt odd, the mood in the room flat and hopeless – but memory stitches could be the very thing to save his family business. He had to tell them.

'Have *you* ever heard of a memory stitch, Nana?' he asked quietly, sliding on to the bench beside her.

She quickly reached out, placed her hand over Hen's and said very quietly, 'I'd leave that subject well alone if I were you.' She glanced at Uncle Bertie. Was she checking that he wasn't listening in to their conversation?

'But Nana, you don't understand what I've found. There's this amazing—'

'No,' Nana said, her voice still quiet but full of power. 'Dangerous, too dangerous. Drop it, Hen. I mean it.'

Dangerous? He'd felt so safe in the memory. So secure. But he knew better than to argue with Nana. Now, clearly, was not the time. Disappointment twisted his stomach but he kept his mouth shut.

Uncle Bertie rose to his feet and wandered into his little cupboard-office, scratching his head and sighing. Nana said a little more brightly to Connie and Hen, 'Why don't you two run along and fetch us all some tea?'

It wasn't a suggestion.

CHAPTER TWELVE

The Memory

Hen couldn't sleep that night. He tried some warm milk. He tried counting shleep. He tried reading his book. But it was no use: his thoughts kept churning away. He was so certain that he had discovered something amazing and yet at the same time Nana had been so adamant he should drop it. She had seemed worried – scared, even – at the very mention of memory stitches. That in itself confirmed that Nana knew what they were – and that she hadn't wanted Uncle Bertie to know Hen knew about them.

Everything screamed to Hen to leave the memory

stitches well alone.

And yet, as the chapel bells sounded midnight, he found himself in the attic with a candle, determined to find out more.

He carefully lifted the silk panel from the tin, making a note to find some tissue paper or muslin to wrap it up in to help keep it safe. Half a heartbeat after his fingers pressed the soft threads of the stitches, he felt the space about him rearrange itself. Night became day. He heard the gulls outside the windows, saw the blue sky and green hills. Milly was sitting exactly as before.

'Hello. My name is Milly. This is my memory of home,' she started.

Hen didn't hesitate; he hurried past Milly and headed for the doorway that led into the rest of the house.

He had goosebumps; he was excited and nervous at the same time. Once out in the narrow, bright corridor beyond Milly's room, Hen wasn't sure exactly where to go. The walls were painted white and a trim of blue and yellow tiles ran along their base. Open doors led off on both sides. Light flooded in through the doors and a large window at the opposite end of the hallway, through which Hen could see orange-tiled roofs and chimneys with thin curls of smoke lifting to the bright blue sky.

As he walked, Hen felt he could stay in this sunshine-filled, lemon-scented memory for ever. He strongly felt that Nana was wrong: there couldn't possibly be anything to be worried about here, in this memory full of light and warmth.

Hen had never felt so safe and at home.

The dark floorboards creaked comfortingly as he walked along the corridor. Through the next door Hen found an old gentleman – or the *memory* of an old gentleman – tending to some plants with bright red flowers. He was humming a tune. The plants filled the room with the most amazing earthy, fresh scent. Hen knew at once this was Milly's grandfather and he hummed along with the tune too.

How amazing that he now knew this tune from this memory, as though he had heard it every day of his life.

The old man didn't look around but carried on tending to his plants. Hen left quietly, though he was sure the old man wouldn't know if he was there or not and he probably could have gone in and jumped on the bed if he had wanted to!

The next room was an empty bedroom, so Hen carried on to the staircase. He walked downstairs, emerging into the main living space: part kitchen, part sitting room. A large copper kettle hung over the hearth and warm red tiles lined the floor.

Outside, he could hear bright music playing. Would he be able to pass through the large front door and on to the street to find its source? Before he could find out, the sound of talking drew him on across the room and through a curtained archway.

He found himself in a small workroom. Milly and her grandfather sat opposite each other, each holding a length of fabric over their laps.

This was a room for secrets. Hen could feel it in the tips of his fingers.

Milly glanced towards Hen without quite fixing her eyes on him, which he found a little disconcerting. 'This is my memory of my grandpa showing me how to stitch memories,' she said before turning back to her grandfather.

Hen felt like he might faint! This was perfect: it was as if the memory had known he wanted – needed – to see this.

He stepped forwards carefully, slowly. He was

afraid he might somehow disturb this moment and it would all vanish.

'My Milly,' Grandpa said gently, reaching out a hand and taking one of hers. 'It is time to show you a new spell stitch . . . this one, though, is not one to use for just any old garment. Save it for something and someone really special. I am going to show you how to memory-stitch.'

Hen looked at Milly, desperate to see her reaction. 'Memory-stitch? What is that?' she asked.

'It is a way to save a memory – its feelings, sights and senses – in a garment for ever,' Milly's grandfather said proudly, and brought forth a crisp white shirt that Hen could see quite clearly was covered in what he now recognized as memory stitches. 'This was the shirt I made to wear the day I married your grandmother – I stitched the memory of our wedding into it.'

Milly leant forward and peered at the shirt and then at her grandfather. Hen could tell by the slight smile on her lips that she didn't entirely believe the old gentleman. 'Is this a joke?' she asked. 'That's not really possible, is it?'

'No joke, my Milly,' the old man said. He reached forward and took her hand, quite gently, and then brought her fingers down to brush the stitches on the shirt.

No more than a few minutes passed, during which Milly was still, though not like a statue, more like she was asleep with her eyes open. Then she let out a little gasp and wobbled forwards slightly. The old man reached out to steady her and chuckled gently as she cried, 'Hestia's needles . . . I . . . I was *there*, Grandpa. I saw it all!'

She hugged the old man tightly and as they broke away, she took the shirt in her hand and held it close to study the memory stitches. 'How does it work? What thread do you use? Oh, I have so many questions!' Milly's voice bubbled with excitement, she could barely stand still and Hen knew just how she felt! He had edged forward, slowly, and was now right in the midst of the conversation. He had to keep reminding himself that they couldn't see or hear him. It was just like watching a moving picture . . . except he could smell the slightly musty air in the room, the fresh cleanness of Milly's hair, the peppermint scent of Grandpa. And he felt the thrill from Milly at being shown memory-stitching for the first time.

'Who taught you how to do this, Grandpa?' Milly asked.

'Some people can do it and others cannot – and our family have a knack for it,' he said. 'I stumbled upon the skill by accident. Then, my mother taught me the rest.'

The back of Hen's neck tingled. He'd discovered it by accident, too!

'So how does it work?' Milly glanced at the shirt again and then at her grandfather.

'Well, you can stitch your own memory or someone else's, if they share the memory with you.' As he spoke, he reached for a large square of sandy-coloured linen, which he handed to Milly, and then he passed her a small fabric wallet. *That must contain their spell needles*, Hen thought. 'Focus on the memory,' Grandpa said. 'It can help if you say it aloud as you sew.'

Milly nodded. She took up her needle, threaded it and straightened the linen square on her lap. Then she took a deep breath and looked at her grandfather.

When he didn't continue, she said, 'That's it?'

He nodded. 'That's it. As you start to sew, your mind sort of . . .'

'Takes over,' Hen said out loud at the same time as Grandpa.

'Well, that all sounds rather vague and unhelpful, Grandpa, thank you!' Milly said, unable to hide her frustration.

The old man chuckled. 'I'm sorry. I don't know how else to describe it. There is no pattern, for each memory has its own unique shape and form. The magic doesn't come from the stitch, it comes from you: the stitch just holds the magic and memory in place.'

'But what if I can't do it?' Milly said. Hen felt her tremor of familiar fear.

Grandpa smiled warmly. 'Well you won't have lost anything, will you? You had no idea these things existed until now. But, you'll never know unless you try.'

'I'm scared . . . I think.'

'Doing anything brave requires ten per cent forethought and ninety per cent imagination!' Grandpa said with a broad grin.

Hen smiled. It sounded just like the sort of thing Nana would say to him. It suddenly occurred to Hen that these people must be members of his family, since their things were in his attic. Perhaps they were distant relatives – great-aunts, -uncles or cousins three times removed.

'OK,' Milly said uncertainly.

'Would you like me to share a memory of mine for you to stitch as practice, Milly?' Grandpa reached out, gently taking her free hand in his own.

'Yes please.'

'OK, are you ready?'

She nodded.

The old gentleman started to tell a story of a boat trip around some islands not far away. Hen didn't quite catch the name of them. Grandpa talked happily about the colour of the water in the bays and coves, the numbers of fish he saw, the warmth of the water. Even more amazingly, Hen watched as Milly began to stitch – at first it looked like she was stitching waves into the cloth and then something seemed to take her over. Her body became still, but for her busy hands, her eyes fluttering not quite open, not quite closed, and her mouth, which seemed to move as though she were talking at the same time as Grandpa.

All the while, the stitches on the linen square grew and grew, radiating outwards from the centre like ripples in a pond or an unfurling flower. It was truly beautiful. She was clearly very skilled, and Hen was impressed at how stunning her first attempt was.

In fact, he was mesmerized by it. Again there was an unmistakable similarity between the stitches he was watching Milly sew, the stitches that had formed the memory he was experiencing at this very moment, and the less elegant and less effective stitches he had sewn into poor Mrs Crab's dress!

Hen wondered what had become of the square of linen that carried the boating memory. Could it be in the attic somewhere?

He yawned.

Despite everything, he suddenly felt overcome with tiredness. He should get back to his bed.

He turned as the memory began to play out again, returning to the beginning of its sequence.

He knew they couldn't hear him, but as Hen reached the doorway he turned and said, 'Goodnight.'

CHAPTER THIRTEEN

ANNOUNCEMENT

Hen slept solidly, exhausted by the excitement of his midnight visit to Milly's memory. When he woke he thought briefly about going straight upstairs and exploring the memory once more. He wanted to see Milly stitching, to see again how it all worked. He wanted his stitching to be as beautiful as hers! He had so many questions and so many ideas. Surely the memory-stitching could change everything for them all . . . if Nana would only let him show her there was nothing to fear.

But at the very least, he would tell Connie. She

was clever and she might just have some ideas about how to bring Nana around.

But Connie sneezed twice during breakfast and was deemed by Aunt Lucia to be suffering from some rare and likely life-threatening ailment. Hen was sent on the morning's errands alone – and when he returned, Connie was tucked up in bed while Aunt Lucia fed her broth and fussed over her pillows and the exact amount of fresh air to let into her bedroom. Hen was instructed to keep away to avoid contamination.

Sitting cross-legged on his bed after lunch, Hen decided to work on the design for his and Connie's garment for the Guild Fair contest. No one had said he wasn't allowed to sketch designs, had they?

He was working out how to combine some of the fabrics he had seen in the attic for the back panel of a coat when he heard Uncle Bertie's shout from downstairs.

'To the sitting room, everyone, please. Quickly!' His voice was high-pitched and full of excitement. 'Mother, Lucia, Hen, are you all coming? Shut up the shop! Quick, quick!'

Hen hurried downstairs. He could see Uncle Bertie by the sitting room door ushering Nana in so fast she nearly tripped over the rug. Even Connie had been dragged out of bed and was sitting in the armchair by the fireplace wrapped in her dressing gown and two blankets.

'All right, Bertie,' Nana said. 'Honestly, is there a fire? An infestation of spell-brats? Or have we won the Ingle lottery?'

Hen slipped into the sitting room and perched on the arm of Nana's chair. She smiled warmly at him and took his hand in hers, giving it a squeeze, and then rolled her eyes, making him laugh. Hen thought perhaps he would try to talk to Nana again about the memory stitches, maybe when Uncle Bertie had finished his announcement?

Uncle Bertie took up position beside the fireplace and beamed maniacally at them all. 'Well, now we're all present I've some VERY exciting news. Or rather –' his eyes darted to Connie – 'we've got some exciting news.'

Hen glanced at Connie. For some reason, she didn't meet his eyes, but stared straight ahead at the fireplace as she slowly got to her feet to stand beside Uncle Bertie. She looked far from happy or excited. In fact, Hen thought she looked as though she was about to be sick.

Connie and Uncle Bertie exchanged a glance and Uncle Bertie actually giggled like an over-excited child. It was pretty weird!

'Go on, then,' Uncle Bertie said, giving Connie a gentle push.

'Oh, no – no.' Connie blushed, and then she *did* look at Hen – but she looked rather wretched and it made a cool coil of worry twist in his stomach. Uncle Bertie stepped away and gestured to Connie, like a magician's assistant.

'Erm . . . well . . .' Connie stuttered. 'There's a . . . competition this year at the Guild Fair . . . for young spell tailors . . .'

Hen's twisting worry turned to disbelief. *No. She wouldn't have done that.*

Uncle Bertie was suddenly at her side and talking over the top of her. 'And Connie is going to be entering a garment for Danelli's. I've just sent off the entry form! The prize is several important commissions, worth about a year's income, as well as the honour of the award of course. Isn't that too marvellous? We shall close and all go for the day. I have to be there anyway, but we could make it a fun day out for us all!' He threw his arms into the air to encouraging noises from Aunt Lucia.

It sounded anything but a fun day out to Hen. He glanced at Nana anxiously, her face pale and drawn.

Hen sat, motionless, as though he had been turned to stone. 'Oh, but I think there's been a misunderstanding,' he said, in a small voice. 'I've been wanting to enter the contest for ages, and actually I suggested Connie and I might enter something together, didn't I, Connie?' He swallowed. 'Maybe we could still do that? Two pairs of hands are better than one!' His hopeful tone sounded grating even to his own ears.

He could feel himself blushing as everyone's attention fixed on him.

'No, I don't think so,' Uncle Bertie said simply.

'But, that's not fair . . . Nana?' Hen turned to her for support but she sat studying her hands intently, and when she finally looked up at Hen her face was quite blank.

'Hen, we've agreed that you're not to do any stitching at the moment, hmm?' Uncle Bertie said, not unkindly.

The sitting room fell silent but for the mantle clock ticking away the awful seconds.

'I . . . I'm going to have a lie down,' Nana said at last. 'I feel awful. Must have a touch of whatever it was poor Connie had this morning. We can chat about . . . about whatever it was later, OK?'

Slowly, everyone else followed – Connie shot Hen a pleading glance as Aunt Lucia ushered her back to her bedroom, but he turned away. Uncle Bertie offered him an awkward pat on the shoulder before he left, too.

Hen sat for a while alone. He felt angry at the unfairness of it all, then sad, then he felt determination grow inside him. He'd show them. He'd make his design for the contest anyway, and he'd use the amazing new memory stitches, and then they'd all see what he could do.

He heard footsteps in the doorway and turned.

It was Connie. 'I'm sorry, Hen, I really am—' she started.

'Oh, don't bother,' Hen snapped.

'I actually brought it up with Dad after we spoke about it because I could see how much it meant to you. I thought I could persuade him to let us enter together.' Her jaw tightened. 'I should have known he wouldn't listen.'

'Well . . . you should have made him listen! You should have refused to enter without me!'

'I know, but—'

'You thought it would be easier if you entered alone? Didn't want to share the spotlight? Or risk working on something with me, the family disappointment?'

'It's not like that, Hen,' Connie said. 'The business—'

'Seems to me it's exactly like that, actually,' Hen replied. He could feel tears prickle behind his eyes. He didn't want to cry in front of Connie. He didn't want her to see he was *that* upset. But he felt so horribly betrayed and cheated. He'd thought he and Connie were becoming friends.

It felt like that was all in shreds and tatters now.

'Just leave me alone.' Hen turned, barged past Connie and raced back up to his room, slamming the door behind him.

He glanced at the photo of Mum and Dad on his bedside table, beaming out happily at him. He wished they were here. Or better still, that he was with them somewhere else. He snatched up his coat design. He'd been so excited to show Connie the design and the memory stitches he'd discovered. He'd so wanted to work on it together. Now, he just wanted to rip the drawing into bits and throw it in the bin.

He slumped on to his bed and thought about pulling the quilt over his head, letting the world just vanish, collapse in on itself. He didn't want to see anyone ever again.

But he did want to go back up to the attics, to feel the safety and warmth of the house where Milly had lived, however many decades ago. He wanted to smell the lemon-scented breeze that danced through that house full of sunshine and love and warmth. He glanced out the window; it was a grey day and rain splattered against the glass.

As he pulled open his door, though, he found Nana standing there.

'Are you all right?' she asked. She still looked a bit ill. Her eyes were watery, her face drained of colour.

But Hen didn't say anything – he couldn't. He just stared past her.

'The contest was my idea,' he said at last, his voice wobbling, fresh tears welling around his eyes.

'I'll speak to your uncle about all of this, I promise. But . . . well, please go and make friends with Connie. She's very upset.'

'No way.' He couldn't believe Nana was taking Connie's side. 'I suggested we enter the competition together. It was all my idea. She told me Uncle Bertie wouldn't go for it – then she went behind my back and asked him to enter on her own!'

'I'm sure it's not as straightforward as that. You know how your uncle can be – Connie would have been saying one thing but he'd be hearing another. I know Connie feels terribly about it all.'

'Good,' he snapped.

'I know you don't mean that,' Nana said.

'Actually, I do.' His words were hot and angry and he regretted them at once.

'OK, you're upset,' Nana said calmly. 'That's completely understandable. But don't let this fester, Hen. You are so stubborn – not the finest Danelli trait, actually. But you can fix this. *You* have a gift for repairing things, unlike anyone I have ever known. And most things can be mended, love – dresses, shirts, friendships ... even family –' her voice caught a little – 'so long as they're not left too long in pieces.' She smiled sadly at the last part. 'So mind you don't leave it too long, Hen.'

CHAPTER FOURTEEN

The Festival

When Nana had left, Hen raced back up into the attics. As soon as he returned to Milly's memory, he headed past Grandpa's room and downstairs. This time, he ignored the voices from the workroom. Instead, he wanted to step through the large door in the sitting room, to find out where that music had come from. Could he explore outside? How far did the memory extend?

He pulled the front door open.

He gasped in surprise as a stream of people surged past. They waved bright banners, sang and laughed. Some wore strange masks, others wore garlands of flowers and leaves. A band headed up the procession – although Hen couldn't glimpse them over the heads of the crowd, he could hear their lively music. It was some sort of festival.

Hen was caught up in the surge of people and soon found himself bustling along the narrow streets beyond Milly's house.

How vast was this memory? He suddenly worried that he might get lost, but remembered Milly saying that if he strayed beyond the edge of the memory he would just find himself back near the aperture.

The street was narrow, shaded from the bright sunshine, and was lined with tall buildings constructed of soft pink or buttery yellow stone. Small wrought-iron balconies jutted out from many of the upper floors, and flags and banners were strung from building to building.

He caught sight of Milly a few steps ahead. Compared to everyone else in the crowd, she stood out somehow – like she was brighter, in sharper focus. Hen supposed it was because this was her memory.

As he was carried along with the crowd – though somehow never stepping on anyone's toes or bumping into anyone! – Hen caught glimpses of small courtyards and narrow alleyways to his left and right. They passed a chapel, the walls covered with row upon row of little pottery saints. Then, the twisting street passed through a tall, broad archway and Hen was spat out into the wide square beyond. The piazza was festooned with fluttering flags – so many that it was hard to see the sky between the brilliant scraps of colour. And at the centre was a circle of large palm trees, their vast leaves swaying in the warm breeze.

Everything was flooded with light. Everyone was happy and smiling as the crowd scattered.

Hen watched as Milly ran towards a boy a couple of years older than her. He scooped her up into his arms and swung her around. The piazza seemed to echo with their shared laughter. Hen hurried forward for a better view. As he did, he realized that in spite of the happy festival mood, this memory was now also tinged with worry and sadness.

As Hen drew closer he noticed that Milly had been carrying a travelling bag, which she now placed at the boy's feet. 'You didn't look inside it, did you?' he asked as he picked up the bag.

'No, why would I?' She sounded a little offended. 'What have you got in there anyway? The family silver?'

It was a joke and yet the boy fidgeted restlessly. He looked as though he was about to say something more but then just shook his head.

Then she softened and said, 'You don't have to go. Grandpa will calm down in a day or two. He's forgiven you. Please stay.'

'I can't forgive myself, though. Besides, he never really thought I had it in me to run the shop, you know that. Especially now after all that's happened.'

'But that wasn't your fault, not really. Perhaps if you just—'

'No,' he snapped. And then more gently, 'Look, I have to find my own path, Milly. The boat's leaving soon. Thank you for fetching my things.' He clutched the bag close.

'Well – maybe – just go back and say goodbye to him first, please.' She sounded more desperate now. 'Don't leave everything broken like this. Mend it.'

The boy glanced away with tears in his eyes. 'Some things just can't be mended, Milly. But how's about a dance before I go?'

And suddenly the music seemed to swell. He grabbed Milly and swirled her into a group of dancers who were just rushing past in a blur of colour and song. Hen watched as they skipped around the square, arms linked, heads raised up to the blue sky and the warm sun.

Suddenly, the dancers paused. The music stopped.

The memory was frozen.

Hen blinked, confused. What exactly had happened? Everyone was like stone – as unmoving as statues. Even their hair and clothes were still. And then, as quickly as it had happened, it was over – the dance resumed along with music and none of the remembered people appeared to have noticed.

Had it been part of the memory, somehow? It hadn't felt that way to Hen; it had seemed *wrong*. As though everything had got stuck!

The sun had dipped down behind the tall buildings that edged the piazza. Warmth was draining from the day and with it the lightness and cheer faded too, leaving a sad, heavy feeling – even as the band packed up and the crowd cheered in appreciation. Hen searched for Milly and the boy again, wondering if they were saying their last goodbyes. Maybe that was why the mood had darkened.

And that was when Hen noticed them.

Two pale shapes.

So pale, they were almost translucent.

Hen swallowed, his throat as dry as sandpaper. The large, pulsating creatures reminded him of huge grubs or maggots but were about the length of the workroom table. They moved around the top of the grand building across the square. And despite their roundness, they were fast.

Hen felt certain they were not part of the memory and shouldn't be there – no one in the square was reacting to their presence. As he watched, Hen noticed how the building and even patches of the sky nearby were withering away, twisting in on themselves like warped cloth or frayed threads.

The creatures were eating the memory.

How is that possible? Hen wondered, staring at the strange darkness filling the space which the maggot-like creatures had destroyed.

He felt chilled to the core.

Suddenly the creatures stopped and swung their blind faces in Hen's direction. Their mouths yawned open and he saw ring upon ring of needle-like teeth.

The creatures made a chilling screeching sound and Hen felt sure that they had sensed him.

He suddenly didn't want to be there any more!

He had to get back to the aperture and out of the memory – fast!

Hen turned and started to move back through the crowd, running. As he passed through the huge arch out of the piazza, he glanced over his shoulder and gasped. Wherever the creatures moved, a churning, swirling, dark vortex of ruined threads grew and grew and grew.

And they were following him. Hen pushed himself faster.

And now he couldn't see Milly any more – or the boy. Had the creatures consumed them?

CHAPTER FIFTEEN

ALDO

Hen tumbled through the aperture, breathless and relieved to have escaped. Golden light swirled and then he was back in the attic again, gulping in the musty air.

He stared down at the fabric panel. Horrified, Hen immediately saw the memory stitches had been damaged: a small portion of the beautiful stitching in one of the outer sections had blackened and frayed. The thread was twisting up like dried autumn leaves, the colours fading. 'Oh, no, no,' Hen whispered. He sat there watching the fabric for another moment, but whatever had happened, it seemed to have stopped for now, thank Hestia.

The creatures – those pulsating, maggoty things – had done this! But what were they, and how could he stop them or get rid of them before they destroyed Milly's beautiful memory for ever?

He jumped when he heard footsteps on the attic stairs and quickly stashed the fabric away. Aunt Lucia peered over the top of the drawers that half blocked the doorway.

'Hi Aunt Lucia,' he said, brightly.

'Hen, sweetheart. Have you seen your nana?' Aunt Lucia asked, her voice a little worried as she peered around the attic, as if expecting Nana to jump out from one of the wardrobes.

'Not for a while,' he said, colouring as he remembered their disagreement. 'What time is it?' He looked towards the attic windows, surprised to find the sun was setting and the bright points of stars had started to dot the sky.

'Nearly dinnertime,' Aunt Lucia said, her voice anxious. 'She said she wanted some fresh air after her nap but that was a couple of hours ago and . . . well, she's not back yet.'

'I'll go and see if I can find her,' Hen said, adding reassuringly, 'No doubt she's got chatting to her friends in the Dragonfly.'

'That would be nice, thank you, Hen.' She smiled. 'It's looking very tidy in here already. Well done.'

Hen walked briskly across the marketplace. The street lamps were lit and shops were starting to close for the day. A few shopkeepers called out brightly to Hen as he passed.

'Chilly out this evening, Hen.'

'You'll catch your death without your coat!'

He headed towards the Dragonfly. What he'd said to Aunt Lucia had been true: Nana liked to go there for hot chocolate and gossip with her friends, and she easily lost track of time when she started chatting. When he found her, he'd apologize too. He'd behaved badly earlier, dismissing her attempts to patch things up between him and Connie.

Somehow, the memory had jolted him out of his bad mood – he'd realized how little it mattered whether he was jealous of Connie entering the contest. Connie hadn't been to blame for her dad forbidding Hen to spell-stitch. And Nana had only been trying to keep the peace.

As he crossed the street, dashing to avoid an oncoming tram, he saw Mrs Mori the librarian waving to him from the partly closed doorway of the library.

'Ah, Hen, I was just coming to find you.'

'I don't think I've got any overdue books, Mrs Mori?'

'No, well, it's your nana. You see . . . she seems a bit . . . muddled.'

'Muddled?' Hen blinked in surprise. Nana was never muddled. 'Where is she, please?' he asked.

'You'd best come inside,' the librarian said gently.

Hen followed Mrs Mori into the quiet library. It was empty, except for a small figure hunched in a seat at one of the reading tables. It took Hen a moment or two to recognize the coat, the hair.

'Nana?'

Nana, who usually sat so erect, shoulders back, looking inquisitively at everything around her, was slumped like a discarded garment. Hen felt a gentle press of worry near his heart, and his breath caught for just a second.

He looked at Mrs Mori. He didn't even know what to ask her.

'She seems to not quite know where she is,' the librarian said, ever so gently.

That was when Nana glanced up and looked at

him . . . and right through him. Her sea-blue eyes clearly didn't recognize him at all. Then, her gaze wandered aimlessly over the surrounding bookshelves.

Hen hurried towards her. As he drew closer, he realized she was muttering to herself, something unintelligible. She plucked at the fabric of her skirt over and over with her long fingers, so like his own.

'Nana?' he said again.

'Who is it?' she replied, turning to look at Hen properly.

'It's me, Nana,' he said, more brightly than he felt.

'Aldo?' Nana asked and her eyes brightened for a second.

Hen's heart sank. He had no idea who Aldo was.

'Is it time for lunch already?' she asked. 'I've not finished my work yet.' She looked at the empty reading table and then around her as though she had lost something. Her voice was unsure and fluttering like a bird's heartbeat.

Hen felt an icy twist of worry deep in his stomach.

'It's not lunchtime,' Hen said carefully. 'Are you still feeling poorly, Nana? Should I fetch Uncle Bertie?' He put his hand to her forehead, but she didn't seem to have a fever.

Her long thin fingers continued to pluck at her skirt. She had pulled away some of the embroidery stitches.

Hen knelt at Nana's feet and took her hands in his own – if nothing else, he could stop her pulling at the threads. Her hands felt limp and bony. He felt a bitter longing for her normal grip – the feel of her strength when she took his hand and squeezed it, usually with a smile or a laugh or a kiss on the top of his head.

She peered closer at him. Curious.

'Who . . . who are you?' she asked. Her own voice was wobbling with fear. Her face was white and drawn, now, her eyes moist with tears.

'Nana, it's me. Hen.'

Guilt snatched at him with sharp, hot hands. He had upset her earlier – and now look what had happened!

Nana stared hard at him. 'I don't know anyone called Hen,' she said. Her eyes swam with tears. 'Aldo, I haven't finished the dress yet. You won't tell, will you?'

'I won't,' Hen said softly. This appeared to calm Nana a little. Hen, meanwhile, could feel his heart thumping inside his chest. Perhaps it was breaking.

He stood up slowly and walked over to Mrs Mori. 'I'll wait here with Nana. Please can you go and fetch my aunt and uncle?' Hen said, his own voice wobbling now.

Mrs Mori smiled and squeezed his hand tight. 'Of course,' she said. 'I'll be right back.'

The doctor had been waiting when they got Nana home from the library and – after examining her – he had called for an ambulance. Aunt Lucia had sent Hen and Connie upstairs out of the way, but from the window they had watched Aunt Lucia climb into the ambulance after Nana. And then it had pulled away.

Now, they heard heavy footsteps on the stairs.

Uncle Bertie entered the room and slumped into the nearest armchair, rubbing his temples.

'What did the doctor say?' Connie asked quietly.

'The hospital will run tests, then we'll know more. She'll be staying there for the time being.'

'And how long will that be?' Hen asked.

'I don't know,' Uncle Bertie sighed. 'Perhaps it's just as well. She doesn't need any more upset.' Uncle Bertie shot Hen a dark glance. 'She's had quite enough – the constant disobedience and disruptions.'

'Dad!' Connie gasped. 'That's not fair. It's not Hen's fault Nana's ill.'

But Hen couldn't entirely disagree with Uncle Bertie. He felt as if he had caused this somehow. 'I'm sorry,' Hen said quickly and then got up to leave the sitting room.

He automatically headed for Nana's room, but then remembered she was gone.

He suddenly felt very alone.

Hen went to his own room but it didn't feel right somehow.

He sat quietly in the dark, thinking of that other house, of those other rooms, filled with warm sunshine and the call of seabirds – the scent of lemons on the warm air. He always felt so wonderful in that memory.

But then he remembered those maggoty creatures, eating its very fabric . . .

There really was nowhere for Hen to go, nowhere that felt right. Without Nana, nowhere felt like home.

CHAPTER SIXTEEN

A Wet Spell

Hen slept badly that night. Every time he drifted off to sleep, his dreams were filled with pulsing glimpses of the strange maggoty creatures from the memory – or the sight of Nana all small and hunched over in the library.

He slept late, missed breakfast and then faced the morning's errands alone as Connie now had to focus on her garment for the contest – *of course she did!*

He had a thank-you note to drop off at the library, letters to post at the post office and bread to collect from the bakery, but there were no deliveries. He realized there hadn't been any for over a week. Even a lovely long letter from Mum and Dad did little to help Hen's agitated mood.

As he returned, crossing the road outside Danelli's, Hen spotted several people waiting on the steps, peering in through the window. One lady even tapped on the glass with the handle of her umbrella and called brightly, 'Hello, Mr Danelli? I'm here for my fitting!'

Hen squeezed through the knot of customers and knocked on the window. Connie hurried across and let him in, but quickly indicated that he should be quiet.

Uncle Bertie was stuck behind the counter as a very angry gentleman shook a Danelli overcoat, which was dripping water all over the counter and floor – though it was dry and sunny outside. 'What sort of a joke d'you call this, then, eh?' the man growled. 'Soaking wet I am, wet through to me drawers and no mistake.'

Hen stifled a nervous giggle. They couldn't risk drowning the few remaining customers they had! Uncle Bertie was desperately trying to calm the gentleman down. 'I'm afraid I don't quite know what the matter is, Mr . . . er?'

'Matlock,' the wet, angry man said. 'Look, this is a

brand-new coat. I only bought it a few weeks ago and when I put it on this morning it was soaking wet and . . . well, look at it!' Mr Matlock lifted the coat so that it dangled from his hand. Hen could see now it was more than dripping; it was as though a hidden tap had been switched on somewhere inside the coat. Water poured from it, covering the counter and floor.

What was going on?

Uncle Bertie gave a huge heaving sigh and then reached for the sopping coat. 'If you can perhaps leave it with me, Mr Matlock, I will look into the situation immediately and ascertain what the cause of the malfunction seems to be,' he said in his calmest and most placating voice. The one he seemed to save for the most awkward customers.

'Just fix it!' Mr Matlock snapped, letting the coat flop wetly into its own self-generating puddle on the floor.

Then he barged past Hen and Connie and out of the shop. They could hear the excited gossip from the watchers outside the door.

'The spell's failed. Look at it!'

'Oh dear. Doesn't look good, does it?'

'Not what they used to be, Danelli's.'

Connie glanced at Hen and hurried to close the door.

'Bolt it, for Hestia's sake,' Uncle Bertie snapped at Connie. 'We don't want anyone else coming in right now! Quickly!'

'I'll fetch a bucket,' Hen said, and hurried through to the back hall where a mop and bucket were kept in the store cupboard. There were another two garments tossed on to the floor of the back hall, both surrounded by a large puddle that was soaking through the carpet.

Three coats, all with their spells malfunctioning?

Hen felt suddenly on edge. Even though he had not worked on any of the coats himself, the fact there was something wrong with them made him feel guilty, as though his strange memory-stitching in Mrs Crab's dress was now somehow also to blame for . . . well, whatever this was.

Hen grabbed the bucket and picked up the two coats, dropping their heavy wetness inside. Then he went to retrieve the third from the shop floor.

A few minutes later the three coats were in a tangled, wet slump in the wide stone sink in the small scullery off the workroom. Hen, Connie and Uncle Bertie stood staring at them and listening to the sound of the water running down the drain. It sounded as though someone had just pulled out the plug. Aunt Lucia, who had returned from the hospital earlier that morning with the news that Nana seemed a little better than the day before, retrieved the ledger from the shop counter and started searching through the records to see when the coats had been sold.

Hen, Connie and Uncle Bertie stared and stared, as though that would somehow reveal what had occurred inside the spell stitches to make them malfunction so magnificently.

'Well?' Uncle Bertie said in a rather accusing tone, his restraint gone now he was no longer faced with the irate Mr Matlock. 'Does anyone have any ideas why this might have occurred?'

Hen could feel Uncle Bertie glaring at him.

'It's not my fault,' Hen offered quickly. 'I had nothing to do with any of those coats.'

Aunt Lucia stepped just inside the scullery door. 'Bertie, dear – one of those coats was made about fifteen years ago. And, ah, well, Mr Matlock's coat ... well ...' There was silence.

'Well, Lucia – spit it out, my love.'

'*You* stitched Mr Matlock's coat, Bertrand.'

Hen could hear the wince in Aunt Lucia's voice. Uncle Bertie charged out of the scullery and into the workroom, Hen and Connie following slowly. He spun the ledger around and glared at it, challenging it to blame him for this latest misfortune.

His cheeks went red. His nostrils flared. He swallowed.

'Three rain-repelling coats, all made at different times and by different – but competent – Danelli tailors, all malfunctioning…' He shook his head and said darkly, 'The spell stitch. Something's gone wrong with the spell stitch.'

Hen's heart sank. He knew sometimes spell stitches stopped working – but normally it was a gradual thing, not a sudden, explosive (or in this case torrential) breakdown.

'So why isn't the spell stitch working?' Connie asked.

'How the devil am I supposed to know?' Uncle Bertie snapped. 'Doesn't anyone else have any work to do around here? Must I do everything myself?' He drew himself up to his full height. 'I'll look into these coats some more. Lucia, I think you had better go up to the shop this afternoon. Constance, stay here and carry on working on your contest garment. And, Hen—'

'Oh, Uncle Bertie, do I have to go to the attics today?' He couldn't shake the thought of the strange memory-eating creatures away, no matter how hard he tried.

'Well, actually,' Uncle Bertie began, and Hen thought for a second he was about to be given a reprieve, 'you'd best mop up all the water in the shop and down here first . . . *then* the attics, thank you.'

Hen was emptying the last bucket of water down the scullery sink when Connie hurried in. She closed the door quietly behind her while Hen put the mop and bucket to one side and washed his hands. 'What's up?' Hen asked.

'It's the stay-dry spell . . . I thought I'd look at the stitch book to see if it might give any clues as to why it had failed. Want to see?' She produced the stitch book from behind her back.

Hen's eyes widened as he dried his hands. Connie had always seemed like such a goody two shoes! 'How did you get that?' he whispered.

She smiled and shrugged. 'Dad's busy and he left his keys lying around. Here.' She put the precious book on the clean, dry surface opposite the sink and flipped it to the relevant pages.

The three waterproof spell stitches folded out across the table – from top to bottom they were oldest to newest.

'Here it is.' Connie pointed to the latest one. 'I'm pretty sure that this is the one my dad used on Mr Matlock's coat, and I'm guessing it's the same one used on the others that went wrong too. Every time a spell stitch is changed, there's a possibility it goes wrong, right? The bigger the change, the greater the risk.'

Hen nodded. That's what Nana had told him, too.

'So I wondered if it had been changed recently . . . except, this latest change to the stitch has only been very small, mostly to strengthen it. And it was done nearly thirty years ago.'

'So how did it go wrong?' Hen asked, not sure he was ready for more bad news. 'It's quite an old one, isn't it? Did the magic just . . . fade?'

'No, but look who updated it last,' Connie said. She turned the stitch book around to show Hen the page with the stay-dry spell on.

'Nana?' Her initials and the date of the change had been stitched in beside the updated stitch.

'Don't you think it's odd, Nana being . . . unwell,

and now this?' Connie asked.

Hen wasn't really sure what he thought, but it did seem a strange sort of coincidence.

'Should I tell my dad, do you think?' Connie asked.

Hen thought for a moment. Whatever had gone wrong, it wasn't going to get any worse if they left it for a day or two. 'I'd leave it for now. Uncle Bertie has had enough bad news for one day. In fact, I think we all have . . .'

'You're right,' said Connie. Then, she picked up the cloth book and held it close. 'Look, Hen, I really am sorry about—'

Hen cut her off. 'No, I'm sorry. I should have believed you – I do believe you, Connie. It's not your fault it didn't work out with the contest.'

Connie's shoulders relaxed slightly. 'Friends, again?'

'Friends,' agreed Hen.

CHAPTER SEVENTEEN

SICKNESS

The next morning, Hen was hurrying from Kaur's Bakers when he bumped into Connie, who'd been to fetch stamps from the post office.

'I just saw your friend's mum, Mrs Henderson,' Connie said. 'She asked if you could drop in and see Simon. Apparently he's not very well. She thought some company might cheer him up.'

'OK, thanks. Do you want to come along as well?'

Connie hesitated for a second, then smiled and said, 'Yes, all right.'

They headed for Brook Lane, where Henderson's

garage was tucked at the end beside the printworks and the high wall of the park.

It wasn't like Simon to be ill, Hen thought, as they went around the side of the garage to the staircase that ran up the outside of the building to the flat above. The door opened into a large space that was kitchen, dining and sitting room in one. One wall was mostly windows that looked over the yard – on the opposite wall, a fire crackled in the fireplace. Simon was slumped on the flowery sofa, his face pale. He sat up straighter at the sight of Hen and offered a weak smile.

'I thought Hen might cheer you up, love,' Mrs Henderson said brightly, waving Hen and Connie inside.

'Who is it?' a wheezy voice croaked from the corner of the room.

Hen hadn't noticed Simon's grandmother, Old Mrs Henderson, sitting in an armchair beside the fire. She leant forwards, adjusted her spectacles that magnified her eyes so she looked rather bug-like and stared hard at Hen and Connie. Her face was lined like an old oak tree.

'Who's that?' She jabbed a knotty finger at them.

'It's Simon's friend,' Mrs Henderson smiled.

'Hen. And . . .'

'I'm Hen's cousin,' Connie supplied, smiling. 'Connie. How do you do?'

'Oh?' Old Mrs Henderson peered at them suspiciously. 'I knew a Connie, once. Quite a long time ago now,' the old lady said, smiling back at Connie.

'Oh, that's nice,' Connie replied, politely stepping closer.

'She was awful,' Old Mrs Henderson wheezed. 'She got run over by a tram doing a sponsored walk, and good riddance, I say!' Her laugh crackled into a sputtering, wheezing cough.

'Ignore her,' Simon's mum said quietly, pulling a face.

'Hi, Simon,' Hen said carefully as they crossed over to where he sat. 'Your mum said you're a bit under the weather.' Drawing closer, he could see Simon's dark-circled eyes – it was like he hadn't slept for days. There was a nasty rash around his neck too, the skin red and angry where the collar of his sweater rested. 'How are you feeling?'

'Not great. This rash really hurts,' Simon said, pulling back a sleeve to reveal patches of inflamed skin with bulging white blisters here and there.

'Pins and needles,' Connie whispered in shock.

'What is it?' Hen asked Simon. 'Allergies?'

'Don't know . . . I thought I'd got the flu when it started a few days ago. But then the rash started up . . .'

'We've tried ointments and all sorts, but it won't budge,' Mrs Henderson said. Hen noticed Connie gazing intently at Simon's sweater . . . it looked brand new. There *was* something about it, but Hen couldn't quite put his finger on it – something at once familiar and different. He struggled to focus on the orange knitted material.

'Is that a spelled sweater?' Connie asked, peering at it more closely. *Of course*, Hen thought. *That's what it was!*

Simon nodded. 'It's got a warming spell.'

'It's not one of ours, though, is it?' Connie pressed.

Mrs Henderson blushed, but before she could speak Old Mrs Henderson sputtered into life again.

'We're not made of money, you know. Not everyone can afford a fancy Danelli sweater. Though quite why anyone would want one is beyond me. Never wore a spelled garment in my life, I'm proud to say.' Old Mrs Henderson jabbed her finger towards Hen and Connie again. 'Magic – nothing but trouble if you ask me.'

'Take it off,' Connie said to Simon.

'What?' He looked rather confused.

'It's the spell in the sweater causing the rashes. Take it off now.'

'Surely not . . .' Simon's mum protested.

'I knew it!' said Old Mrs Henderson. 'Nothing but trouble!'

Simon looked at Hen.

'Do as she says!' Hen said quickly, and reached forward to help Simon pull the sweater over his head. As soon as Hen touched the material, he could feel how the magic in the sweater felt wrong – somehow spiky and unbalanced.

Connie quickly snatched the sweater away, turning it over in her hands. Simon sat on the sofa in his vest watching Connie as though she was totally barmy. There didn't seem to be a patch of skin on Simon's arms or torso or neck that wasn't covered in angry sores and blisters. Hen wondered how he didn't cry in pain from it.

After just a few moments of handling the sweater, Connie must have found the spell stitch. 'There,' she said, and then yelped and dropped it.

'What's wrong with it?' Mrs Henderson asked.

'The spell stitch is defective,' Connie said, shakily. They all stared at the sweater bunched up on the rug, as if afraid it would suddenly explode. Then Connie leant towards Hen and said quietly, 'Look at the label.'

Hen carefully turned out the sweater's collar to read the label:

Pepper's Affordable Fashions

The fizz of magic against his fingers was suddenly too much and Hen dropped the sweater as if it were a stinging nettle.

'Is there anything you can do?' Mrs Henderson asked.

'You can't repair a spell stitch, certainly not one in another tailor's garment,' Connie explained sadly. 'Spell stitches are closely guarded secrets.'

'Sounds about right,' Old Mrs Henderson grumbled.

'My boy's in pain,' Mrs Henderson said, placing a gentle hand on Simon's back. 'If that sweater can hurt him, do you have one that can heal him?'

'I told you, Dotty, that no good would come of wasting good money on such a frivolous article,' Old Mrs Henderson said, before turning away and picking her nose with great enthusiasm!

'I'm so sorry,' Connie said gently. 'But I don't know if there is anything we can—'

'Wait!' Hen said suddenly. 'I have an idea.'

He hadn't been into his parents' bedroom in some time but he knew where his mother kept the quilt – in a small pine chest under the window, where extra blankets and eiderdowns were neatly folded for chillier nights. There was a particular quilt that she had often tucked Hen up in that had a very old spell stitch in it. One that was never used on clothes any more, she said, but still had its uses. And whenever Hen had been wrapped up in it, if he had a fever or a stomach ache, after a while he had always felt better.

The quilt was tucked at the bottom, and Hen fished it out and hurried back to the Hendersons' as fast as his legs would carry him.

'Here.' He offered the quilt to Simon and when his friend just blinked back at him, Hen unfolded it and wrapped it gently around him.

'What's this?' Old Mrs Henderson asked, peering across the room at them.

'A quilt with an old healing spell stitched into it. It might help,' Hen said.

'Huh, more magic,' muttered Old Mrs Henderson.

'Thank you, Hen,' Simon's mum said loudly. 'That's really thoughtful of you.'

'Will it work?' Connie asked, lifting a corner of the quilt and examining it carefully.

'Should do,' Hen said.

Simon sat back in the chair beside the fire. His face already looked more relaxed and he let out a small sigh. 'It feels nice,' he murmured.

Old Mrs Henderson continued to mutter to herself and picked up her newspaper.

'I'll check back later,' Hen said as Mrs Henderson showed them both to the door.

They waved as they headed towards home through the park.

'Hestia's needles! That's terrible. Poor Simon, how can that awful Tiberius Pepper be allowed to get away with making clothes like that?' Connie asked as they walked down the tree-lined path back towards Beacham Terrace.

'I don't suppose he knows or cares.' Hen sighed. 'He tells everyone his garments are cheaper than a spell tailor's, even when it's not true at all. And this is the result of making stuff without care and attention—'

'—and love,' Connie added.

Hen nodded. It was the vital ingredient in any garment or spell. The love of making it.

'Mass-produced magic.' Connie shook her head. 'It's not right.'

CHAPTER EIGHTEEN

SECRETS

When Hen emerged from the attics later that day, he found Marjorie fast asleep hanging from the bannister rail. She stirred a little and gave a low, dreamy call, then twitched and whimpered. Nana always said she was probably dreaming about a lovely rocky meadow or a cliff when she did that. 'A happy dream, love,' she would say. But what if the dream she was having wasn't nice at all? What if she was searching for him, or Nana? What if Marjorie was scared and alone somewhere? Hen's instinct was always to gently reach out to her, not to wake her entirely but to let her know he was there. Even in her dreams.

He stepped across the wide landing and reached out to place a gentle palm on her warm side, his hand vanishing into her cloud-like coat. Her twitching stopped at once and she made a soothing trill that was half snore, half whistle.

But she really shouldn't be up here in the apartment. Uncle Bertie would flip his lid if he found her.

'Rule number whatever,' Hen said, in his best Uncle Bertie voice. 'No fun for anyone ever again!'

Hen moved his hands to scratch behind Marjorie's huge curving horns, which she always liked. 'Wake up, Marjorie, wake up, little sleepy-shleep,' he said gently.

She stirred, her large green eyes blinking at Hen, mouth creasing into a smile. She purred, leaning forwards to lick Hen's hand.

'I know, it's nice to see you too. But we'd better get you back down to the workroom or Uncle Bertie will have you turned into a rug!'

But she didn't move. Just held tighter to the bannister rail and closed her eyes again, feigning sleep.

'Marjorie, come on. Please.'

Hen knew that if Uncle Bertie found Marjorie

upstairs he would somehow get the blame. And then he would never be allowed back in the work-room ever.

'Hey, Marjorie. Do you want a . . . *biscuit*?'

The usually sedate animal's head snapped straight up. Her eyes wide, her nostrils already flexing, sniffing out the treat.

'Come on, then, we need to go downstairs to get it,' Hen said gently and headed for the stairs.

It took Marjorie a second to catch on but then she slipped down to the floor and followed him, her clawed toes clicking on the floorboards.

He paused in the kitchen to retrieve three oatmeal and raisin biscuits (two for Marjorie and one for himself) before carrying on down, Marjorie following and getting a little bit of biscuit every few steps.

He could hear busy voices in the shop and hoped everyone was in there so he wouldn't run into anyone in the workroom.

He pushed open the basement door and listened out for any sounds that might indicate the room was occupied, but it was quiet.

'OK, let's go.' Hen snapped off another bit of biscuit and Marjorie surged forwards. In another few seconds they were in the workroom and

Marjorie was climbing back up on to her beam and eating the last cookie. Hen leant back against the wall and bit into his own. A job well done.

'Hen?'

Connie stepped out of the shadows at the back of the workroom. She had coiled a length of ribbon around her hand, tidying it away.

'Are you working on your garment for the contest?' Hen asked, and felt bad that he was unable to hide the jealousy in his voice, even though they'd made up.

'Would you like to see it?' Connie asked.

He shook his head. 'Do you mind if I don't, just now?' He wasn't sure he could face it. 'I only came down to bring Marjorie back.'

Connie smiled gently. 'Well, don't let my dad catch you in here!' She nodded her head towards Uncle Bertie's cupboard-office. The light was on and Hen could see the familiar shape of his uncle silhouetted in the small frosted window.

It sounded like he was on the telephone – that was good. It meant he probably hadn't heard them chatting.

'I'd better go,' he whispered to Connie – she was right, he really didn't want to get caught.

Connie followed him quietly across the work-room, back towards the stairs. But as they passed the door something in Uncle Bertie's tone made Hen pause and listen.

'Yes, yes. Well, I am certainly interested in visiting to see exactly what you do. It would be most illumin-ating to see how the factory works on such a . . . grand scale.'

Hen and Connie stared at each other and both mouthed, *Factory*.

Uncle Bertie continued, 'Well, I'm not sure we are quite ready to discuss that at this precise moment, as I told you on your visit – well, yes, that's very gener-ous, very interesting.'

Hen knew that Connie was thinking the same thing he was. The only factory that sprang to mind was Tiberius Pepper's. But surely Uncle Bertie wouldn't think about even talking to him, after that article in the newspaper?

Uncle Bertie was speaking again, his voice low and confiding. 'No, no need to send a car. I'll drive myself. Yes, well, thank you. I look forward to seeing you again tomorrow morning. Goodbye.'

Hen heard the click as the receiver was put back in place and suddenly Connie was dragging him away from the door and up the basement stairs.

'If he catches us, he'll know we were eavesdropping,' she hissed.

They quickly and quietly made their way past the fitting rooms, dashing by Aunt Lucia as she walked through with a customer. She looked rather startled. 'Careful, you two!' she called.

They didn't stop until they were in the kitchen, the door closed firmly behind them.

'Twist it, Hen,' Connie said, grabbing his arm. 'He's not really going to go and visit that man's factory, is he? Why's he doing that? No wonder he's keeping it quiet! Should we tell my mum?'

'I don't know,' Hen said quickly. He was trying to straighten it all out in his head first.

Uncle Bertie visiting Tiberius Pepper's new factory?

They were quiet for a few more moments and then Connie said, 'We have to follow him tomorrow.'

Her voice was low and serious.

'Follow him?' Hen gasped. 'You're kidding, right? How would we even do that?'

'I have an idea. Just meet me downstairs by the back door as soon as it's light tomorrow morning.'

As soon as he saw the first flush of light in the dark morning sky, Hen pulled on his duffle coat and hurried downstairs. Connie was already waiting by the back door, her hat pulled low, her scarf wrapped up high so Hen could only just see her eyes.

'Is that a disguise?' he whispered.

Connie pulled the scarf down just enough to poke her tongue out at him.

They left almost silently through the back door and then raced down the garden path to the brick sheds that stood behind the slightly scrappy rose bushes. Hen followed Connie to the larger shed, which Uncle Bertie was currently using as his own garage. They stood, looking at the car.

Hen tried a door. 'It's locked.'

Connie smiled, moved around to the back and fiddled with the catch on the boot of the car, which opened with a quiet but satisfying *chunk*.

'It stopped locking months ago and Dad never had it fixed.' Connie grinned.

Hen couldn't help grinning back.

'After you,' Connie offered.

Once he had settled himself in the boot, Connie followed and pulled the lid closed after her.

'Won't your mum think it's off we're not at break-fast?' Hen asked, after a few quiet minutes.

'I left a note,' Connie said. 'Said we went out early to Simon's.'

'You really did think of everything,' Hen said. They lay in the dark for what felt like ages. 'What's the plan when we get there?' Hen whispered, eventually. 'We can't exactly follow him into the meeting, can we?'

'I suggest we have a look around, find out more about what that man does in his factories.' Connie's voice was grim. 'The spell stitch in Simon's jumper . . . it was so *wrong*.'

It all sounded a bit too risky to Hen, and he was about to suggest they get out when they heard the shed doors being dragged open, and then the car door too. They felt the car shift as Uncle Bertie climbed in. The next moment the car sputtered into life and then they were moving.

It was too late to back out!

CHAPTER NINETEEN

The Factory

They jostled and rolled about in the inky dark of the car boot, elbows and knees jutting into heads and backs for about half an hour. Then they felt the car slow. It juddered across a rough surface – cobbles, perhaps? – and came to a stop, though the engine was still running. Hen could just make out muffled voices, but he didn't know what was being said.

The car moved off again, slowly, gently, and then stopped a few moments later. This time the engine was turned off.

They lay in the dark, waiting for Uncle Bertie

to move, and at last the car rocked as he climbed out and shut the door. They heard his footsteps move away.

Connie shifted, obviously wanting to get out, but Hen held her back. 'Wait. Just have a little peek before we get out, OK?'

'OK.' She lifted the boot so a narrow line of light sliced through the darkness, making Hen blink.

Connie pressed her face close to the gap. 'I can see my dad. He's heading to a building with someone . . . Oh, they've gone inside. OK, I think it's safe.'

'Are you sure?' Hen asked, nerves hitting him again.

'Yes,' Connie hissed. 'There's nobody else about, look.'

And with that she threw open the car boot and clambered out, stretching away the aches of the short but cramped journey. Hen followed and as he gazed about, he saw they were in a wide courtyard. A few large, wheeled wicker baskets stood about, only slightly smaller than Uncle Bertie's car. A network of narrow metal rails, like train tracks, criss-crossed the cobbled courtyard, and a brick ramp disappeared off somewhere through a high archway. The air was thick with dust and smoke that made Hen cough. A thin ribbon of an acrid yellow dye ran across the cobbles from a cracked downpipe. Tall red-brick walls rose up all around them. A few windows looked down into the courtyard, but they were high up and smudged with dirt and grime or painted over.

At the far end of the courtyard, above the door Uncle Bertie must have gone through, was a large freshly painted sign, the only new or well-tended thing in the courtyard.

Pepper's Affordable Fashions

Connie sighed. 'Now we're here, I've got absolutely no idea what to do, Hen.' Her voice wobbled with anxiety.

Something Milly's grandpa had said sprang into Hen's mind. 'Doing anything brave requires ten per cent forethought and ninety per cent imagination!'

'Wherever did you hear that?' Connie asked.

He briefly thought about telling her everything but decided they had quite enough to be dealing with already. 'Um ... I'll tell you some other time.'

'Well, it sounds good to me,' Connie said with a small smile. 'Let's go this way!'

And she raced off towards the nearest set of doors.

The doors opened on to a long empty corridor,

walls panelled halfway up and painted a rather dingy brown colour that was dusty and flaking here and there. The floor tiles were dull and the air was heavy with the tang of smoke and chemicals.

Hen's stomach knotted with worry. 'We can't just go wandering around the factory willy-nilly, Connie. What if someone sees us?'

'Ten per cent forethought, ninety per cent imagination!' Connie reminded him brightly.

Hen squashed down his ominous feelings as Connie started rummaging through one of the wheeled wicker baskets. It seemed to be filled with dirty rags – one of which Connie pulled out and threw at Hen, saying, 'Put this on.' She grinned at his confused expression. 'This is the ninety per cent imagination part!'

Hen wished he'd never said it!

The rag was in fact a rough, greyish, tatty and rather smelly warehouse coat that fell past Hen's knees.

'I bet this is what the workers here wear,' Connie said. 'See? We'll blend right in.' She was fastening the buttons on her coat as another set of doors along the corridor swung open and a small group of people, adults and children, came walking . . . no, marching along. And they *were* dressed in the same grey coats that Connie and Hen had just put on – Connie glanced at Hen and raised her eyebrow as if to say *See?*

The workers all looked rather tired, fed up, hungry and in need of a good wash, Hen thought. Was this how Tiberius Pepper treated his employees? Surely if Uncle Bertie saw even a glimpse of this he would leave straight away, no matter what his business at the factory. As much of a pain as Uncle Bertie was, he wasn't cruel, and Hen felt to his bones that he would never get involved with a man who treated people so badly.

It gave Hen an odd glimmer of hope.

The workers marched in two straight rows in total silence, except for their boots on the tiles. They passed Hen and Connie without a word or a glance and went through the next set of doors.

'Let's follow them,' Hen said before he had time to think too much about it.

He grabbed Connie's hand and they hurried after the group.

They kept their distance but stayed close enough that anyone looking would assume they had just fallen slightly behind. Thankfully nobody tried to stop them or asked them where they were going.

They passed rows of internal windows that looked into largely empty offices – though occasionally they saw someone stooped over a typewriter with a tall stack of papers beside them. Other rooms had piles of wooden shipping crates, some labelled and ready for delivery. Just before they passed through another set of double doors, Hen glanced into the room on their right and he saw rail after rail of finished garments. He stopped, pressing his face against the glass panes to see. He turned to call Connie over, but she was peering through a window a little further along.

'Hen, look at this . . .'

Something in the tone of her voice worried Hen. He hurried to her side and peered into the dark room beyond the glass. At first he couldn't see anything much at all.

It looked like the room was filled with piles of earth for some reason. Then he saw movement. It was as if the whole floor was moving.

Hen gasped and jumped back away from the window. He gaped at Connie. 'Are those . . .'

'Spell-brats,' Connie said. 'Looks like a pretty big nest of them too.'

'Why would you keep a nest of spell-brats in a clothing factory?' Hen asked and peered closer. The room must have been filled with thousands of spell-brats and their larvae. Hen could even see empty, translucent, papery chrysalis cases discarded in piles in the corners. They reminded Hen of something, but before he could put his finger on what, Connie asked, 'What did you find?'

'Some of the famous Pepper garments. Look.' Hen turned away from the spell-brat room and pointed through the glass of the door to the racks of sweaters.

'Let's get a better look, shall we?' Connie asked, and before Hen knew what was happening she had hurried inside the room.

Hen followed her, closing the door quietly behind them. Wheeled racks held hundreds upon hundreds of the same style sweater, in three different colours. Hen lifted one out to get a better look. It was similar to the one that had made Simon so unwell.

He peered at every seam, every buttonhole, every cuff, looking for a defect.

But everything was done perfectly, as far as he could tell. Even the spell stitches, although unfamiliar to Hen since they weren't Danelli stitches, were neatly executed and uniform from garment to garment.

He had to admit that the work was technically flawless. And yet ...

He walked up and down the racks of garments, his hand trailing over the sweaters, letting the fabric shift under his fingers. The sweaters didn't sting him, as Simon's had, but they still felt somehow wrong.

'Oh, Hen, look here. This looks like an Uckman's stay-clean spell to me, I'm sure of it,' Connie said. 'How would they have got hold of the Uckmans' spell stitches, do you think?'

From out in the corridor, they heard a loud, sharp voice. It rang off the walls and made them both jump. 'Why isn't this consignment ready to be shipped? It's been waiting here for three days now ... well, it's simply unacceptable! Spelled garments they may be,' the voice added with a sneer, 'but they aren't going to walk themselves to the stores, are they?'

The double doors flew open with a bang. Whoever was outside was now coming in. Hen grabbed Connie and dragged her under the cover of one of the garment rails.

As they peeped out a figure strode into the room. A tall woman, dressed in a smart (unspelled) suit, her hair pinned back from her face and tucked under a small hat with a large feather sweeping out of the top of it. She had a pouty mouth, the sort that rarely smiled or opened to laugh, Hen guessed. It was a bit twisted, like she was chewing a rock. Her jet-black eyes scanned the room, looking for something else to complain about. Hen ducked back under cover. He had seen this woman before. He was sure of it. But where?

'I'm not going to be the one to go to Mr Pepper and elucidate why shipments are behind,' the woman's voice rang out again.

'But, Mrs Thackerey, we're tryin' to sort it, I promise.' Another, very nervous, voice could now be heard too.

Thackerey? Wasn't she the woman who had been at the shop – the one who'd left the gift basket?

'Trying is not achieving, Mr Hertz,' Mrs Thackerey said coolly. 'I want these ready by the end of the day or your employment here will be terminated. Is that clear? And not just you, Mr Hertz. Your wife and your children will similarly be dismissed. And before you leave you will go to Mr Pepper and explain why you are leaving his employ. Is the situation graspable for you, Mr Hertz?'

She made it all sound quite horribly reasonable, and Hen could hear the fear in the man's voice when he replied, 'Yes, Mrs Thackerey, of course, Mrs Thackerey.'

Hen heard the sound of booted feet hurrying away.

'Well, I don't like the look of her,' Connie hissed quietly.

'Don't you recognize her?' Hen whispered.

'Who, that giraffe woman, Mrs Thackerey? Oh!'

Hen watched the penny drop.

'She was at the store that day with my dad,' Connie whispered, her eyes wide.

Hen nodded.

'Vile woman,' Connie hissed.

'Perhaps we should go now?' Hen said. 'We can explain all this to your dad. It should be enough to put him off Tiberius Pepper and whatever's going on.'

'No,' Connie said. She grabbed one of the garments and shook it at Hen. 'This is just the tip of the needle, Hen.'

Suns blazed in her eyes – Hen was reminded oddly of Milly.

They heard the approach of another set of feet, slower, heavier, and then a deep voice said brightly, 'Must you terrorize the workers quite so much, Agnes?'

'Oh, Mr Pepper, I didn't see you there,' Mrs Thackerey said. Although she didn't sound bothered by the slight reprimand, her whole demeanour changed – a sickly smile spread across her lips, her shoulders softening, though her eyes remained hard.

'Pepper?' Hen and Connie mouthed at each other.

'I'm so sorry you had to see that,' Mrs Thackerey said. 'You know our staff welfare is so important to me but when it comes to something like this, something that could seriously tarnish your reputation and business, I'm afraid that a dose of good old-fashioned discipline is necessary.'

Hen peered through the rack. He had only ever seen the man's photograph in newspapers or on the posters advertising his garments – photographs in which he always looked quite severe. He was smaller than Hen had expected, shorter than Mrs Thackerey. But in his dapper suit and with his snow-white hair and silver glasses, he was still impressive and commanding. And very real. Not a made-up person at all . . . worse luck!

'Is this another shipment of the new sweaters?' Mr Pepper asked, stepping towards the racks.

'Yes, and all just waiting to be sent off,' Mrs Thackerey said.

'Any issues with this batch?'

'Of course not, Mr Pepper.'

'We don't want things to be shoddy just because they're cheap, do we? The Pepper brand is afford-able, quality clothing! I couldn't help noticing a couple of unfavourable reports . . .'

Mrs Thackerey smiled again. 'A business as large and profitable as yours, Mr Pepper,' she said, 'is bound to attract jealousy and negativity from those less fortunate. I would steer clear of the papers if I were you – for your own health. Nobody ever read anything good about themselves in print! And besides, I am here to manage things so you could take a step back and enjoy the fruits of your labours and be our illustrious leader, the face of the brand!' The sharp-ness in her tone was now barely perceptible.

'Quite . . . quite. Thank you, Mrs Thackerey. What would I do without you? Oh, but I would like to have a look around the new work hall now, if it's convenient?'

'Mr Pepper, you have a meeting, don't forget.'

'Oh – of course, who is it this time?'

Mrs Thackerey checked her clipboard and said, 'A Mr Bertrand Danelli, from that little spell tailor's in Sparrow Down.'

Connie gripped Hen's wrist.

Mr Pepper paused briefly and then said, 'Danelli . . . are you sure?'

'Quite sure,' Mrs Thackerey replied. 'He will have arrived by now.'

'Well, I, er – shouldn't keep him waiting then, should I? See you later, Agnes.'

She bowed her head. 'Mr Pepper.'

Hen and Connie waited a few moments to be sure they were alone, but as they slipped out of the shipping room and into the corridor, they walked straight into Mrs Thackerey, who was studying her clipboard again. She looked more than a little startled and thoroughly annoyed, as though nobody had ever dared to accidentally bump into her in her whole life.

'And just precisely what were you two doing in there?' she said, towering over them both. 'What section are you from? Not shipping, I know that much.' She peered closer at them both. 'Hang on . . .

I know you two . . .' she said slowly. 'What are your names?'

Hen was frozen to the spot with fear – and it appeared Connie was too. Had she really recognized them from that day on the steps outside the shop?

'Well?' Mrs Thackerey asked again, her eyes narrowing, her pouty mouth twitching – a hawk anticipating its prey. 'You're not from the factory at all, are you?' she said.

Hen reached for Connie's hand and gripped it tight.

'Run!' he hissed.

CHAPTER TWENTY

The Work Hall

Mrs Thackerey lurched forwards, trying to grab them, but they skidded around her on the tiled floor and pushed through the double doors into the next section of corridor. They ran and ran, their feet pounding on the hard tiles. Each time they found themselves in a dead end or near too many people, they swerved off into empty offices or storerooms. But obviously, Mrs Thackerey knew the building better than they did, and no matter what they tried, she never seemed to fall far behind them.

'Come back here, you verminous little brats!' she

screeched. 'I'll have your unsanitary skins for a new pair of boots after this, mark my words.'

Hen and Connie raced down another corridor, widening the gap between them and Mrs Thackerey – she might know the building, but they were faster. The corridor looked like all the others – half-panelled, half-glazed walls on one side, tiled walls on the other with high windows.

Had they already been along here? No, Hen didn't think so. From somewhere he could hear the chug and whirr of machinery. They turned left and found themselves at another dead end. Frantically they tried each of the doors leading off the corridor.

'What's that noise?' Connie asked as she tried a second and third door.

'I don't know,' Hen said as he ran towards a smaller door, sending up a silent prayer to Hestia as he did. Mrs Thackerey's boots clicked along the tiled floor, gaining fast. She would be on them any second. Hen pulled the handle and nearly cried with relief when it swung open . . .

Except, it opened on to some sort of narrow chute, not a room. Hen peered in but the chute vanished into darkness.

'It's wide enough for us,' Hen said, 'but not for

her.' He was already climbing inside.

'I'm not going down there!' Connie said, hanging back. 'We don't know where it goes!'

'It's the only way!' Hen replied. Mrs Thackerey was close, now – Hen could hear her flinging open the doors in the corridor. He hovered on the edge of the chute. 'Look, I'll go first and call you to follow if it's OK.'

Not waiting for Connie's reply, Hen wriggled down until he felt himself start to slide. He picked up speed, thrown to one side as the chute curved, his breath stolen from his lungs.

Down.

Down.

Drop!

His stomach somersaulted as he fell out of the bottom and dropped through the air before landing in a pile of fabric in one of the large, wheeled wicker baskets.

The noise hit him first – the loud clanging of machinery, the roar of engines and the occasional shout of a command. The cacophony reminded Hen of the station when a train was about to set off; how the metal parts clashed and clanked, building and building to a crescendo.

'Connie!' he called up the chute, grateful for the general noise muffling his voice. 'It's safe!'

He peeked his head over the rim of the basket. His eyes widened. He was in a huge work hall filled with people and vast machinery. The scale of it was unbelievable!

A few seconds later, a whooshing noise sounded over Hen's head and Connie landed in the pile of fabric beside him with a *whump*. Hen reached out, pulling her to her feet. 'You OK?' he asked, all but shouting over the noise of the machines.

Connie nodded and put her hands over her ears, her eyes widening as Hen's had as she took in the magnitude of the place.

They climbed out of the basket and stepped cautiously forwards. The ceiling arched high above, supported by strong iron beams and dotted with dirty skylights. Hen peered closely at the machinery, which was part mechanical loom, part vast sewing machine. Huge spools of thread, bigger than a grown man, spun overhead on long metal poles. The drone of a hundred spinning belts filled the air like a huge, angry swarm of bees. The machines moved in unison, creating a rhythmic sound, *clackety-clack*. Noise seemed to fill every molecule in the vast hall.

Men, women and children wearing their uniform of shabby coats or overalls tended to the machines, pushed the heavy wicker baskets and occasionally untangled or replenished the great spools of thread. The younger workers scurried underneath the clanging machinery to clear debris – which Hen thought looked quite dangerous. Everyone had a role and a purpose. But Hen noticed the workers' anxious eyes constantly searching the walkways that ran along the edge of the hall, high above. The men and women up there were dressed more like guards and watched the workers below avidly. They carried short truncheons like the local policeman in Sparrow Down.

Hen and Connie watched in horror as a huge set of doors opened a few feet away and Mrs Thackerey stepped inside – quickly, they ducked behind a bundle of empty sacks stacked on a large barrow. Despite having pursued them around the factory, she didn't look out of breath – there was not a hair out of place, not a wrinkle in her skirt. She was the vision of calmness and control and she strode into the room like a queen. Almost at once, a bell rang. Everyone and everything came to a halt.

The machines.

The workers.

Even the motes of dust, dancing in the shafts of light, seemed to freeze for Mrs Thackerey.

Everything was silent except for Mrs Thackerey's boots as she marched across the work hall.

In the centre of the hall, she stopped and said, 'Attention, everyone. There are two children running about the factory and I am quite certain they are somewhere in this very hall.' She scanned the room slowly, adding, 'Come forward now, children, and your punishment will be lenient.'

Hen silently prayed none of the workers had seen them enter. He was quite sure Mrs Thackerey had no idea what lenient meant and she would delight in punishing them both, even though they didn't work here.

Not to mention the heap of trouble they would then be in with Uncle Bertie!

He felt Connie grip his hand tighter. She was shaking . . . or was it him?

When no one came forward, Mrs Thackerey said, 'Very well. Then I have no choice but to waste yet more of my precious time in finding you. And I *shall* find you.'

At her signal, the bell rang again, in two short blasts this time. The sound of shuffling feet filled the hall as the workers filed to stand before Mrs Thackerey in rows so straight and neat they would have shamed a brigade of fusiliers. Then, carefully, Mrs Thackerey walked the rows of people, scanning each face as she passed. Hen and Connie held their breath.

Mrs Thackerey gave the hall one last assessing look before she turned and strode away, flicking a piece of lint from her skirt. She walked back through the double doors, which one of the overseers locked behind her. Then the bell rang once more, the workers scattered like ants, and moments later the machines whirred back into life.

'We should wait here for a second and then head back to the car,' Hen said, his heart racing.

'How are we going to get out?' Connie said. 'The doors are locked, and we can't climb back up the chute!'

She gazed over his shoulder. Then, she grabbed his arm and shook the sleeve of his coat.

'Hen . . . isn't that . . .'

Hen turned. A tall girl with straggly blonde hair was pushing one of the large wicker baskets right towards where they were hiding, its narrow tracks running past the stack of sacks.

She was thinner, her hair was matted and dirty and she looked as though she had all but given up. But Hen would recognize her anywhere. 'Lottie?' he said, his voice catching in his throat.

'I had no idea she'd come to work here. My dad said she'd handed in her notice because—'

Hen shot her an exasperated look and Connie fell silent.

'Oh. Oh, Hen, he didn't?' she said quietly.

Then, Connie was on her feet. She'd grabbed a pile of the empty sacks and was marching across the workroom towards Lottie before Hen could do anything to stop her. 'Connie!' he hissed.

She carried on towards Lottie and her huge wheeled basket.

Hen broke his cover to follow her, grabbing a couple of sacks himself as he ran. Thankfully everyone else was back to work and too busy to notice the three of them converge at the edge of the hall. Luckily, the small area of the workroom near the chute wasn't in view of the guards high up on the balconies.

Lottie's face was a picture of surprise when she caught sight of Connie and Hen. Then, she broke into a broad grin, pulling Hen into a tight hug.

'What are you doing here?' Hen asked her.

Lottie started to explain. 'After I lost my job at Danelli's . . .'

Hen shook his head. 'I'm so sorry, Lottie.'

'Me too,' Connie added.

'Not your fault,' Lottie said. 'Anyway, after that, my whole family thought it would be a good idea to come and work here together but . . . well . . . you've seen for yourself. Oh, but it's mighty good to see you!' Lottie reached out and took Hen's hand.

'Oi, get back to work, you three!' The shout from an overseer on the balcony overhead startled the trio – but the man didn't hang about to check they'd listened. He carried on along the walkway, tapping his truncheon against the railings.

Even so, Hen and Connie made a big show of stuffing their empty sacks into Lottie's basket as they carried on talking. 'There's something weird about the stuff that's made here,' Connie said. 'A jumper from here made one of Hen's friends poorly. Do you know what's going on?'

'An old gentleman who works here, Mr Addison, has a theory. He's a spell tailor who used to have his own shop, so he should know,' Lottie said. 'He thinks the spell stitches go wrong because the garments aren't made with any particular wearer in mind – *and* because they definitely aren't made with love. They're all made by machines.'

'Nana always says spelled clothes have to be made with love to work,' Hen said.

'That's right. And because the spell stitches keep going wrong, Mr Pepper keeps having to find new ones,' Lottie said. 'He's buying up failing spell tailors and their stitches. Quite a few seem to end up working for him, too.' Then Lottie frowned. 'But hang on, why are you two here, anyway? You haven't gone out of business too, have you?'

'No,' said Connie. 'Not yet. We're just on a little ... reconnaissance mission.' Lottie was visibly relieved – but Connie and Hen exchanged a glance. Was Tiberius Pepper attempting to buy Danelli's? Could that be why Uncle Bertie was here today?

'We have to find Uncle Bertie,' Hen said.

'Lottie, can you get us out of here ... and show us where Pepper's office is, please?' Connie asked.

Lottie glanced back into the hall at the workers and overseers. 'I can't be away from my post for too long but, yes, quick – follow me.'

CHAPTER TWENTY-ONE

PRISONERS

Lottie helped Connie and Hen into one of the huge wheeled baskets in the corner of the work hall, glancing nervously at the guards overhead. They burrowed down into the fabric inside, completely covering themselves.

'OK,' Lottie whispered. 'Let's go!'

She heaved and the basket trundled along. Hen held his breath to avoid sneezing as some tweedy fabric tickled his nose.

Lottie paused and Hen heard voices beside the basket.

'Another batch ready for delivery already?' a gruff

man asked.

'Yes,' said Lottie brightly. 'Productive day, isn't it?'

The man grunted doubtfully – but, to Hen's relief, he heard a door opening and the basket trundled on. After a few moments it stopped. 'The coast's clear!' Lottie said.

Hen and Connie scrambled out. They were in another long, bare corridor – the sounds of the work hall muffled.

'You two are heavier than you look,' Lottie whispered, rubbing her arms. 'Come on – you can help me push now!' They hurried on, pushing the wicker basket along the metal rails.

Eventually, they found themselves outside again in a small service yard full of rubbish. Connie jumped as a rat scuttled for cover. A narrow alleyway led off to the right and on their left was a long slope with yet more of the metal rails for the baskets running along it. In the distance, Hen caught sight of Uncle Bertie's car.

He felt a flood of relief that Uncle Bertie hadn't left and they wouldn't be stranded in this awful place. The slope would take them back to the first courtyard – and home!

'This way,' Lottie said, pointing to the alleyway in

the other direction. They abandoned the basket and hurried down the alley into a larger, neater yard, ringed with windows. Lottie signalled for them to keep low and close to the wall – out of sight of anyone at the windows – and led them to a door at the far end. Cautiously, she pulled it open.

The hallway inside was sparkling, hospital clean. The tiles gleamed and the walls were painted in bright cheerful colours. There were paintings and framed designs for outfits from the Pepper lines on the wall.

'Here,' Lottie said. 'This is where Mr Pepper's office is, where he greets all his guests. He never shows them the factory. In fact, I don't think I've ever seen him in the factory at all.'

Connie and Hen exchanged a glance – Lottie's observations seemed to fit with what they'd overheard.

'Lottie, come home with us,' Hen said. 'We can't leave you here like this.'

Lottie squeezed his shoulder. 'That's sweet of you, Hen. But I can't leave my family behind.'

Then, a voice boomed from behind them: 'What the grot do you three think you're doin' in 'ere?' They all turned but the beefy overseer was already on top of them. 'You bleedin' kids ain't supposed to be in 'ere.'

Before they could move, the overseer had reached out and grabbed Hen and Lottie by the collars of their overalls.

'Get off!' Hen scrabbled, trying to twist himself free, but the man was too strong.

'Leave them alone,' Connie growled, suddenly springing into action. She grabbed the man's arm and tried to free Hen from his grip. But he was clearly used to dealing with wriggling children. The thought made Hen feel rather sick.

Connie's face grew hard with determination. Hen watched as she drew her leg back and kicked him in the shin. The overseer yelped in mingled pain and surprise. His grip loosened, and Hen and Lottie were able to squirm free as the man doubled over, clutching his leg. The three of them raced back the way they had come.

But as they hurried down the alleyway, Lottie gasped and shoved the others quickly into a dark doorway. Hen caught a glimpse of Mrs Thackerey storming towards them.

'Stay here, I'll lead her off,' Lottie said. And before either Hen or Connie could protest, she slammed the door, leaving them both swathed in darkness.

A sickening smell enveloped them like a heavy blanket, all filth and disease and sadness.

'What is that?' Hen gagged, covering his mouth and nose.

'Smells like something died.'

From outside, Hen heard hurried boots on the cobbles and sounds of a brief scuffle. Something thumped hard against the door. He sent a silent prayer to Hestia to keep Lottie safe.

Were they about to be discovered? He reached towards where he thought Connie was, and was reassured when she gripped his hand and squeezed it tight.

The footsteps moved away from the door at last. Hen let out a long sigh of relief but coughed as the awful smell overpowered him once again.

'Where are we?' he choked.

He heard Connie scrabbling about and there was a sudden chink of brightness as something moved, letting in a narrow shaft of light. Connie had found a boarded-up window.

'That's better . . .' she said, turning to Hen, but then she froze.

'What is it?' Hen's mind raced as he turned slowly

to see what Connie was looking at.

His heart broke. Behind the rusty metal bars of a makeshift pen was a small pod of shleep, chained together and shackled to the filthy stone floor.

'Oh, Hen,' Connie said, a tear trickling down her dirt-streaked cheek.

The shleep glanced up at the sudden sliver of light. Hen could see fear in their eyes, and his own vision swam with tears.

'It's all right,' he said gently, reaching towards them. 'It's OK, we're not going to hurt you.'

He reached towards the chain around the nearest shleep's leg, but it was fastened tight, locked. Hen could see where the metal clasp had rubbed against the poor animal's leg, its fine creamy-white fleece gone, the skin underneath sore and red and swollen.

'They shouldn't be chained to the floor like this,' Hen sobbed. 'They like to be up high, like Marjorie.'

'Pepper is a monster,' Connie spat, and she was suddenly beside Hen, helping him try to loosen the immovable chains. 'How could he treat people and these poor, gentle creatures so badly?'

'I'm not so sure he even knows, not that that's an excuse.' Hen sniffed. 'But Mrs Thackerey seemed pretty keen to keep him away from the truth.'

'You think she's the really evil one, then?' Connie asked.

'Maybe . . .'

Connie got to her feet and started searching through the piles of junk in the small room. 'If only there was some way to show my dad all of this, then we could prove what's really going on here. If Lottie's right, he won't have any idea of what's really happening – he'll only see that lovely painted and clean side over there. He wouldn't do business with Tiberius Pepper if he knew even a little bit of this. Oh, if only we had a camera.' She kicked out at a pile of rusted, broken tools in frustration.

But as he stared at the lock and chains in his hands, Hen realized they had something better than a camera.

Hen could record all of this in a memory, couldn't he? He could stitch his or Connie's memory and show Uncle Bertie. He would have to believe them then, surely?

'Oh, Hen – look!' Connie said, and hurried back to the door where an old key, spotted with rust, hung on a nail in the rotten door frame. She grabbed it and held it aloft like a trophy. As she did, a sharp voice cut through everything like a blade.

'Search everywhere, you simpletons. I want those beastly little brats found.' It was the unmistakable voice of Mrs Thackerey. 'Mr Garvy said he pursued them down here, heading back towards work hall seven and the loading yard.'

Connie crouched beside Hen as they listened to Mrs Thackerey snapping orders in the alleyway. She must be right outside. 'And get this door open. IMMEDIATELY!'

There wasn't any time to hide. In a heartbeat, the door burst inwards, flooding the room with light. Connie squeaked in terror. Two figures were silhouetted in the doorway – the taller was clearly Mrs Thackerey.

'You two,' she hissed with venomous delight.

They were stuck.

There was no way for them to get past now. She had them penned in, just like the poor shleep.

Hen felt something cool and solid press into his palm as Mrs Thackerey took slow steps into the room, her hand covering her nose at the smell.

The shleep!

Connie was passing him the key. And Hen realized he was still holding the lock and chains behind his back.

'I suppose you two think you've been very clever?' she asked.

Hen fumbled with the lock and key and chains. He hoped that Mrs Thackerey was so busy gloating that she wouldn't notice.

'When the pair of you start working for me, you will be on rat duty for a year.'

Hen carried on fiddling with the lock.

'You'll not see daylight for six months. Then we'll see whether you feel so clever!'

It just wouldn't budge. Had it rusted shut?

'I am so going to enjoy having you both here!' she smiled.

CLICK!

Hen heard the lock give and the chains snaked to the floor. In one hurried movement, he grabbed Connie's hand, pulled her up and dragged open the rusty gate of the makeshift shleep pen before Mrs Thackerey could get an inkling of what was going on.

Shleep, though usually docile and calm creatures, had the ability to move fast when they needed to, and they were also incredibly strong. Hen guessed you had to be, to hang upside down all day long every single day of your very long life.

The shleep charged straight for the door. Just as Hen hoped they would.

Mrs Thackerey was knocked off her feet as the creatures barrelled into then trampled over her. Her companion gave a shriek of dismay and ran as fast as he could, his cries echoing down the alleyway.

'Stampede! Stampede! HELP!'

Holding tight to Connie, Hen ran, leaping over Mrs Thackerey's sprawled form. They raced along the alleyway, following the shleep, who seemed to have an inbuilt compass for space and freedom.

In the small yard, Hen saw the basket they'd abandoned earlier and another idea blossomed.

'Push the basket!' he called to Connie. It moved easily on the tracks and as they reached the brick and stone ramp leading down towards Uncle Bertie's car, Hen jumped up, scrabbling inside, Connie right behind him.

The basket zoomed along. Hen saw the building whizz past through the gaps in the basket. And then . . .

CRUNCH!

They were suddenly toppling over, Hen and Connie spilling out on to the dirty cobbles.

The basket lay on its side, its little iron wheels still

whizzing around. Off to their right waited Uncle Bertie's car – and safety.

Hen never thought he would be so happy to see it!

They clambered into the boot, dizzy with terror and excitement and relief. No one had followed!

But Hen's relief soon faded. They had escaped Mrs Thackerey this time, but what if Uncle Bertie agreed to sell the business to Tiberius Pepper? In his mind, Hen replayed images of the haunted faces of the workers and the poor shleep chained to the floor and covered in their own filth. There was so much more at stake than Danelli's going out of business.

But Hen knew they would *show* Uncle Bertie what they had seen. And once he understood what was really happening, he'd surely never work with Tiberius Pepper.

CHAPTER TWENTY-TWO

Secrets Shared

Somehow, Hen and Connie made it back home and into the house without anyone seeing them come from the garage. Hen was exhausted and yet he still knew he had work to do. And he was going to have to tell Connie everything!

'Did you have a fun morning with Simon?' Aunt Lucia called from the kitchen as they climbed the stairs.

'Yes, thank you,' Hen called out.

'Well, lunch is nearly ready. Bertie just got back too, though I've no idea where he's been!' Aunt Lucia said.

'Any news from the hospital?' Hen asked, desperate to change the subject of where everyone had spent their mornings.

'Dr Skelton called about an hour ago – Nana is doing a little better but still needs to rest. But she'll be allowed visitors in a few days. Now, off with you both for a wash – you're absolutely filthy, whatever have you been doing?'

'We were—' Hen faltered.

'—playing in the park,' Connie supplied quickly.

Aunt Lucia wrinkled her nose. 'Well, you both smell like shleep dung! Hurry along.'

Hen and Connie cleaned up in the kitchen after lunch – Aunt Lucia was out for a walk and Uncle Bertie was shut in his cupboard-office. Finally, it was safe to talk.

'Are you OK, Hen?' Connie asked.

'Um . . . yes. I think so. What a morning, eh?'

Connie nodded slowly. 'I keep thinking about poor Lottie. I hope she'll be OK.'

'Me too. She was so brave to help us like that.'

Connie put the stack of plates she had been drying down on the counter and turned to Hen. 'We can't let that happen with us, with our family,' she said. 'And we have to find some way to help Lottie and the others working there.'

'I was thinking the exact same thing,' Hen said. 'And, well, there's something I've been meaning to tell you ... it might help ...'

Connie's eyes widened. 'Well spit it out then, Hen!'

'Memories!' Hen said quickly.

'What?' Connie asked. Then her eyes widened. 'Is this what you were talking about before, in the workroom?'

Hen nodded. 'Connie, you need to come with me to the attic now.' He was already heading for the door. He jangled with excitement and nerves at the thought of sharing the stitched memories with Connie, but it felt right.

Minutes later, Hen was retrieving the old biscuit tin from the back of the wardrobe. He watched Connie take in the makeshift workspace he had created. She ran her fingers over the open trunks of discarded, never-finished garments, dresses, jackets and sweaters. Her eyes widened at the bolts of unused fabrics, old reels of cotton, and pin cushions full of pins.

'These could have been beautiful,' she said. 'Why are they all shut up in the attics?'

'Who knows?' Hen said. 'Fallen out of fashion, probably.'

Then she saw the designs and sketches for Hen's coat pinned to the wall – the ones he'd been working on for the competition. 'But these are yours?' she asked, looking back at Hen.

He blushed and suddenly couldn't speak.

'This was what you wanted to enter for the contest?'

Hen nodded. 'I know you're entering now . . . but I still really wanted to make it. I wanted to show your dad I know what I'm doing.'

'But it's wonderful, Hen,' she said after a few quiet moments studying the sketches and the swatches of fabric Hen had gathered up. 'You were going to use these bits and pieces you found up here?'

He nodded, unsure how she was going to react.

'That's a brilliant idea. It's so *you*, Hen.'

He felt warm with pride – but cleared his throat. 'It'll have to wait now, there's something more important we need to do,' Hen said.

He was worried about those creatures he'd seen

on his last visit to Milly's memory, but he decided they would stay close to the aperture, in the bedroom. Then they could leave quickly if they needed to. He just had to show Connie what was possible.

Hen placed the biscuit tin on the makeshift worktable.

'It's a biscuit tin, Hen . . . how is that going to help exactly?'

'It's not the biscuit tin, Connie.'

He was so nervous, but excited and relieved to be sharing this at last. Finally, he could show Connie that what he had done with Mrs Crab's dress wasn't something wrong or awful, but magical and wonderful.

'OK, now try not to freak out,' Hen said as he started to lift off the lid.

'That's reassuring,' Connie replied. But she stayed put.

'Ready?' he asked.

He lifted the lid and carefully picked up the panel of fabric. The sunlight caught the memory stitching. Connie peered closer.

'What's that? What sort of spell stitch is that, Hen? It looks sort of like . . .'

'The stitching in Mrs Crab's dress?'

Connie nodded. 'Did you do this too? What sort of spell is it supposed to be anyway?'

'No,' Hen said. 'I found this up here in the attic, it's years and years old. And . . . it's a memory stitch. Look . . .'

Hen reached gently for her hand and pressed it and his own against the bloom of stitches. Barely a flicker of a moment passed before Milly's memory began to shimmer to life. Hen watched Connie carefully as their attic above the shop in Sparrow Down became Milly's attic room filled with the warmest summer sunshine and the tang of sea air.

He heard the gulls outside the windows, saw the blue sky and green hills and then Milly was there, bent over her work as usual.

Hen felt Connie move back, startled by Milly's sudden appearance. 'It's OK, just listen,' Hen said quickly as Milly began her greeting.

'Hello, my name is Milly. This is my memory of home.'

Hen watched as Connie's eyes widened and her mouth dropped open. He could see her breathing faster, feel her pulse race under his hand. Was this how he had looked that first time the memory had unfolded around him?

'Oh my – what in the wide world – Hestia's needles!' Connie gasped – but she didn't scream, she didn't run like Hen had the first time he had encountered the memory.

That felt like a lifetime ago now.

Connie stepped forward to get a better look at Milly. She moved around her carefully, as though afraid to disturb her.

She seemed to already be relaxing. She looked as though she was trying to see how it all worked, like peering behind a clock face at all the gears and cogs and levers.

Connie moved around the attic. She went to the window and peered down at the narrow winding street below, across to the tree-covered hills and up at the bright blue sky.

'I can hear the sea,' she said with wonder and then fell silent for several long moments.

'Are you OK?' Hen asked eventually. 'We can go back if you want.'

'This is all a memory?' Connie asked, her voice heavy with wonder.

'Yes.'

'And it's all . . . in those stitches we saw before?'

Hen nodded.

'But why hasn't anyone ever told us about this?'

'I don't know.' He shook his head. He'd had the same thought so many times since discovering Milly. 'I tried to tell Nana – I think she knows about it somehow. But before I could really explain, she told me to steer clear, she said it was dangerous.'

'Really? Dangerous?' There was more quiet as Connie took it all in. Hen decided not to tell her about the strange creatures – not now. He needed her to help and if she knew about them, she might not. Then, she said, 'Is this what you did to that awful woman's dress? Was that a memory?'

'Yes, I think so.' Hen scratched his head. 'Or . . . the start of one maybe.' He explained about Milly's grandfather teaching her to memory-stitch. 'He said that some people find out that they can do it by accident. I think that must be me.'

'I wonder if I can do it,' Connie said.

Hen blinked. She really was taking this all much better than he'd ever imagined. She wasn't scared in the slightest, like he had been. Her curiosity seemed to have taken over completely! She had changed so much . . . or perhaps he hadn't really known her properly to begin with?

Finally she turned to Hen and said, 'OK, what's the plan?'

CHAPTER TWENTY-THREE

STITCHING

ack in the attic, Hen put the memory-stitched silk back into the biscuit tin. 'I was thinking we could stitch the memory of our visit to Tiberius Pepper's factory and show it to Uncle Bertie. It's our best shot, Connie. If we just tell your dad, he's never going to believe us, or even listen – you know that. But if we *show* him the memory, well, he won't be able to argue with that, will he?'

'It sounds like a good plan to me,' Connie said.

'So you'll help?' Hen asked.

'Yes, of course.' She smiled. 'What should I do?'

'Well . . . Perhaps we could try to stitch your memory? I saw how Milly stitched her grandfather's memory, so I think I know what to do . . . roughly! All you have to do is tell me what happened – in detail.'

'All right,' said Connie. 'Well, you'd better get the bits you need. I'll find somewhere for us to sit!'

Hen hurried nervously about the attic workroom, gathering his materials: a piece of fabric, needle pouch and thread.

Connie arranged two of the least wobbly chairs so they were face to face before the dusty windows. They sat down.

'Ready?' he asked, his voice wobbling just a bit, his hands more.

'Yes.'

Connie crossed and then uncrossed her ankles. She sat on her hands and then stuffed them deep in her pockets before taking them out again and folding them in her lap. 'Sorry,' she muttered.

Hen's hands were shaking and it took several attempts for him to pass the thread through the eye of the needle. He lifted the square of grey linen and then nodded at Connie.

She took a deep breath and said, 'So we hid in the

boot of my dad's car and—'

'No, wait. Wait!' Hen called. 'Sorry. I've dropped the needle.'

It took him a few seconds to find it then a few more to rethread it, his hands shaking more than ever.

'Are you OK, Hen?' Connie asked gently.

Was he? This was so important! Hen didn't know how he hadn't realized before that the future of Danelli's, his home, his family, his own future as a spell tailor all seemed to hang by a single thread!

'Yes, yes. I'm fine,' he lied. He closed his eyes and imagined Nana was there, saying gently, *Why don't you just try, Hen? It doesn't matter if you get it wrong. Just try.* 'OK, let's go . . . again.'

'Deep breath,' Connie offered calmly.

Hen nodded.

'OK. Well . . . We arrived at Pepper's factory in the boot of my dad's car . . .'

As she spoke, Hen pushed the needle through the linen and felt the tug of the fabric as he pulled the thread through for the very first stitch. His first few were regular, as though he were starting the very centre of a spell stitch. But as Connie began to recall racing along the never-ending corridors and through the work halls and offices, seeing the spell-brats, Lottie, the poor shleep, he felt his work becoming more random, freer. The stitches spread out this way and that across the fabric, leading Hen's hand, capturing the memory in the thread and cloth. And as Connie spoke it was almost as if he was back at the factory, running alongside her, hiding with her from that awful Mrs Thackerey. He could smell the stench from the poor chained-up shleep, see the fear in Lottie's eyes. But now he saw everything was linked, connected with a stitch of silvery thread which all threaded back into the needle held in his right hand. He stitched these threads into the air before him, into the cobbles of the dirty work yards and even into the clothes and hair of each person Connie recalled from their memory. Was this what it was like when Hestia stitched the universe into being? It felt as though it was taking an eternity and mere seconds all at the same time.

'And that was when we left,' Connie finished and looked across to Hen.

Hen was sitting, his hands suddenly quite still in his lap, staring at Connie.

He shook himself. He felt as though he had been underwater and had just resurfaced. Or woken from the most vivid of dreams. Had he nodded off? 'Oh, sorry. I think I must've missed a bit there,' he started, guiltily.

But Connie was already on her feet in front of him. 'Hestia's needles,' she breathed, lifting her hand to her mouth. She leant forward and rested her hand against the square of grey linen on Hen's lap. 'Oh, Hen, look – it's ... beautiful.'

'What?' Hen glanced down, quite sure Connie was playing some sort of joke.

And then his breath rushed away from him in a gasp of shock.

Across the square of cloth was a gorgeous swirling pattern of stitches – almost as fine as the one that made up Milly's memories. The threads all connected to each other but spiralled, bloomed across the fabric like a cloud. But within them he saw patterns from the memory itself – the metal rails for the huge wicker baskets, the chains that held the poor shleep, plumes of filthy smoke, even cogs and gears that drove the machinery.

'Did ... did I do that?' he stuttered. His hands felt tingly.

Connie nodded silently.

'How?' Hen asked and took in the stitches again.

'It was like you were in a trance,' Connie explained. 'Your hands were moving so fast, like a blur, and you looked like you were talking when I spoke but you didn't say anything at all. It was kind of weird actually. A bit spooky.'

'I listened to you but then it was like I was—'

'Back there?'

'Yes, exactly. But this time everything was connected by threads . . . it was amazing, Connie. I wish you could have seen it.' He looked down at the stitching again. 'Do you think it works?' he asked.

'Let's hope so, but I guess there's only one way to check.' Connie smiled.

She took hold of Hen's hand and pressed it and hers against the memory stitches on the square of linen.

The attic around them faded as the memory unfolded about them – just as it had when Hen visited Milly's memory. The swirling threads of the aperture (silver in this memory, rather than gold) waited near Uncle Bertie's car, where they watched their memory-selves clambering out and taking in the scene. Hen could even smell the acrid tang of the factory smoke.

They had done it! Together, they had stitched a memory.

CHAPTER TWENTY-FOUR

INDECISION

'What is this?' Uncle Bertie asked suspiciously, glancing down at the square of linen that Connie placed in front of him after dinner. It glistened with Hen's beautiful memory stitches. 'Is this something of yours, Hen?' He lifted the linen square with a careful thumb and forefinger, as though it were a dirty, stinky sock or slimy, damp hanky. He brought it closer for a better look. 'We've talked about this . . . creative stitching of yours, Hen . . . and what is it stitched on to? A rough old piece of linen, is it?' He pulled a face as though a bad smell had wafted in from somewhere.

'You mustn't sell the business to Tiberius Pepper,' Connie said quietly but firmly, taking Hen by surprise. He hadn't thought she was going to come straight out with it like that. 'This stitching will explain.'

Uncle Bertie's eyes widened, his face coloured and he shifted in his seat as though something were prodding into his bottom.

'I . . . um . . . well, what a notion! I don't quite know what games you two have been playing, but—'

'Dad, we know you had a meeting with him,' Connie said. 'We know you went to the factory.'

'Sounds as though someone has been snooping when they really should know better, Constance.' Uncle Bertie kept his voice light, but Hen could tell he was angry.

'Please, Dad, please don't even consider it. If you touch the stitching, you'll see the conditions he keeps his workers in and—'

Uncle Bertie started laughing. 'Heavens. You two really have let your imaginations run wild, haven't you?' He shifted in his seat again. 'I, er . . . was simply asked on a tour of the factory along with other members from the Tailors' Guild. Naturally I was curious to see how our main competitor runs his business. There was nothing more to it than that.' Uncle Bertie swallowed hard.

He was lying. Hen was sure of it. It was like he could smell it in the air.

'We saw poor Lottie there,' Connie explained. 'Her whole family went to work there after you fired her and now they can't leave. You'll see if you just—'

'And just how do you know all this?' Uncle Bertie asked.

Connie looked at Hen. A wave of uncertainty crashed against him. This was a mistake. Uncle Bertie wouldn't understand, wouldn't listen.

But Connie powered on. 'You have to listen to us, Dad. Please.' She reached out to him but he stood, brushing her off.

'I have to do no such thing – thank you. What I do with the business is up to me.' His face softened ever so slightly. 'Look, Constance, Hen. You're worried, I know. It's a hard time, with Mother being sick. But the best thing you can do for the business – for the *family* – is stay out of all this, understand? I really don't have time for children's games.' He cast his newspaper aside like scraps from a pattern cutting.

'Dad, wait. Please. We can show you.' Connie's eyes flicked back to the linen square on the coffee table. 'Just try it. It's a memory. Hen has figured out how to stitch memories!'

Uncle Bertie stiffened but quickly disguised his unease with a scoff. *He knows about memory stitches*, Hen realized, certain now. *And like Nana, he doesn't want anything to do with them*. 'This all sounds like the result of an overactive imagination and a bad influence –' he glanced pointedly at Hen – 'if you ask me.'

'You're right. Sorry, Uncle Bertie. We heard some-where that you can stitch memories, but this . . . this was just . . . just some practice stitches for a design I wanted you to look at. But you're right, they're no good so don't worry about it – I'll keep trying.'

'Hen?' Connie said, clearly at a loss as to what was going on now.

'Oh, for heaven's sake, you two,' Uncle Bertie grumbled. 'Enough of this. Constance – erm – go to your room.'

'What? Why?' Connie asked.

'Please just go!'

Connie kicked the armchair nearest to her, growled and stormed out of the room muttering to herself angrily. A moment later Hen heard her bedroom door slam, making the whole house shake.

'Oh Henryton, you have to stop this nonsense.'

'But—'

'Please just listen to me.' He put a gentle hand on Hen's arm. 'I am going to tell you something extremely important. And I hope, once you understand, you will never do this again.' Uncle Bertie straightened himself in his chair, lifted the memory stitching up and held it towards Hen.

'This is dangerous, seriously dangerous, Henryton. You see, monstrous creatures are drawn to these types of stitches. They infest the magic in memory stitches and then they feed off it and the memory, and destroy both. They're called alcuri.'

Hen went cold. 'Monstrous creatures' sounded a lot like the maggoty things in the memory. Suddenly he remembered the husks he'd carelessly swept away from around the memory-stitched garment. Had they been alcuri husks?

'This was very nearly the ruin of the family back in Scillia,' Uncle Bertie went on. 'Great-uncle Maximus vowed never to let a Danelli memory-stitch again.'

No wonder Nana had looked so concerned at Mrs

Crab's dress! And yet – aside from the alcuri – hadn't the memory been the most wonderful thing? Even now Hen could feel the warmth from Milly's memory, the love and tenderness that existed in that little house.

'But surely there is some way?' Hen started. 'We can repel spell-brats, so why can't we—'

'No,' Uncle Bertie said firmly. He picked up the swatch of fabric on the table. 'The only way to be safe is to destroy the stitching altogether.'

'NO! Please don't, Uncle Bertie.' Hen reached forwards. But Uncle Bertie stood and turned away from Hen, towards the fireplace.

'Go to your room, Henryton,' said Uncle Bertie, tiredly. 'And promise me to never, ever memory-stitch again. In fact, promise me you'll never mention it again . . . or even think about it.'

But Hen ran from the room, sobbing, unable to bear the sight of the bunched-up fabric being dropped into the flames.

The next time Hen saw Connie was on the way home from deliveries and errands the next afternoon. She was ahead of him, walking through the marketplace, clutching a stack of library books.

The rain splashed down as Hen ran to catch up with her, trying to get her to stop and listen to him. 'Connie, wait!'

She ignored him, upping her pace. She was clearly still angry with Hen about how he'd doubled back on their plan – and she had successfully avoided him until that point. She had not been at breakfast and had eaten lunch in her room. It was strange how quickly he had got used to having Connie as his friend. Without her, the world felt out of balance. He couldn't blame her though: it was all his fault, after all – and for nothing. Pretending the memory stitches were innocent practice hadn't worked and Connie's memory had gone up in flames.

Hen darted around the puddles, gaining on her. 'Connie!'

He was still trying to get his own head around the fact that Uncle Bertie and Nana had known about memory stitches all along. He *had* to tell Connie.

She couldn't ignore him for ever. 'Connie! Wait! I'm sorry.' She slowed her walk, but she didn't stop. And she didn't turn to face him.

'It was no good,' Hen continued, finally reaching her side. 'I shouldn't have chickened out but your dad knew about memory-stitching anyway. And he really wasn't happy. There's no way he would've touched it. Hestia as my witness!'

Connie didn't respond. She just carried on walking, her eyes fixed on the wet pavement ahead as they both wove in and out of people dashing for cover from the downpour.

'He burnt the memory, Connie.'

Connie stopped suddenly, shoppers darting around her, some moaning at her to move out of the way. She turned. 'What?'

'He threw it in the fireplace and told me not to try to do anything like it again.' Hen ran through his fraught conversation with Uncle Bertie after she had been sent away. 'It's all to do with these dangerous creatures . . .'

'Oh, Hen . . . all your beautiful work!' Connie said, stepping forward. 'I'm so sorry . . . wait, what did you say about dangerous creatures?'

'I saw some in a part of Milly's memory – not the part I took you to, though, I promise. They looked like horrible big maggots. Your dad said they're called alcuri. They feed off the magic and memories.'

'Worse than spell-brats then,' Connie said with a small smile.

'When I thought about it, I remembered seeing

some husks on the attic floor near the memory . . . I thought they were ancient and didn't think anything of it.'

Connie sighed. 'So now what? That was our only plan, wasn't it? If we can't convince my dad to view the memory of the factory, who knows what will happen.'

She was right. Hen wished they could tell Nana, but they didn't know when she would be back from the hospital and whether she'd be all better. Even if she was, he really didn't want to add to her worries right now. It felt like they were right back where they'd started!

'Come on, let's head home,' said Connie softly. 'We're both getting soaked.'

CHAPTER TWENTY-FIVE

DELIBERATE DAMAGE

A week later and the shop and house were in excited disarray – with just two days until the guild contest, Uncle Bertie and Aunt Lucia were focused on helping Connie complete her garment, a pale yellow dress which Hen had only caught glimpses of once or twice.

He wasn't allowed near it in case something awful happened to it, of course.

To distract himself, Hen spent every spare moment he could escaping to the attic and working on his coat designs. After deliveries, before breakfast. He even sat up late at night, secretly sorting and cutting sections from the various old garments in the attic – even bringing bits and pieces down to his room so he could continue planning the coat in bed.

Which was how he found himself waking up with the various coat sections covering him like a drift of leaves! He clambered off the bed, stretched, and gazed down at the most recent sketches of his coat. It would be long and more fitted than was currently the style, but still with a fashionable wide, high collar. It would also have a small, short cape attached to the back, inspired by the shape of the panel that held Milly's memory. It would be made from a variety of different fabrics, all in shades of green, his favourite colour.

Hen knew he'd never actually get to make the coat. He had started it to prove to Uncle Bertie that he *was* capable of being a spell tailor; to show him what could be achieved with all the so-called junk in the attic. He'd probably never convince Uncle Bertie to let him make it now – especially after what had happened with the memory stitches. Whenever he thought of Uncle Bertie throwing them into the fire, a fresh wave of shame crashed against him.

Yet, he couldn't *not* think about and tinker with the coat panels and designs – after all, he wasn't sewing. He had promised not to *sew*, but no one had told him not to cut fabric or make a pattern, had they? And he was really pleased with how it was all coming together . . .

Hen yawned and pulled back his curtains. Light flooded the room.

Glancing at his clock, he realized he had over-slept. Everyone else would already be hard at work in the shop. He was surprised nobody had woken him for breakfast – but he supposed it was just as well really, as they would have found the coat pieces. He pulled open his bedroom door as a shriek of horror rang through the house, followed by the clanging of the bell in the back hallway.

'Not another drill,' Hen yawned.

He headed for the stairs, following the shrieks and shouts that rang up from downstairs. What was going on? It sounded as though it was coming from the workroom! He hurried, skipping two or three stairs at a time, starting to feel worried.

Hen had thought the shrieking was Aunt Lucia at first, but as he raced down the workroom steps he saw her standing beside Uncle Bertie, who was clutching a tattered yellow garment to his chest and wailing, 'It's ruined, ruined! Look at it!'

Connie stood at the bottom of the stairs, backed up against the cupboards, watching aghast as Uncle Bertie went into full meltdown.

Not a drill, then!

'What's happened?' Hen asked Connie.

'Spell-brats,' she whispered.

A shot of horror raced through Hen. So the tattered thing Uncle Bertie was clutching so desperately was Connie's lovely dress for the contest? 'Oh, Connie. I'm sorry,' Hen said, reaching out a hand.

Now, Hen spotted six or seven crushed spell-brats on the workbench and more on the floor near Uncle Bertie's boots.

Connie was pale with anger, her face wet with tears as she clutched Hen's hand tightly. But she was clearly taking it much better than poor old Uncle Bertie.

'Dad's really upset,' she said, which seemed like the understatement of the century.

Hen glanced at Uncle Bertie again. He held Connie's dress to him as if it were a precious, injured bird, fat tears rolling down his pale cheeks as he mumbled to himself. And then as Uncle Bertie looked up, he saw Hen for the first time. He raised his free hand and pointed straight at him. A slick chill of fear ran through Hen.

'This is all your doing,' Uncle Bertie said quietly.

'Bertie!'

'Dad!'

Aunt Lucia and Connie gasped together.

'You were supposed to check the spell-brat traps, Henryton,' Uncle Bertie said, his voice wobbling.

'What? Me?' Hen asked. 'How could I? You said I wasn't allowed in the workroom.'

But Uncle Bertie wasn't listening. 'It was your responsibility to check the traps. I was quite, quite clear about that. And now look what's happened!'

He lifted the ruined dress again.

Hen could see where the spell-brats had gnawed away at Connie's chosen fabric, her careful spell stitches. The dress would have been so beautiful. 'I'm sorry, Uncle Bertie, but you never asked me to check the traps. You banned me from the workroom, remember?' Hen shook as he spoke, not quite able to look at Uncle Bertie directly.

'This might have cost us . . . *everything*!' Uncle Bertie wailed. He seemed on the verge of jumping up and down in frustration. 'We needed to win that prize at the Guild Fair. Connie was our only hope. Don't you see? Those commissions could have saved our business – for another year at least!'

Uncle Bertie truly thought Hen was so useless that Connie was the only hope for Danelli's? The realization was like a hard slap. 'Thanks,' Hen said quietly.

'Bertie,' Aunt Lucia said carefully. 'Hen's right: you did ban him from the workroom. And let's face it, if you hadn't made us throw out your mother's shleep-dung remedy perhaps this might not have happened.' Hen glanced up. It wasn't like Aunt Lucia to disagree with Uncle Bertie like this.

'But, Lucia!' Uncle Bertie said, holding the ruined dress up again and staring at her in dumb shock.

'It's a terrible shame, of course. But this is not Hen's fault. It's no one's fault. And besides, the traps are empty. They didn't work. You know they're not reliable.'

'Mum's right,' Connie added. 'I should have stored the dress away properly, anyway. It didn't need to be left out.'

Hen was so touched at how Aunt Lucia and Connie were both standing up for him – his eyes felt a bit watery. As he glanced away from Uncle Bertie, he noticed the basket in the far corner of the work-room. It was mostly empty now but it had been filled to the brim with treats about a month ago when Uncle Bertie had accepted it from the hands of – his eyes widened – Mrs Thackerey!

His mind clicked. The huge nest of spell-brats they had seen at Pepper's factory, the mysterious outbreaks at spell tailors' shops putting so many of them at risk, and the random gift from Mrs Thackerey . . . they had smuggled spell-brat chrysalises in the basket of treats, Hen was certain of it! And now Danelli's was in grave danger, he was certain of what would happen next . . .

'That woman,' Hen said quickly. 'That Mrs Thackerey gave you that basket – I bet the spell-brats were in there.' He looked across at Connie, who seemed to quickly catch on.

'Who's Mrs Thackerey?' Aunt Lucia asked.

'Just a business acquaintance.' Uncle Bertie blushed.

'And you think she might have brought spell-brats into the shop? Why?'

'She's from Tiberius—' Connie started.

But Uncle Bertie was having none of it. 'Henryton, Connie, go to your rooms!' he blustered, his face pink and sweaty.

Hen was torn. He wanted nothing more than to

be out of the workroom, but at the same time he wanted to stay to make his point.

Aunt Lucia, ever the peacemaker, smiled over to the children. 'Go on up, sweet Hen, Connie,' she said gently. 'Poor Bertie's upset. Let me deal with this, please.'

The cousins hurried upstairs. Moments after he shut his door, there was a gentle knock and Connie called, 'Can I come in?'

Hen pulled his door open and Connie hurried in. They both started talking at once.

'Are you OK? My dad isn't thinking straight.'

'It was Mrs Thackerey who brought all those spell-brats in, Connie, in that gift basket.'

They both fell silent, then Connie nodded. 'I think you're right. There was that huge nest of spell-brats at the factory – this must be what they were for. I'm not sure if that helps, though,' she said. 'It's all too late, now.'

But it certainly did help. Somehow it made Hen feel lighter, as if some of the worry had lifted, now that the burden of it was shared. 'I'm sorry about your dress too, Connie. I really am.'

She picked at Hen's bedspread and then shrugged. 'It wasn't the best.'

'Connie, it was really great.'

'Well, that's sweet of you but . . . I'm no designer really. That's your department! And my dress was nowhere near as good as your coat could be.' She nodded at the garment pieces on the bed.

Her eyes sparkled.

'You should enter your coat for the contest, Hen. It should have been you all along,' she said seriously. 'We could win with your coat! And I have the entry forms signed by my dad! We'll just need to switch your name for mine.'

'But it's nowhere near ready,' Hen explained. 'It's just bits!'

'Then let me help.' Connie smiled. 'This might be our last chance.'

CHAPTER TWENTY-SIX

HELP

Minutes later they were in the attic, the pieces of Hen's coat spread out on the makeshift workbench.

'Can you do the sleeves please, Connie?' Hen asked, indicating a mound of material pieces in front of her.

Hours passed, both of them lost in blissful quiet as they stitched, occasionally talking, studying each other's work or suggesting a way to fix a problem with a different stitch or needle. Neither of them mentioned Tiberius Pepper, though it felt to Hen like he lurked in the shadows of the attic like a spectre.

'If you could stitch a memory, Hen, save it for ever, which would you choose?' Connie asked. Hen had thought about this more than once since he had encountered Milly.

'I remember one afternoon, it was grey and cold out and I was bored. Nana suggested we go for a walk in the park, so we did,' Hen said. He remembered he'd been wearing his good winter coat, one of the many red scarves that Nana was always knitting and new green wellies. 'She was doing her best to cheer me up but for some reason I just wanted to grump. And then she said "Well, suit yourself then, Hen" and she ran off down the path and when she reached a lamp post she grabbed it and swung around it like she was in a musical or something. Then she ran to the next and did the same thing again. It was the funniest thing I had ever seen and it certainly helped to cheer me up. But that wasn't even the best bit! It started to rain, and I mean it was really pouring down. You could hardly see more than a few feet ahead. We were drenched but Nana was loving it, she was splashing in puddles and still swinging around the lamp posts! When we got back home she made us tea and toast, and we sat by the fire in the sitting room and listened to the radio and played cards. It was the best day ever.'

Hen glanced up at Connie. At first he thought she wasn't listening, as she was intently bent over the sleeve she had been stitching. But she seemed strangely still, statue-still, except for her hands which were moving fast. Her eyes were half-closed as if she was drifting off to sleep. Her mouth moved as though she were speaking or singing, though she made no sound. She was memory-stitching!

Her needle stabbed in and out of the fabric, the thread flowing through after it, in and out, in and out, as she stitched the sleeve together. Her stitching had left the seams and bloomed out across the fabric like clouds, all the stitches connected, linked to each other.

She was doing it! Connie was memory-stitching and it was beautiful work.

Connie's actions slowed as Hen stopped talking, as though she were a machine winding down. Her eyelids fluttered like someone waking from a deep sleep.

'Sorry, what did you say?' she asked. And then, she glanced down and gasped. 'Oh, Hestia's petti-coats. Oh, Hen, I'm so sorry! What have I done. I've ruined it.' Connie promptly burst into tears.

'It's OK, Connie,' Hen said soothingly, and he took her hand and pressed their two hands against the stitches she had just sewn.

He felt the welcome sensation of all the air in the room suddenly being rearranged. And then he heard the most wonderful sound – laughter. His and Nana's shared laughter as they raced through the pouring rain in the park. It was as though he had forgotten the wonderful sound of her laughter. His breath caught in his throat. He was afraid to speak in case he cried. He missed Nana so much.

He could feel the rain splashing down on him. Feel the chill nip in the autumn air that smelt of woodsmoke and damp leaves.

'You did it!' Hen said, gesturing to the memory that was still unfurling about them. 'You stitched a memory, Connie.'

They sat beside the fire with the memory Hen and Nana as they ate their toast and sipped their tea. As the rain battered the sitting room window, it felt like they were all safely cocooned inside this memory. It was so hard to leave that cosy, happy room, to leave Nana, happy and well and smiling, just as Milly's memory had been hard to leave too.

Hen realized as they approached the aperture that

he hadn't thought about the alcuri before he entered the memory, which was silly of him really. He glanced about, looking for telltale signs, remembering the way they had affected Milly's memory.

'The alcuri?' Connie asked as though reading his thoughts. 'Are they here?'

'I don't think so,' Hen said with a reassuring smile. 'But let's get back anyway, just to be on the safe side.'

Hand in hand, they stepped through the aperture, out of the memory and back into the attic.

'Exactly *what* is going on up here?'

Uncle Bertie stood inside the attic doorway, squeezing between the wardrobe and chest of drawers that still partly blocked the staircase. His face was the colour of beetroot.

Everyone froze.

Hen.

Connie.

Uncle Bertie.

Hen saw the attic through Uncle Bertie's eyes. It looked like a workroom. A rather clumsily put together one, but still recognizable as a workroom with its large worktable and piles of fabric. Hen swallowed.

'Constance, come here at once, please. And

you—' He pointed a shaking finger at Hen.

Connie stepped in front of her father, holding her hands up. 'Dad, I can explain.'

But Uncle Bertie stepped around her and quickly over to the worktable. With his hands behind his back he leant forwards and peered ever so closely at the partly assembled coat.

'What is this?' he asked.

'Hen had an idea for a garment to enter for the contest and I was helping to—'

'Henryton, I asked you a question,' Uncle Bertie said, ignoring Connie altogether.

'It's a coat. I was making it to show you what I could do, Uncle Bertie. But we thought, Connie and me, well, that maybe we could enter this for the Tailors' Guild contest. In place of Connie's dress.' Hen's voice sounded suddenly so small. 'Connie was helping to get it finished.'

'You were not given permission to enter the contest, Henryton,' Uncle Bertie said as he walked around the attic taking in every little detail. 'Because of your ... peculiarity.'

'But it's safe, we've just been into a memory,' Connie argued. 'There are none of those alcuri in there.'

She lifted up the coat sleeve she had been working on, the sleeve that held Hen's rainy afternoon memory. Hen could see the shape of dark rain clouds and curtains of rain stitched into the spell, and the ripples from rain falling into puddles. Connie placed it ever so gently into her dad's trembling hands.

Uncle Bertie studied her work carefully. His fingers hovering, almost touching the stitches.

'Who did this?' At first he looked at Hen.

'I did,' Connie said quickly, clearly aware what her dad was thinking. 'It's my work, Dad. Not Hen's. *I* stitched that memory.'

The attic was silent but for Uncle Bertie's breathing and the far-off sounds from Beacham Terrace. It was closing time. Hen could hear shopkeepers sweeping the steps and pavements outside their stores, the last few shoppers hurrying home for the evening.

'We can still enter the contest with Hen's coat,' Connie said pleadingly.

Hen now saw his coat through Uncle Bertie's eyes like he had seen the attic. It was nothing but scraps, cast-offs . . . rubbish.

'You know what, it's a bad idea really—' Hen reached for the pieces of the coat but Uncle Bertie was quicker (and had longer arms too), and in a few seconds he had swept the pieces up and held them to his chest. He stepped back, purposeful, away from the workbench. Away from Hen. Away from Connie.

'I, um . . .' His eyes flicked back and forth from Connie to Hen. He looked so sad. 'This, er . . .' He looked back at the crumpled pieces in his hands and said very definitely, 'NO.'

And without another word, he turned and headed for the attic stairs faster than you could say 'stitch', taking the half-assembled coat with him.

'Dad, wait. What are you doing?' Connie called. She stumbled past the chest of drawers and the wardrobe again.

'Uncle Bertie!' Hen called.

They hurried after him.

Uncle Bertie muttered as he headed down the stairs. 'Knew this would happen. Only a matter of time. I warned them. No one listens to Old Bertie though and now look – calamity! We're doomed – the good Danelli name, ruined!'

Hen and Connie reached the bottom of the narrow attic stairs a second after Uncle Bertie stepped through the door. He held the door half-open.

'Dad, please. Hen's design is amazing, and not just the memory stitches – reusing the old garments and all that stuff . . . it could be wonderful for us.'

Uncle Bertie took a deep, shuddering breath and rested against the door frame.

'Dad?' Connie tried again.

'Uncle Bertie?'

'It's not safe,' Uncle Bertie said sadly. He started to close the door. 'You'd best stay here for now. I, um . . . I have to go and get ready for the Guild Fair.'

'No, Uncle Bertie, wait!' Hen threw himself at the door but it was no good, Uncle Bertie was larger and stronger. The door closed easily and a moment later they heard the click of the lock being turned.

'He's locked us in?' Connie asked, half giggling, half crying with nerves.

Hen tried the door even though he was sure it was useless.

Uncle Bertie had his coat. The coat they were going to enter for the contest. He would probably throw it in the fire, like he had the factory memory.

They tried banging on the door and calling – but there was no answer.

Hen had worked so hard on the coat, the idea, the design sketches, finding the different fabrics in the attic and of course stitching it all together with Connie. He had been so close . . .

'My mum will come and look for us when we don't go down to dinner,' Connie said certainly.

Hen wasn't so sure. But he smiled in the gloom and said, 'Well, shall we go back up and wait, then?' He tried to stay calm even though he was more worried now than he could say. It felt as though everything was suddenly collapsing around them both.

They trudged back up into the dark attic and waited.

CHAPTER TWENTY-SEVEN

Rescue

It was dark.

Hen was nodding off to sleep even as he sat upright on the packing crate. Thoughts and dreams tangled and knotted together. Flashes of real things knitted with the imaginary. He saw Tiberius Pepper and Mrs Thackerey striding up the steps of Danelli's and through the door as everyone else filed outside carrying suitcases and odd bits of furniture. Then Hen opened his suitcase for some reason only to find it filled with spell-brats that swarmed over everything.

He jumped awake to see Connie's round face

peering at him through the darkness, a little light coming from the attic windows.

'Hen, what was that noise?'

He felt groggy from his half-dreams. But a noise had certainly sounded somewhere at the back of the attics.

Rats?

Hen's mind filled with thoughts of the alcuri, but they couldn't escape from a memory, could they?

The noise sounded again.

A squeak.

A scrape.

A scratch.

The dry sound of something moving, for the first time in a hundred years perhaps. Then there was a glimmer of light: a gentle, flickering, warm light in the dark.

Hen and Connie exchanged a look and moved closer to each other. Connie held a pair of shears from the workbench in her shaking hands.

'What is it?' she whispered, her voice trembling as much as her hands.

'I don't know,' Hen answered.

The light fluttered more. There was another loud scrape followed by some muttered words that Lottie had often used when frustrated. And then the light caught silver braids, spectacles perched on the end of a large but loveable nose, sea-blue eyes.

'Nana?' they both called.

She stood in a doorway that hadn't been there just moments ago, the light from her oil lamp illuminating her face. She looked tired but well: there was colour in her cheeks and sparkle in her eyes. 'Oh, my dears,' she said as she stepped into the room properly at last. In her other hand she carried a large wicker basket. Marjorie was at her side and the shleep raced to Hen and Connie for horn scratches and neck rubs as Nana put the lantern and basket on the makeshift workbench.

'Are you both all right?' Nana asked, pulling them both into a tight hug that Hen hoped would never end.

'How did you get up here?'

'When did you come home?'

'Are you better now?'

They fired questions at her and she smiled, chuckled and then held up a hand. 'OK, can you give me a second before you continue the interrogation?' She grinned.

It was so lovely to see that smile again. 'I used the

old servants' staircase,' Nana said. 'Nobody uses it any more. I'm not sure anyone knows it's even there, apart from me.' Her eyes twinkled with mischief. 'As for hospital, Dr Skelton said I had improved enough to come home, though she's still no wiser as to what made me ill. So I've to carry on taking things easy for a bit longer until they can run more tests and get me sorted out!' She took a hand each from Hen and Connie and squeezed tight. 'Now, don't you two worry a jot. I'm a tough old bird!'

'Is my dad OK?' Connie asked. 'He was acting really strange.'

Nana sighed. 'Poor Bertie. He's very anxious at the moment. But yes, he's OK.'

'He locked us in,' Hen said.

'I know. He's very muddled.'

'Are you going to let us out?' Hen asked quietly.

'Well, I think you're better off staying up here just for now. I've fetched you some food.' She lifted a covered dish out of the basket and the aroma of Aunt Lucia's spiced dumplings made Hen's stomach rumble.

Nana smiled and then took a few steps around the workbench, taking in all Hen's efforts. 'I haven't been up here in years and years. It's much tidier than

I remember. Good job, Hen. Looks like you've set yourself up a little workroom too.'

He blushed. 'We were working on my coat for the guild contest. But Uncle Bertie took it away—'

'Ah yes. The coat,' Nana said carefully. 'I saw it.'

'What's my dad done with it?' Connie asked.

'Can you get it back for us?' Hen added hopefully.

She didn't say anything or look at them, but studied the open dresser and the biscuit tin where Milly's memory was stored away.

Hen went cold with a certainty that Uncle Bertie had destroyed the coat. Burnt it, shredded it with shears. He didn't know which, but he felt sure the coat was no more.

'Oh, Hen,' Connie said quietly. 'All your hard work.' She clearly thought the same!

Nana turned then and said carefully, 'It was beautiful work. Who did it?' Her quick quizzical eyes flashed from Hen to Connie.

A current of electricity rushed through him – beautiful work! 'We both did,' Hen and Connie said together with a smile at each other.

Nana smiled back at them.

'It's all Hen's design,' Connie added. 'I was just helping with putting it together.'

'And who . . . stitched the memory into it?'

Nana had seen it, sensed it; she knew there was a memory stitched into the coat – the realization hit Hen like a wall.

'I did,' Connie said quietly but firmly, her eyes fixed on Nana.

'But she didn't know what she was doing, it's my fault – I'm sorry, Nana,' Hen said. 'Uncle Bertie explained how the memory stitches ruined your family, how Great-uncle Maximus forbade anyone from stitching them ever again—'

'That's right,' Nana said, though her face gave nothing away. 'I tried to warn you, Hen. But you have a stubborn streak. Hestia knows where you get that from,' she said with a twinkle in her eye.

'But why didn't you say any more? Why didn't you tell me what was wrong with Mrs Crab's dress from the start?'

Nana looked suddenly very tired. She sat down heavily in an old seat and folded her hands in her lap. Her long fingers laced over one another. She looked over to the windows and it seemed to Hen that she wasn't just looking out on to the night, but back to another time and another place.

'Because . . . I was scared.' She looked up at them

both. 'I didn't want to believe that it was happening again. So many lives ruined and all because of one tiny insect.'

'The alcuri?' Connie said.

'Yes – though we didn't know at the time. My brother had never been the greatest spell tailor in the family and then a memory garment he had stitched made a young man dangerously ill. Poor Grandpa was desperate and I'm afraid it caused a rift between him and my brother, Aldo.'

Aldo! Nana called me that in the library, when she was confused, thought Hen. She had thought Hen was her brother!

'Aldo decided to leave Scillia,' Nana continued. 'To find his fortune elsewhere, he said. But not long after he left we found that all of Grandpa's very best designs – and the collection of family memory garments – were gone. Poor Grandpa. He had no way to pay back the customers whose outfits had been stolen and he couldn't afford to buy new material to replace what had been lost.'

'Your brother . . . stole them?' Connie asked.

Another connection was forming in Hen's mind. He remembered the festival in Milly's memory, how she'd begged the boy not to go, how she'd told him that their grandpa would calm down . . . and how Milly had handed over the bag to Aldo without knowing what it contained . . .

Nana nodded sadly. 'I took him a bag the day he left. I thought it was his own clothes and things but, after, I realized what must have been inside. Grandpa was ruined. He wouldn't show his face in town. He sent me here to Sparrow Down to stay with my Uncle Maximus, promising to follow after. But then Grandpa got sick and . . .'

Hen wasn't really concentrating now; his mind fizzed with an idea: a huge, magnificent idea.

Nana continued, 'Uncle Maximus was very clear about one thing: memory-stitching was not something he would ever allow under his roof.'

'He sounds like my dad,' Connie said with a small smile.

'He said if I tried it he would burn the stitches and turn me out of the house.'

Hen's heart started to race as he reached for the biscuit tin that held Milly's memory and carefully lifted it out. 'Which was why you hid your memory of home up here in the attics, where no one could find it?' Hen asked as he placed the panel that held Milly's memory into Nana's lap. She smiled wide even as tears ran down her cheeks. 'Oh,' she breathed.

'It *is* you,' Hen said, certain now. For a second he thought his heart had stopped beating. He had to take a deep gulp of air. 'It was always you. You're Milly.'

She smiled. 'That's what my brother used to call me – when I was born he couldn't manage Amelie. And it sort of stuck. It's been here all this time ... the memory ... I'd forgotten how beautiful it was,' Nana murmured.

And then she fell silent. Her face altered as though it had suddenly been covered by clouds. Her mouth drooped sadly. Her eyes darted nervously and she started to pluck at her skirt. Like she had in the library.

'It's OK, Nana,' Hen muttered, reaching towards her.

'Hen?' Connie looked worried. 'Is Nana OK? Is this what happened before, in the library?'

'Yes,' Hen said. 'And I think I know why.'

He reached gently forwards, lifted Milly's memory out of Nana's lap and laid it on the work-table. 'It's the alcuri,' he said, peering down at the bloom of stitches.

'They're affecting Nana?' Connie asked. 'But how?'

Hen fixed Connie with a level gaze. 'Because this is her memory,' he said, suddenly so sure. 'The alcuri are in Nana's memory and they're affecting her in the real world. This must've been what happened before, when the memory stitch made a customer ill. And that's why the stay-dry spell stitch failed: it was Nana who updated it.'

Connie nodded slowly. 'So what are we going to do?'

'Stop the alcuri, of course.'

'But how?' Connie asked, getting to her feet. She looked across at Nana, worried.

'The alcuri aren't part of the memory, they're intruders.'

Connie looked at him blankly. 'And?'

'If they got in, then they can be forced back out again!' He looked down at the memory with its patch of damage. 'Are you coming?'

'Surely someone else could help . . .'

'No. It's my fault, don't you see?' Hen said quietly. 'By opening the tin in the first place, I let the alcuri get into the memory and I put Nana in danger. And if that wasn't bad enough, when I saw them last time I didn't even try to do anything about them. I just ran away.'

'But you weren't to know, Hen.' Connie reached out and took his hand.

'I have to help Nana,' Hen said. 'I have to stop running away from things that scare me.'

Connie nodded. 'You don't have be scared, Hen. I'm here with you. Let's go!'

CHAPTER TWENTY-EIGHT

CAPTURE AND ESCAPE

Hen and Connie raced down through the memory of Milly's house and flung open the front doors. Bright, cheerful music filled the street; the steady beat of drums, the jingle of bells and the lively chatter of the festivalgoers. Hen fizzed with the excitement that filled the memory but now it was mingled with fear, especially now he understood the very real danger the alcuri posed to Nana.

'Are they here?' Connie asked, her eyes wide as she stared about her. 'What do they look like?'

'You'll know them. They're kind of like big maggots – last time they were up on the rooftops,'

Hen said grimly. He took Connie's hand and they hurried on.

Together, they plunged into the narrow, shady street alongside the memories of people dressed in their finest and brightest clothes, carrying instruments, banners or flags.

Eventually, the crowd slowed and everyone crammed in closer as they reached one of the narrow archways that led into the square where Milly had met Aldo.

'So, Hen ... what happens when we take the alcuri out of the memory?' Connie asked. 'Do they turn back into whatever those things were that left the husks behind ...' She gripped Hen's arm and shook. 'What if ... what if the alcuri are actually spell-brats, Hen?'

He turned and gaped at her. 'What? You think spell-brats and alcuri are the same thing?' he said, confused. 'I know what spell-brat husks look like, Connie. I just told you the alcuri were like huge maggoty things.'

'They could be the same, though. You know, like caterpillars and butterflies. The spell-brats are like the caterpillar and the alcuri are ...'

'Really ugly butterflies?' Hen finished.

'I bet they got in after Mrs Thackerey delivered her gift basket – you didn't see the alcuri before that, right? I bet they don't transform until they've got memory stitches to feed on. Or when they get inside the memory itself.'

'So spell-brats feed on memory stitches, and turn into the alcuri?'

'That's my guess. And because so few spell tailors can memory-stitch, that's why only a few have encountered the alcuri.'

They stood staring at each other for several moments, the enormity of Connie's theory seeming to rumble between them like a gathering storm.

She could be right.

Anger bubbled up inside Hen, fighting against the emotion from the memory. Not only had Tiberius Pepper and Mrs Thackerey tried to ruin Danelli's, they had put Nana in hospital!

'So if we drag the alcuri back through the aperture and out of the memory, they might turn back into spell-brats, right? In which case . . .' Connie mimed stamping down on an imaginary spell-brat. 'Hey presto!' Connie beamed.

Hen prayed to Hestia she was right!

They passed through the archway and into the

wide square with the palm trees, where the alcuri had been before.

Connie froze. 'What's happened? Is this . . .'

'The alcuri,' Hen said grimly. They had clearly been hard at work.

The square felt and looked very different from the last time Hen had been here. The strings of bright bunting that hung across the square were still; no warm breeze moved here now. The colours seemed less bright. Hen remembered how, on his previous visit, the music and dancing had paused and restarted so oddly. Now there was no music and the people moved as if through treacle or underwater. And around the central palm trees, things were even worse. A twisting darkness lurked there and it was spreading. Damage crept into the stones of the square, wrapping itself around the palm trees like rotten ivy. And at the edge of this ever-expanding ruin were the alcuri.

Hen watched in horror as their almost translucent, grub-like forms undulated this way and that in the ruined parts of the memory. They were bigger than before, clearly well fed! Hen thought they were slightly larger than Marjorie. He could see their sharp rings of teeth, which seemed to be chewing at thin air, but he knew were actually slowly but surely destroying Nana's memory.

'That's them?' Connie asked quietly. 'The alcuri?'

'Yes. This is what's affecting Nana,' Hen said, unable to hide the panic in his own voice. How were they supposed to drag them from the memory? His eyes caught again on their teeth, many-layered and needle-sharp.

But they had to do this. If Nana was so unwell with just this amount of damage, what would it be like when they spread beyond the square?

Hen wasn't going to let that happen! He had already caused enough trouble for everyone. Now, it was time to start repairing things.

He was shaking as he walked towards the alcuri – but determined.

Unlike the last time, the alcuri didn't appear bothered by Hen and Connie's presence – even when they were standing a few feet away, on the edge of the darkness, the grubs didn't even glance over.

'So what do we do now?' Connie asked.

Hen had thought the alcuri would attack, or at least give chase like last time. But they just carried on eating away at the memory. 'I don't know. I guess we need to get their attention somehow . . .'

The music from the festival suddenly burst into life and a loud but slow cheer echoed eerily around the piazza. Startled, Hen turned to see what was going on and as he did Connie rushed past him, waving her arms over her head. Every few feet she leapt into the air and hollered, 'Helloooooo! Alcuri! Come and get us!'

'Connie!' Hen hurried after her. 'Are you crackers?'

'You said you wanted to get their attention,' Connie called back. 'So I'm getting their attention.' She waved her arms again and blew a huge raspberry at the maggoty creatures.

'Connie, I don't think that's going to—'

Hen stopped. The alcuri had paused in their eating and had now lifted their heads, their blank, blind faces fixed on Connie. 'Oh, Hestia help us!' Connie said. She took two tiny steps backwards but stumbled.

At once, the alcuri launched themselves forwards. They lolloped and slithered clumsily towards Connie, hissing angrily. They were surprisingly fast!

'Come on!' Hen tried to help Connie up but it was too late to run now – the alcuri were too close!

Without thinking, Hen darted forwards and grabbed the one closest to Connie by the back of its body. It was like wrestling with a sack of wriggling meat! The alcuri struggled and hissed in anger, desperately trying to turn itself so it could bite Hen with its needle teeth.

Hen fell, bashing his arm on the ground. Pain spiked through his shoulder. He lost his grip for a second and the alcuri wriggled away. He grabbed its rear end but it swung back around hissing, its mouth full of ring upon ring of sharp teeth that clicked and snapped.

Connie was back on her feet and doing much better. She had her alcuri by the tail and was dragging it as fast as she could towards the archway, muttering, 'Awful, horrid creatures. You brought this on yourself!' She gave it a swift kick for good measure.

Hen gritted his teeth, jumped out of the way of his alcuri's bite and grabbed it by the tail again – but even dragging it a few feet was a chore. They were so heavy and wriggly!

'It's too far to drag them back to the aperture, Hen. This will take for ever!' Connie called. 'Isn't there a shortcut?'

A shortcut!

'Connie, you're a genius! We just need to find the

edge of the memory!'

Hen looked around – there was only one way in and out of the square, which was through the tall archway. So the edge of the memory must be close by, perhaps the opposite side of the square.

'When we get to the edge of the memory, it will automatically take us back—'

'To the aperture,' Connie gasped. 'Oh, Hen, that's brilliant!'

The hope seemed to give them both a burst of energy and they hurried as fast as they could, dragging the struggling alcuri towards the far side of the square – avoiding the dark mass of destroyed memory at its centre.

They reached the large buildings that lined the far end of the square. Hen sweated as he wrestled the alcuri towards the nearest door. He gulped – it certainly looked very solid. 'Here's hoping this works,' he said to Connie, 'or I'm just going to throw myself at a locked door.'

He gripped the struggling alcuri tighter and leapt straight at the door, bracing for a hard crash.

The expected impact didn't come.

Instead there was a flutter of light, and Hen felt a wooden floor beneath his feet with no more of a jolt than if he had jumped off a low step.

He was back in Milly's room, and right before him swirled the golden threads of the aperture. The creature in his hands seemed to sense what was happening and redoubled its efforts to be free, but Hen managed to hold on tight – just!

He heard a strange wobbling, popping sound and Connie was suddenly beside him, still wrestling with her alcuri.

It was now or never.

Nodding once at each other, Hen and Connie leapt into the rippling circle of threads that formed the aperture.

The alcuri screamed so loud Hen was sure he would go deaf. It was as though they were in his mind and his mind was about to split open like a cracked egg.

Musty air rushed about them. The light shifted and changed as Milly's memory faded and Hen and Connie found themselves back in their attic, Nana sitting in front of them.

Home again.

But where were the alcuri?

CHAPTER TWENTY-NINE

Repair

Nana stirred in her chair, Marjorie laid across her lap. The shleep blinked up at Hen and Connie, perked up at once and dashed over to them, jumping up at Connie.

'Oh, Marjorie – what is it?' Connie sighed. 'Get down.' She gazed around the attic forlornly. 'Hen. It didn't work,' she said. 'They're not here.'

Hen sighed. She was right, there was no sign of the alcuri in the attic. They'd failed ...

But then Hen realized what Marjorie was jumping up at! He gasped, surprise mixed with wonder and delight. 'Connie, look!'

He pointed at her shoulder. Clinging to it was, unmistakably, an alcuri – except now it was some way between its original spell-brat form and its alcuri shape, which only made it more disgusting.

'Urgh!' said Connie, freezing and screwing her eyes shut. 'Get it off me!'

Though exceptionally large for an insect, Hen realized with relief it could still be easily squished under his shoe . . . or maybe both shoes!

But before he could do anything, Marjorie stood on her back legs and snaffled the alcuri from Connie's shoulder. There was a crunching sound as Marjorie ate the alcuri whole!

Hen shuddered, but at the same time a bubble of laughter erupted from him.

Seconds later, Marjorie had tracked down his alcuri (now dangling from the bottom of his jumper!) and snacked on that, too. She smiled up at Hen with a satisfied expression on her face, her dark green, marble-like eyes blinking.

'Did . . . did Marjorie just eat the alcuri?' Connie asked, sounding every bit as fascinated, amused and disgusted as Hen felt.

Hen nodded slowly. 'Yes, she absolutely did. Good girl, Marjorie! Who's a good shleep?'

And they both burst into laughter and fell to the floor, hugging Marjorie tight.

Then, Hen remembered Nana. He sat up and turned, hoping it had all been worth it. She still sat in the chair, blinking and confused as she studied Hen, Connie and Marjorie. She clutched tightly to the scrap of material that held Milly's . . . no, *her* memory. Hen could see that despite their efforts it had been damaged beyond repair. At the heart of the spell stitch, the threads were blackened, shrivelled and ruined.

Hen's joy died as fast as it had erupted. It had all been pointless. Whatever the alcuri had done to Nana's memory, it was permanent.

'Can you remember the square, Nana? The festival? Aldo?' Hen asked hopelessly.

Nana's lips pursed and she looked off to one side as though she was searching for something on the floor of the attic. 'Aldo?' Her voice sounded lost, faraway. 'Who is that?' she frowned. 'Who are you? Aldo?'

Connie looked at Hen. 'It hasn't worked, has it?' Her voice trembled.

'I'm so sorry, Nana. This is all my fault.' Hen turned away and wiped the stinging hot tears that coursed down his face.

He couldn't look down at the mess of threads on the fabric or at Nana. It was too hard.

Would he ever stop failing at everything?

Then, something caught his eye near the window. It was the spider; the one he had been trying to ignore since that first day in the attic. Its web lay in straggles, torn by a breeze from the window or who knew what. But as Hen stood watching, fascinated and scared, he saw the spider move this way and that, gently lifting the damaged strands of the web and mending them with new silk.

'Fix.'

Hen turned back. 'Nana?'

She seemed to be trying to raise her hand and point at the web. She had noticed it too! 'Fix . . . it,' she said, each word clearly an effort. She was pointing at the spider mending her web and then at the fabric and her ruined memory stitches.

'The memory stitch! She wants you to repair it,' Connie said.

'But you can't fix a spell stitch,' Hen said quickly. 'That's the first thing you learn about spell tailoring. Once a spell stitch fails, that's it – isn't it?'

But, if nothing else, the past few weeks had shown

him that there was so much that they didn't really understand about the true magic behind their spell stitches.

'Hen . . . fix . . . anything,' Nana said with great effort, but then smiled.

'She's right, Hen. You have a gift for mending. Isn't it worth a try?'

He was squeezed by doubt, a cold tight fear that pressed against him. 'But what if I do it wrong? This is Nana's memory, Connie.'

They both looked back at her. Nana was clearly not herself – might never be her old self again. 'Try,' Connie said. 'Please try.'

Hen leant over the square of fabric and studied the memory stitch, even though he felt he knew every single stitch by heart already. He could feel himself trembling. His thoughts were all jittery and jangly. He didn't know what to do. Didn't know how to even begin to fix this.

Connie and Nana were wrong. This was beyond him.

'You can do this.' Connie smiled as though she had read his thoughts. 'If anyone can, Hen, it's you.'

You have a gift for fixing things.

How many times had Nana told him that over the

years? He seized a needle and thread from the work-bench and knelt before Nana, gently taking the panel from her.

But as soon as Hen touched the memory stitches, before he had even brought the needle near enough to even attempt to sew anything, he found himself tumbling back into the memory itself, back into Milly's – Nana's – room. 'Hestia's needles,' Hen spat, and hurried back through the aperture into his attic. He tried again.

And again.

And again.

But each time he wound up back in the same place. He kicked out at the leg of Milly's bed – he wouldn't be able to fix the memory from inside it!

Or could he?

He was still holding the needle he had picked up to repair the stitches. Was it possible he could repair them from inside the memory itself?

He left the memory again, this time to retrieve Connie. 'Grab a needle and come with me!' Hen said quickly.

Seconds later they were back in Nana's memory and hurrying again through the crowds of festival-goers who wound their way through the narrow, shadowy streets. They were soon back in the square, standing before the ruined area of the memory.

'How do we do this, Hen?' Connie asked, looking at him and then at the ruined threads that were all curled in like autumn leaves, blackened like something half destroyed in a fire.

Where the alcuri had destroyed the memory, Hen could see the ragged edges of something that looked like fabric and loose thread. So perhaps that was something he could work with. As Hen reached up towards the ruined area, something strange happened. His needle suddenly fizzed in his hands, buzzed, quivered as though electricity had passed through it. It made him startle for a second. But then he leant forwards and ever so carefully pierced the ruined memory with his needle. It was hard at first, like the toughest, coarsest material, but then as the thread finally passed through, a thin stream of light fluttered from the end, like thread. It glowed with a light so brilliant Hen was sure he would need to shield his eyes. Connie copied him as soon as she saw what he was doing.

At first it was just bringing the gaping, ruined area back together. The silvery, glowing thread pulsed with power and seemed to be repairing the damage quickly. 'There were two more palm trees just over there,' Hen called to Connie as he stitched the crowd of dancers back into existence beside the leaping fountain – they swirled into life again as though they had never stopped dancing even for a second.

When the square was repaired – or as close as they could make it from their own memories – Hen used his needle to stitch Aldo, Nana's mysterious brother. He closed his eyes and pictured him, the rounded shoulders and large blue eyes and the dark sweep of thick hair. The threads shifted and the boy moved back into the memory – he fiddled with his bow tie and straightened his shirt cuffs, apparently none the worse for wear.

'So that's Aldo?' Connie asked, coming to Hen's side. 'He looks sort of familiar.'

'He looks like Nana,' Hen said.

'And you,' Connie replied. 'I wonder what happened to him? She's never mentioned him – ever.'

'Let's go and find out,' Hen said.

CHAPTER THIRTY

Nana's Secret

As Hen stepped through the aperture he sent up a silent prayer to Hestia that Nana would be herself again.

They passed through the swirling, golden threads and back into the attic above Danelli's.

Hen had no idea how long they had been gone.

It was still dark outside, but perhaps a whole day had passed? Nana had fallen asleep in the seat beside the makeshift workbench. Hen looked down at the memory stitches in the fabric panel. He thought they looked the same as they had before the spell-brats and alcuri had ruined them, but he couldn't be sure. 'Nana?' he said gently. His hand on her shoulder. 'Nana, it's Hen, wake up . . .'

He looked at Connie, more scared than ever.

What if it hadn't worked?

What if she was now worse than before?

Nana's eyes blinked huge and clear behind her silver-rimmed spectacles. She licked her lips and stretched a little, then stared blankly for a moment at Hen and then Connie.

Icy fear rushed against him. *It hadn't worked.*

'Oh my dears. I think I must have nodded off,' Nana said with a yawn. 'Are you all right? You look quite pale, the pair of you.'

Hen reached forwards and grabbed her hands. 'Do you remember? Do you remember the festival, do you remember . . . Aldo?'

She looked rather shocked. 'What the . . . well of course I do . . .' She fell silent as it all sunk in. 'Oh, you did it? Hen, you fixed the memory stitch!'

She leapt up from her seat and caught Hen and Connie in a tight embrace. 'I knew you could do it, Hen. I knew it.'

'Connie helped too,' Hen said, struggling to catch his breath in the grip of Nana's hug.

'You are both too wonderful for words!' Then she

was spinning them around, laughing and dancing on the spot. 'My clever grandchildren!'

'So, Aldo was your brother, Nana?' Connie asked once they were gathered back around Hen's work-table, Marjorie settled beside them. 'Did you ever find out what happened to him?' There was a cautious edge to her voice.

Nana sighed. 'I thought perhaps I knew where he was once. But when I wrote to him, he never replied.'

'I can't believe he stole the garments,' Hen said. 'Your family's memories, too.'

'Sometimes years of silence can be more damaging than any words spoken in anger. I was angry with him for so long . . . but I still miss him.'

'Nana, I . . .' Connie stopped abruptly and then asked, 'Is that why you kept this?'

Nana patted her memory-stitched panel. 'Yes. I stitched this when I first came to Ingle as a girl. These are all my favourite memories of home. I wanted to be able to go back, walk the streets and see the town . . . the memory-stitching allowed me to do that. That was all. It was nothing more complicated or simple than a child's wish to see home again, to relive the important moments that happened there

– even the painful ones, like the last time I saw Aldo. But dear old Uncle Maximus was dead set against memory-stitching, because of the trouble with the alcuri and what it did to my grandpa's branch of the business, so I kept this secret and hid it up here.'

She smiled weakly and glanced over to the windows of the attic. The sky beyond had changed from inky black to dark grey. The sun was rising. 'Isn't it the day of the Guild Fair?' Nana asked.

'Yes . . . but what's the use of that now? Connie's dress is ruined and my coat is ashes now,' said Hen sadly.

'Oh, is it?' Nana asked, her eyes shining. She hurried to the basket she had been carrying when she came into the attic, reached in and brought out the sections of Hen's coat!

'You saved it!' Connie gasped.

Hen felt tears prick his eyes. He couldn't believe it! That Nana had so much faith in him meant so much. He ran his fingers over the soft material . . . but it was still no use. 'We don't have time. I'll never get it all stitched together now.'

'Well, *we* can help.' Nana looked at Connie.

'Oh, yes!' Connie clapped her hands together in excitement. 'Let's get to work!'

Bright morning light filled the attic and the first sounds of the new day in Sparrow Down were rising up from the street.

Hen's coat hung from the dressmaker's dummy. Hen, Nana and Connie took it all in. The square of fabric that held Nana's repaired memory had been carefully added into the back cloak panel of the coat. Two more memories, one from Hen and one from Connie, had also been added. Hen's rainy afternoon memory sewn into the sleeve by Connie. And Connie's favourite Nana memory, of Nana singing a Scillian lullaby, stitched by Hen, had been added into the front of the coat. It seemed the right thing to do.

'A prize-winning coat if ever I saw one,' Nana smiled.

'I don't know, Nana. I'm not sure it's a good idea.'

He had flip-flopped as they worked, about whether to still enter or not.

Was he really going to do it?

What if the judges wouldn't let them enter?

What if they were horrified by the memory stitches?

What if everyone just laughed at him?

Nana laughed. 'No, it's a *fantastic* idea.' She was already lifting their finished coat off the mannequin. She placed it carefully on to the workbench, her keys jingling as she moved. Next, she unfolded a large piece of clean white muslin.

Nana laid out the coat with such care Hen felt sure he would cry. She folded it all quickly but delicately and precisely, humming as she worked. This was something Hen had watched her do a thousand times, yet it was still mesmerizing. He could have watched Nana work all day long.

She tied the bundle with ribbon and then produced a large velvet sack from her basket. Once the coat was tucked away, Nana rested her hands on the top and whispered a quick, silent prayer, then she handed it all to Hen. 'Now go,' she said. 'And good luck, my loves.'

She planted a big Nana-kiss on Hen's and Connie's foreheads and beamed proudly at them.

'Wait,' squeaked Connie all of a sudden. 'How will we even get there? My dad will have already left and the bus won't get us there in time now. We'll miss registration.'

They stared at each other.

They'd come so far and now they were going to be

scuppered by the district council's bus timetable of all things. 'Twist it!' Connie spat.

'Oh, wait.' Nana grinned. 'I have just the thing! Come with me.'

They followed her back down the attic steps and into the house, Marjorie close behind them.

'I finally got it to work in hospital,' she said mysteriously.

Nana went to her bedroom and emerged with her vast bundle of knitting trailing behind her. She pulled out two of her signature incredibly long red scarves. 'I've been working on this for years!' she said proudly.

'Another red scarf. Lovely.' Connie glanced at Hen, her eyebrows raised.

'It's a flying scarf, of course,' Nana explained, as though that were all too obvious.

'A flying scarf?' Connie repeated, flashing Hen a look of concern.

Perhaps they hadn't been quite as successful as they'd thought with fixing the memory stitch?

'Yes,' Nana said as she looped one of the scarves twice around Connie's neck, the ends of it trailing across the carpet and their feet. She quickly wrapped the other around Hen's neck the same way.

Connie and Hen exchanged more worried looks.

'Erm, they don't seem to be working, Nana,' Hen said gently, lifting one limp end of his scarf.

'Well, they won't work inside – imagine the disaster that would be!' Nana grinned. She beckoned to Marjorie and marched towards the stairs. 'Come on!'

CHAPTER THIRTY-ONE

The Fair

They headed downstairs, Hen deciding to go along with the whole flying scarf thing for now. They'd work out what to do once they were outside. Nana unlocked the back door carefully and they stepped out into the garden, Connie nearly tripping over her trailing scarf once or twice.

Almost at once Hen felt a movement, something flapping nearby, as though someone had wafted a bolt of cloth near him. He glanced right and left and saw that the long trailing ends of the scarf had started to move. They rippled in the air beside him, undulating, fluctuating like the tendrils of some strange plant or . . . like wings!

Connie's scarf was doing exactly the same thing. And that was when Hen realized he wasn't on the ground any more. He was about thirty centimetres above the lawn and so was Connie! It was working. Marjorie let out a little purr of excitement.

'Oh, blimey,' Hen gasped. 'Nana?'

'That looks like it's doing the trick perfectly well, doesn't it? I've been practising that flying stitch for years and years but it never worked – until now!' She beamed and rocked back on her heels. 'And Bertie said it would never work – pah! Far too much of your grandfather's side of the family in him, they were a miserable lot.' Nana rolled her eyes.

Connie giggled – a little nervously – as Nana handed Hen the velvet bag that held the coat and beamed. 'Now, you two,' she called as they floated up and up, past the kitchen window, past the bathroom window, 'you're like me – a bit more gumption, thank Hestia!'

'I'm not sure this is a good idea,' Connie squeaked. 'What will our parents say?'

'Oh, never mind your parents,' Nana laughed. 'I think it's high time you two had an adventure. Does everyone the power of good to have an adventure every now and then, you know. Someday I'll tell you the real story about sewing that wedding dress for the Queen of the Giants!'

They were floating higher and higher, the ground gently slipping away. The wall and windows of the house rushed past them and then they were above the rooftops, Nana and Marjorie growing smaller and smaller below them on the back steps.

'See you there, my loves!' she shouted and waved, dancing a jig on the back steps. 'Good luck!' she called, and Marjorie joined in with a low but loud squeak that set Dr Hunter's dog barking a few doors down. 'Oh, look out for that tree!'

As they cleared the rooftop and chimney pots, a gust of strong wind caught them and propelled them forwards. They sailed over Beacham Terrace, early morning shoppers pointing and waving at them. One lady dropped her shopping basket, the contents spilling out across the street as she shrieked and ran for cover. Another gust of wind sent them speeding off, fast enough to knock the breath out of Hen for a second!

And then they were leaving Sparrow Down behind, roads and streets and houses slipping away, turning to lanes and fields, hedges and trees.

They were on their way.

Fear gave way to fascination and excitement as Hen and Connie flew on, realizing after a few minutes that every small move of their bodies steered them, made them fly faster or slower, banking left and right, dipping down and soaring back up again. The long tail ends of their scarves rippled gently in the air beside them. Occasionally people saw them and pointed, open-mouthed, then stared up and waved.

After several minutes it suddenly occurred to Hen that he had no idea if they were headed in the right direction.

'Are we going the right way, Connie?' he called out, his voice tight with panic. It was all but swallowed up by the rushing air around them.

'Yep!' Connie replied and pointed down at the thin ribbon of black that wound beneath them. 'That's the main road and that's Brackwood Moor coming up. Just the other side is Brackwood town and then we carry on to Hampston.'

Hen was relieved Connie seemed to know where they were. 'Did you think these would work?' he asked, pointing at his scarf as it flapped away.

'Not in a million years.' Connie laughed. 'But here we are, flying! I think they're pretty great!'

It made Hen wonder what other tricks Nana had up her sleeve . . . and what other magic lurked within the family that people had been keeping secret for who knew how long! He clutched the velvet sack tight to his chest, terrified he might drop it as they soared over a large pond, and then a wild thatch of woodland before the expanse of Brackwood Moor opened below them. It was all patches of copper, brilliant yellow and bright green with great lumps of rock that seemed to surge upwards from the depths of the earth like searching fingertips. Hen even spotted a few pods of wild shleep roaming near the rockier parts, their calls carrying to him on the wind.

Connie suddenly banked to her left, following the snaking road below. Hen followed, but turned a little too sharply and flew off in the wrong direction for several panic-filled seconds before he righted himself. Whoever thought flying by scarf was going to be easy? They flew over Brackwood, Hen's stomach clenching when he saw the billows of yellow smoke rising up from Tiberius Pepper's factory. A few people in the streets saw them, and there was more pointing and waving. Hen and Connie waved back with delight.

As they cleared Brackwood, Hampston came into view in the next shallow valley.

'Do you know the way to the Cloth Hall?' Hen called to Connie.

She laughed and pointed ahead.

Hen soon saw why. The huge rectangle of gleaming, creamy yellow stone was hard to miss. People flooded in through the gates at the south end and then into the vast courtyard, which already looked packed. As Connie and Hen started to descend, people began to notice them, pointing and waving and calling out in delight.

'So much for going unnoticed!' Hen said as they dropped lower.

'Let's make a grand entrance, shall we?' Connie called, swooping over the high walls of the Cloth Hall.

They dropped lower and lower, the crowds below moving to make a space for the amazing flying children to land. They must have thought it was some sort of spectacle, arranged just for the fair. As they finally touched the floor, a loud cheer rose up around them. Their scarves rippled one last time before falling still.

Hen could feel himself blushing but Connie clearly thought it was a good idea to take a bow, and the crowd cheered again! As they looped up the trailing scarves people crowded closer, patting them on the back, shaking them by the hands, dozens of questions being asked all at once.

'Wonderful! Ingenious!'

'Is there a spell stitch in the scarf?'

'Wherever did you get them?'

'Danelli's!' Connie called proudly.

Hen held up his hand before more questions rushed in and asked, 'Can you tell us where we go to register for the contest, please?'

'My cousin is entering a garment,' Connie explained, brandishing the entry form.

'*We're* entering a garment,' Hen corrected. 'It's a family effort.'

A kindly woman pointed through the crowd. 'The desk for registration is over by the door of the Cloth Hall itself. Best you hurry, though, dears. Registration closes at ten – not much time left.'

'Thank you!' they chorused, already dashing away as fast as they could.

As they hurried through the crush of people, they saw various stalls with cloths and fabrics and garments from all over Ingle and even some from further afield.

'These are beautiful!' Connie said, pausing by a stall covered in the brightest coloured fabrics Hen had ever seen. As Connie brushed her hand over the fabric it shimmered with light.

'Come on, we need to hurry,' Hen said, pulling her along. But it *was* hard not to be distracted!

It was Hen who slowed his pace next, when he glimpsed a stall covered in strange plants with long, dangling roots that the merchant appeared to be knitting. He had never seen or heard of anything like it.

Hen was about to move on when Connie shoved him hard so that he stumbled between two stalls.

'Ow, Connie!' Hen gasped. 'What are you play-ing at?'

But Connie threw him a look that told him to keep quiet. 'I just saw my dad!'

Seconds later, Uncle Bertie strolled past. He paused and lifted some fabric for a closer look, made a few notes and then carried on.

'It's OK, I don't think he saw us.' Connie sighed.

The stallholder peered down at them, a puzzled look on her face. 'What are you doing?'

'Sorry, I dropped some money,' Connie said. She pulled Hen back up and whispered, 'That was too close.'

They hurried past more stalls overflowing with all manner of fabrics, some they recognized, but many they didn't. They both kept a careful watch out for Uncle Bertie as they made their way towards the Cloth Hall.

As the stalls ended and the crowd thinned, they could see the huge arched doorway into the Cloth Hall at last, and just to one side was a long table with a sign above it that read:

GUILD FAIR YOUNG TAILORS' CONTEST REGISTRATION

But as Connie headed for the table, it was Hen's turn to let out a gasp. He had spotted Mrs Thackerey next to the registration desk, carefully scrutinizing a clipboard which she then thrust back at the man behind the table, before staring off into the crowds again.

'We can't let her see us,' Hen said. 'She might recognize us!'

'Oh, knots!' Connie grumbled. 'We don't have time for this, look!'

The clock on the tall spire above the guild hall showed it was nearly ten o'clock, and they were already starting to tidy things away on the table.

Before Hen could think of a plan, Connie squeezed his hand and then darted towards Mrs Thackerey, shouting, 'Over here, you rickety old broom handle!'

Hen couldn't believe it.

It took Mrs Thackerey two seconds to realize the jibe was aimed at her. Her eyes widened. Her nostrils flared and her bony cheeks went pink as summer apples. Onlookers gasped as Connie ran up to her, kicked her hard in the shin and blew a massive raspberry at her.

Mrs Thackerey lunged to grab Connie, but Connie was fast, and she darted into the crowd before Mrs Thackerey had thought to follow. But follow she did.

Leaving the registration table clear.

Sending up a silent prayer for Hestia to watch over Connie, Hen hurried forward, pulling the completed and signed registration forms from his pocket, which he slammed on to the desk in front of the clipboard man. His name had been printed next to Connie's at the top in his neatest handwriting.

'I'm Henryton Danelli,' he gasped. 'I'd like to enter a garment for the contest, please.'

The clipboard man peered at the papers and then lifted them up for a better look, just as the Cloth Hall clock struck ten.

CHAPTER THIRTY-TWO

JUDGES

The clipboard man glanced at the clock and pulled a face. Hen worried, for one heart-stopping moment, that he wasn't going to let him enter. Then he sighed and brought down a rubber stamp on to the entry forms. A bright blue guild crest now filled most of the bottom left-hand corner of the form.

'Hurry along, then,' the clipboard man said, and pointed in a rather bored fashion at the huge arched doorway.

Racing through, Hen found himself in a wide aisle between rows and rows of chairs, many of which were already full. The chairs ran all around the outside of the guild hall itself, and the space in the centre was empty except for a line of mannequins and a small group of young spell tailors, though all of them were still a good few years older than Hen and Connie. He could feel the curious glances from the audience as he walked into the centre of the space. An official hurried over. He wore a blue sash and clutched a clipboard like the man at the registration table had.

'Are you OK, little boy?' he asked in an overly sweet voice he obviously thought was kind. 'Are you looking for your mummy and daddy?'

'No,' Hen said rather crossly. 'I'm an entrant for the contest.'

'Oh, really?' the official said. 'Papers, then, please.' He gave a little laugh, as though he wasn't expecting Hen to have an entry form, so Hen was quite pleased when he handed over the stamped forms and the man gaped at them for a second. 'Oh, I see,' he stuttered. 'Over there with the others, please.'

Hen thanked him and went to join the other entrants. He could see now that most of the garments were already on display. The other young entrants were busy making last-minute adjustments.

Stitches were stitched, loose threads were snipped, fabric gently pulled this way and that. Another sashed official smiled at Hen as he cautiously approached, a wave of doubt crashing over him. She checked his forms and then pointed to the dummy at the far end of the line, the furthest away from the judges' table and slightly out of the glare of the spotlight. Hen wasn't sure if that was good or bad.

He rested the velvet bag by his feet and stared at the dummy. He tried not to look at the neighbouring garment, a long dress that cascaded across the floor in layers of ruffles and flounces.

'Will you need any help, young man?' the official asked kindly.

Before Hen could reply, a voice sang out behind them. 'No, it's OK. I'm here.'

'Connie!' Hen spun around as Connie raced up to him, her hair all sweaty and flyaway, her eyes alight with adventure.

'What happened to Mrs Thackerey?' Hen asked as they hugged tight.

'Oh, well, despite her giraffe legs, she really couldn't keep up with me this time,' Connie laughed.

The sashed official returned with a large card

label with 'H & C Danelli' written on one side in huge letters. She handed it to Connie before hurrying away again, checking her clipboard and calling to someone they couldn't quite see. 'No, don't leave that there, Pascal, or someone will break their neck!'

Connie looked at the other entrants and then said quietly, 'We'd better get a move on.' She untied the cords of the velvet sack and they both reached inside to lift out the coat.

Soon the coat was on the dummy, and Hen could feel the curious glances from the other entrants and the officials, who walked past a few times muttering quietly and pointing. Hen was worried, but Connie said, 'It's fine, Hen, it looks amazing. It's the most original thing here. Everything else looks ... *dull*!'

'Hmmph.' The neighbouring entrant sniffed and aggressively flounced the many ruffles of her dress.

'My lords, ladies and gentlemen, Tailors' Guild members and honoured guests. We are delighted to welcome you to the two hundred and eleventh Ingle Tailors' Guild Fair, and our very special contest this year for the most original garment from a young spell tailor aged under eighteen.' Hen turned and saw one of the officials was now speaking into a large, red metal cone that amplified her voice around the hall. 'We have received nineteen entries from students and apprentices from some of our most respected and long-established spell tailor houses.'

There was a spattering of applause from the assembled crowd as even more people squeezed into the hall.

The announcer continued, 'Our judges for the contest are . . . Sophia Bakewell of Bakewell's Pins and Needles, Sir Hugo Horrocks of Horrocks and Daughter's Cloth Merchants, and Emeline and Edward Avis of the House of Avis.'

The judges stood and waved at the crowd, who answered with more applause.

The next forty minutes were painstaking, as the judges, clipboards in hand, made their way along the row of entrants. At each garment they stopped, walking around it once or twice, looking closely but not touching. Then they took it in turns to chat with the creator and to handle the garment, lifting hems, cuffs and collars to study stitching. Every little detail was under scrutiny. Hen watched as the other entrants were quizzed by the judges. Faces turned various shades of pink or purple, or drained of colour completely. Hands twiddled nervously, lips were chewed, brows beaded with sweat. Hen felt quite awful for them all and sick with worry about what the judges would say when they reached him. He suddenly couldn't even look at the coat.

And then it was their turn!

The judges all introduced themselves and shook Hen's and Connie's hands first. Sophia Bakewell was first to ask, 'And who created this?'

'Hen,' Connie said brightly.

'We both did,' Hen corrected.

'But Hen designed it, see.' Connie was suddenly showing the judges Hen's design of the coat. When had she taken it off the wall in the attic?

'A true family effort.' Sophia Bakewell smiled. 'That's nice to see.'

As she said this, Hen saw Uncle Bertie standing in the crowd at the edge of the hall. He was trying to get through but there were too many people blocking his way. They locked eyes briefly and then Hen looked away again, pretending he hadn't seen him.

The judges passed the drawing back and forth, muttering quietly to each other and pointing out different things on the design.

'It's quite ingenious.' Sir Hugo Horrocks smiled. 'Like a sort of patchwork, is it?' He peered closer, his nose almost touching the fabric as he squinted at the stitches.

'Patchwork is about to make a *huge* comeback, darlings, mark my words,' Emeline Avis purred.

'Hen used lots of old, unfinished garments that he found in our attic,' Connie said proudly.

Hen winced. He'd rather hoped that detail wouldn't come up.

A quizzical look passed between the judges. 'Old garments?' Sophia Bakewell asked, and peered at the coat again as though seeing it for the first time.

Hen felt rather sweaty and a bit sick. He wondered what shade of pink he had turned.

The judges were hurriedly making notes on their clipboards and exchanged whispered words that Hen couldn't make out.

They turned back to the coat, studying the memory stitches more carefully. 'Now who was responsible for this spell stitching and what is it for? It's not one I recognize from Danelli's,' Emeline Avis said. Her fingertips brushing against the threads ever so gently.

She gave a small, delighted gasp of surprise followed by a husky, dry laugh. 'Whatever was that?' she asked, looking at Hen and Connie.

Now or never!

'It's a memory,' Hen said carefully, proudly.

'A memory?' Emeline Avis asked, tentatively reaching out again to brush the memory stitches.

Hen imagined what she saw when she did. Milly in the attic room looking out across the rooftops to the tree-covered hills, the scent of lemons in the air.

'Amazing,' Emeline Avis said, smiling at Hen.

'Would you like to try it on?' Connie asked.

Emeline Avis seemed to consider this for a moment. She looked at the other judges, who all nodded, clearly intrigued.

'Well, I'd be delighted,' she said, smiling at Connie and Hen.

Ten minutes later, each of the judges had tried on the coat and the hall was buzzing with chatter.

Hen had risked a glance across at Uncle Bertie, who seemed to have gone quite pale and wasn't really watching.

'Enchanting!' Sir Hugo said as the judges finally

moved away from Hen and Connie and back towards their table. 'Very interesting to note the effect of the memories on the wearer,' he murmured to the other judges. 'It's like being wrapped in a big, warm, lemony hug.'

'Imagine,' Sir Hugo continued, 'you could hold your favourite memory always, experience it as many times as you like, relive those feelings just by pulling on a jacket or sweater.'

'Or experience how someone else felt in their memory,' Emeline Avis murmured, thoughtfully. 'Remarkable.'

'I think they really liked it, Hen,' Connie said, gently nudging him.

Hen felt rather stunned. He didn't know what to say. Or if he could even actually speak. That had gone so much better than he had expected.

The official announcer spoke into her megaphone again. 'The judges will now withdraw to make their final deliberations. We will have a thirty-minute intermission. Refreshments are available from the Cloth Hall kitchen, located at the right of the main entrance just near the lavatories—'

'STOP!' A sharp, scraping voice ripped through everything else. 'Stop the judging! Those children have no right to be entering the contest under the Danelli name!'

It was Mrs Thackerey.

She hurried across the hall, followed by Tiberius Pepper himself!

CHAPTER THIRTY-THREE

Tiberius Pepper

Mrs Thackerey charged towards the stage, a large piece of paper flapping like a flag in her hand. 'The Danelli store and their spell stitches belong to Mr Tiberius Pepper. And so does . . . well, whatever that thing is.' She sneered at Hen's coat. Hen noticed that as Tiberius Pepper himself drew closer, he slowed and hung back. He clearly left all his dirty work to Thackerey. 'Look!' She flapped the paper at the judges as several sashed officials hurried towards her.

Hen swallowed and glanced at Connie, who was staring intently at Tiberius Pepper for some reason.

He searched the crowd for Uncle Bertie, Nana or Aunt Lucia, but couldn't find them; the room was on its feet, everyone straining for a clear look at the unravelling drama.

One of the officials came over to Hen and Connie and said quietly, 'I'm sorry, but these papers do seem to indicate that Tiberius Pepper is now in possession of the Danelli family business and *specifically* the family spell stitches. Is there someone with you – a grown-up – that we could talk to, just to clear things up?'

Hen and Connie stared at each other in horror. They were too late. Uncle Bertie had already sold the business to Pepper!

The official continued, 'It's just that, well, if the garment entered under the Danelli family name contains registered family spell stitches it will have to be re-entered as a . . . Pepper garment.'

'No!' Connie cried.

But Hen was shaking his head. 'There aren't any registered spell stitches in the coat,' he said firmly and fixed his gaze on Tiberius Pepper. 'The memory stitches aren't registered.'

Was it Hen's imagination, or did Pepper's eyes widen slightly when he'd said 'memory stitches'?

The official looked utterly puzzled. 'Well, that's rather . . . unusual,' she said. 'But if you're certain, you'll be happy for the coat to be examined further to confirm that?'

Hen nodded. He could feel himself shaking with nerves, even though he knew he was right; the memory stitches definitely weren't registered among the family spell stitches, which surely meant they *didn't* belong to Tiberius Pepper.

But his mind was spinning. Even if they entered the coat under the Danelli name, even if they won, everything else now belonged to Pepper! Hen glanced over at Connie, her face caught between anger and shock.

The official carefully lifted the coat off the dummy and hurried away. As she did, Mrs Thackerey stalked towards Hen and Connie where they waited next to the now bare mannequin. She was pale with rage. 'You two little brats are going to be mighty sorry about—'

'You, madam, shall leave my nephew and daughter alone!' Hen turned to see Uncle Bertie fighting his way through the audience. 'Will you *please* get out of my way?'

Hen felt light with relief.

Uncle Bertie jogged towards them, flapping his arms as though trying to take off. Connie's face was thunderous! 'You didn't really sign a contract with that awful man, did you, Dad?'

He took a gasping breath, swallowed and said, 'Well, I did, yes – but—'

'Oh, Dad. No!' Connie stepped away, horrified as Uncle Bertie collapsed to his knees in exhaustion.

The audience were loving every second. People were whispering to each other and pointing excitedly. Hen even saw a few camera flashes.

Tiberius Pepper watched from just behind Mrs Thackerey with a curious expression on his face, as though he wasn't sure how he had ended up here, while Mrs Thackerey waved the contract at Uncle Bertie. 'You signed a contract!' she said, relishing her triumph. 'You had no right to let these children enter a garment under the Danelli name!'

But poor Uncle Bertie suddenly didn't look very well at all. Hen knelt beside him. 'Uncle Bertie, are you OK?'

His uncle gasped, clutching at his throat.

Connie had turned away, clearly too angry to even look at her dad. But she *was* staring at Tiberius Pepper again.

Hen called over to the officials, 'Would someone please fetch my uncle some water?'

'I'm . . . all right,' Uncle Bertie said, finally catching his breath.

Then another angry voice snapped through the hubbub of the Cloth Hall.

'Bertrand Archibald Danelli. What by Hestia is going on here?'

'Oh knots!' Uncle Bertie mumbled.

Hen followed the shout and saw Nana walking briskly across the hall towards them, dark skirts flaring out behind her, boots clicking across the wood floor, keys singing as they swung this way and that. Aunt Lucia and Marjorie were just behind her.

Everyone fell quiet, even Mrs Thackerey.

'Tell me you haven't signed a contract with that –' she pointed at Tiberius Pepper though she didn't even glance at him – 'despicable creature!'

Uncle Bertie sighed. 'Mother, I *can* explain. I promise.'

'Bertrand, if I thought it would do any good, I'd ground you until Christmas!'

Aunt Lucia reached Uncle Bertie and knelt beside him, taking his hands in her own. 'Poor Bertie,' she cooed.

Hen inwardly cheered for Nana as he glanced over to see Tiberius Pepper's reaction.

But Pepper didn't look angry at Nana's arrival – he looked surprised, shocked and confused. It was such a puzzle.

'Don't you even look at me. I know all about your business!' Nana snapped.

Hen had thought he might scowl or argue back but he stood dumbfounded beside Mrs Thackerey.

Nana continued her tirade and stepped towards him. She prodded a long bony finger at him as she spoke. 'Shoddy spells making people ill, throwing us hard-working folk into disrepute! And putting good honest people out of business. You are a cheat and a liar and you can't stitch a spell for toffee!'

There was a collective gasp from everyone in the hall.

'Nana, don't,' Connie said, coming between Nana and Tiberius Pepper. *Why is she defending him? Just because he lets Mrs Thackerey do his dirty work, doesn't mean he's blameless!* Hen thought.

'He's a bully, Connie,' said Nana, 'and sometimes in life we have to stand up to bullies and tell them what's what.'

'Now just a moment,' said Mrs Thackerey, stepping forward, 'you will treat Mr Pepper with the—'

'Oh, do be quiet!' Nana lifted her chin in defiance, fixing her eyes on Pepper's and ignoring Mrs Thackerey altogether. 'Have you nothing to say for yourself then? Or does that old bag of bones do all your talking for you as well as conducting your slimy, sly, shifty business?'

What Connie said next was in such a small quiet voice that Hen wasn't sure he'd heard correctly at first. 'But he's your brother, Nana,' Connie said. 'He's Aldo Danelli!'

Silence fell over the hall. Tiberius Pepper stared wide-eyed at Nana – he looked like he'd seen a spectre!

'Nonsense!' Mrs Thackerey scoffed, breaking the tense silence.

'Connie, I hate to agree with *her* on anything but . . . what are you on about?' Hen asked in a small voice.

'*Look at them*,' Connie said, gesturing to Nana and Tiberius Pepper. 'Don't you see the similarities? You said it yourself that day outside Fancy's, how he looked like Great-great-uncle Guido! And what kind of a name is Tiberius Pepper, anyway? It sounds made-up because it *is*!'

Two pairs of brilliant blue eyes were staring intently at Connie.

Hen felt dizzy. Nana and Tiberius Pepper were sister and brother!

Nana stared again at Tiberius Pepper. And he stared back at her.

'I think we need to talk,' Tiberius Pepper said, blinking. 'All of us.'

The small side room off the main hall looked like it was generally used for storing extra chairs and folding tables. It was dusty and the single light was rather dim. At Pepper's firm request, Mrs Thackerey waited just outside the door, her lips pursed in thought.

'Will someone please tell me what in sweet Hestia's name is going on?' Aunt Lucia asked, once the door was shut. 'Bertie? Constance?'

Uncle Bertie raised his hands as if in defeat. 'I . . . I did sign a contract for a merger when I visited the factory. But . . . then . . .' Out of his pocket he pulled the square of linen that held Connie's memory of visiting Pepper's factory.

He hadn't burnt it at all! Hen realized with wonder that he'd never actually seen Uncle Bertie throw it into the fireplace – he must've changed his mind!

'When I saw the memory, the awful conditions at the factory, I knew Hen and Connie were right. I tried to stop it all and speak to Pepper directly. But that Thackerey woman, who had been so charming at first, refused to allow me to see him, or even speak to him on the phone. I got it all badly wrong, I'm so sorry.' He cleared his throat. 'And . . . I was worried about Hen and those strange . . . wonderful stitches of his. Father always said there was danger in those memory stitches, that they shouldn't be done, he . . . threw mine into the fire . . .'

'You can memory-stitch too?' Hen, Connie and Nana said together.

Uncle Bertie nodded sadly. 'I'm sorry Hen, I'm sorry I doubted you. I suppose in my way I was trying to protect you . . . the alcuri . . .'

'Hen and Connie found a way to stop them, Bertie,' Nana said softly. 'They're just spell-brats transformed in the memory by the magic. Our shleep-dung repellent should do the trick.'

Uncle Bertie blinked. 'Well . . .'

'Hen even managed to mend my memory,' Nana continued. 'The one stitched into the back panel of the coat.'

His uncle's eyes widened. 'Is that why you fell ill? Because—'

'We'll explain everything properly later,' Connie said. 'It's a pretty long story.'

'Whatever the story,' Uncle Bertie said, 'that coat . . . it's truly wonderful.'

Hen felt like a shaken bottle of pop. He could feel Nana's strong hand squeeze his shoulder gently.

Uncle Bertie got to his feet and came to stand before Hen. 'I'm very sorry, Henryton. I've not been kind. I don't deserve it, but I hope if nothing else that you can forgive me.'

Aunt Lucia and Connie hugged Uncle Bertie tight and Nana sighed, 'Oh, Bertie.'

'That's all wonderful but, oh, I'm so confused,' Aunt Lucia said, scratching her curls. 'Tiberius Pepper is . . . Aldo Danelli?'

Everyone turned and looked at Tiberius Pepper. He had been so quiet that Hen had nearly forgotten he was there! He filled the space by the door like an out of place wardrobe. Connie had been right – there was something about those brilliant sea-blue eyes, the silver hair, even the way he held himself so tall and straight-backed, that reminded Hen of Nana. Hen couldn't believe he hadn't connected the dots!

'Yes, he is,' Nana said flatly, sadly.

'You knew?' Hen and Connie gasped together.

'Oh . . . blimey!' Aunt Lucia said, leaning against the wall and fanning herself.

Everyone looked at Nana. 'I didn't know where Aldo was going when he ran away,' she said quickly. 'I waited and waited for a letter. He'd promised to write. I thought after a while he must have died. And even though it had been years and years, when I saw *Tiberius Pepper* starting to appear in the papers . . . well, I recognized him instantly. You *do* look just like Great-uncle Guido! My only brother had come to Ingle, assumed a new name and new life, and clearly he didn't wish for me to be a part of that.'

Hen gazed at Pepper expectantly, but he appeared to be speechless. Pepper opened his mouth, closed it, then stared at his shoes.

'Didn't you ever try to get in touch?' Connie asked, taking Nana's slightly trembling hand. 'Back in the attic you said you'd written to him?'

'Oh, I did. Several times. But he never wrote back. And that silence was stronger than any other message he might have sent, had he bothered.'

'I never received any letters from you,' Tiberius Pepper said at last, meeting Nana's eyes. Then he studied them all, as though he had found something he had lost a long time ago but now wasn't certain if it belonged to him or not, or if he even wanted it. 'If I had known you were here in Ingle, well of course I would have tried to . . . You have to believe me – I thought Grandpa had stayed angry, and that you'd grown angry too. I never dreamt I'd be forgiven, by any of the Danellis.'

Everyone looked at the door. Hen could hazard a guess at who was to blame for the missing letters!

'How could you do it?' asked Nana. 'Why? Put my friends out of work, nearly destroying the spell tailors' industry. That's our history. And then stealing others' spells—'

A voice objected sharply from beyond the door. 'Excuse me! All the spell stitches we possess were legally acquired and properly purchased!' Mrs Thackerey had clearly been eavesdropping the whole time. Pepper pulled the door open to allow her inside.

'That's a load of shleep poopy!' Uncle Bertie said, puffing out his chest. 'Henryton and Connie saw the spell-brat nest in the factory. You purposely infested businesses in order to cripple them before swooping in and offering a contract. And then they come and work for you – in those appalling conditions.'

Pepper turned to Mrs Thackerey. 'Is this true?' His voice was deep and dangerous. 'Is this why you keep me away from the factory floor? And the staff? Why it's always too "inconvenient" to visit the work hall?'

Mrs Thackerey's face hardened. 'Oh don't play the innocent now, Tiberius – Aldo – whoever you are! You were happy to gather up all those shops and spells. When we first met all those years ago, you said you wanted a spell-tailoring empire. You wanted to be the biggest, the best, the most famous spell tailor in the world. "I'll show them all," you said. But you didn't want to get your hands dirty, did you? You didn't have the spine for it – that's what I was for. And I made it all happen.'

Pepper's cheeks and forehead went pink with shame.

'How did you think your empire came about, Tiberius?' She scoffed. 'Your remarkably good business sense?'

'You're fired, Agatha! Make no mistake about that!' Tiberius Pepper said, his voice dry and hot and full of anger and sadness.

Mrs Thackerey scoffed again. 'Oh, so you turn

away from me now because you're having a cosy family reunion? You coward.' She glanced down suddenly. 'Ah, will someone get this wretched beast off my leg!'

Hen stepped forward and lifted Marjorie away from Mrs Thackerey, noticing that she had peed all over the woman's skirt and boots.

'Oh what a shame.' Nana smiled. 'Shleep urine is quite pungent, my dear. Your skirt will be quite ruined now. But I can recommend somewhere to get a lovely new one – properly made and spelled by the finest tailors in all of Ingle.' She smiled and shoved the door closed, forcing Ms Thackerey to jump backwards as it swung shut in her face.

Connie gave Nana a round of applause.

'I didn't know the lengths she was going to,' Tiberius Pepper began. 'But she was right about one thing: I buried my head in the sand.'

'Not a way to run a business, but then it started with a lie and with stolen things, didn't it? Like the garments you had me help you steal from Grandpa the day you left?'

Tiberius Pepper looked at the dusty floor and fiddled again with his tie and shirt cuffs.

Nana moved towards him now, his silence clearly

just making her angrier.

'I could have forgiven you that. But why did you never come to find me?' Nana asked. 'In all those years . . . you could have come for me. You *should* have come for me.'

Tiberius Pepper blinked and cleared his throat – Hen thought his eyes looked shiny. Tears perhaps.

'If you have nothing else to say, then perhaps you had best leave,' Nana said at last.

For a moment it looked as though he would speak, but what could he really say now to make things right? Eventually he bowed his head, turned and walked slowly out of the room.

'Are you OK, Nana?' Hen asked.

She smiled, perhaps a little sadly, but eventually said, 'Of course, I have everything I need right here with me, love. Maybe some things *can* be too broken to be mended,' she said, staring after her brother.

There was a gentle cough from the doorway – an official was there, fiddling with a clipboard and pencil. 'Ahem, the judges are just about to make their announcement, if you would like to come back through, please?'

*

The whole family gathered in the centre of the hall alongside the competition garments. The other young spell tailors were already waiting nervously to find out who had won.

Sophia Bakewell stepped out of the tangle of judges and officials. 'First, we'd like to confirm that the stitches used in the Danelli coat are unique and do not match any stitches recorded by the guild for the Danelli family, and are therefore separate from any business transaction with Pepper's Affordable Fashions.' She smiled.

Hen smiled back, feeling Connie squeeze his hand. He'd known it was true, but it was still a relief to hear it.

Now, Sir Hugo took the red cone megaphone and started to speak to the whole hall. 'Furthermore, we are pleased to announce that the winning garment of this year's Young Tailors' Contest is . . . Henryton and Constance Danelli's most remarkable memory coat!'

The hall erupted with a loud cheer and a roar of applause.

Everyone seemed to rush at Hen in one go. A loving crush of family surrounding him, holding him and Connie close.

As they separated from their family hug, Hen turned to see the coat was now back on the mannequin, and pinned to it was a golden guild rosette.

CHAPTER THIRTY-FOUR

DANELLI'S MARVELLOUS MEMORY GARMENTS

en and Connie were walking back along Beacham Terrace with Simon after a morning in the park. It was early summer, bright and warm but not yet the baking heat when all you want to do is hide under a tree.

As they reached Dr Hunter's offices, just a few doors down from Danelli's, the pavement became totally packed and they had to squeeze through the crush of people to carry on along without walking in the road itself.

'Blimey, is it always like this?' Simon asked as they

battled through the crowd.

'More and more!' Connie said.

'I guess everyone wants a memory coat now then?' Simon asked. 'I know exactly what memory I want sewn into mine . . .'

'Ah, well – the guild is still investigating the memory stitches to make absolutely sure they are safe,' Hen said. He hadn't been surprised when they had insisted on this, and Uncle Bertie and Nana had agreed it was for the best – especially given their strange and tangled history. But since they'd discovered the truth about the alcuri – and Hen and Connie had been able to describe precisely how to fix the memory stitches if needed – everyone was hopeful the Tailors' Guild would give them the OK. It was just a matter of waiting, Nana reassured Hen.

'So what's the massive queue for then?' Simon asked.

Hen blushed and glanced away as Connie said, 'Well, everyone went mad for Hen's design and his ideas for using old garments to make new ones! That's pretty much all anyone wants these days. Oh, and Nana's flying scarves! We've had people booking appointments from as far away as Andil. And that actor, Gloria Garden, she's coming in next week for a fitting.'

'You'll have to put a new sign up: *Danelli's – spell tailors to the stars.*' Simon laughed.

'Don't even joke about it,' Connie said. 'I caught my dad sketching one yesterday on a scrap of paper!'

'How are things with Uncle Bertie?' Simon asked Hen.

'A lot better than before,' Hen said quietly. Uncle Bertie had taken himself away for a little rest after the Guild Fair, and when he had returned he had been nearly unrecognizable!

And life seemed to have fallen into a new pattern. A better one.

'And what happened to that Tiberius Pepper guy?' Simon asked. 'Is he really your great-uncle? And did he really buy Danelli's? That's crackers!'

'Well, he's definitely our great-uncle,' Hen said. 'But no one knows where he is. After the Guild Fair he vanished – and Mrs Thackerey, too! When they searched his properties they found he'd just abandoned everything. But he left instructions for the factories to be closed down at once and he'd torn up the Danelli's contract. So I guess he tried to make things right in the end … a bit.'

'My dad says some of the families affected may take over the factories themselves,' Connie explained. 'To see if there is a way to make spelled garments on a larger scale.'

'I wonder what became of Mrs Thackerey after she was fired?' Hen asked.

'Old giraffe-face?' Connie asked. 'I hope she's in a zoo! Hateful witch!'

'Don't cross Connie, ever,' Hen warned Simon.

They had reached the pavement outside Danelli's now, and if anything the crowd was even denser. They saw customers hurrying away, clutching boxes with *Danelli's* printed in elegant lettering across the lids, broad smiles on their faces.

They tried to go up the steps, where they could see Uncle Bertie by the door. He was adjusting a new sign, which Hen couldn't quite see because of all the people, while also fending off two rather overeager shoppers who were desperately trying to get past him and into the shop.

'I'm sorry, ladies,' Uncle Bertie said calmly. 'But Wednesdays are now half-day closing.' He pointed to the sign beside the front door.

Connie and Hen exchanged a look of amazement. *Half-day closing?* The old Uncle Bertie was truly gone for good, it seemed.

'But, Mr Danelli, I've been waiting several weeks for an appointment,' one of the ladies said. She sounded on the verge of tears.

'Yes, I understand, and we are doing our best to fit everyone in but there is a huge demand just now.' Uncle Bertie beamed.

'Isn't that Mrs Crab?' Connie asked, pointing at the woman with her foot jammed in the half-closed door.

Sure enough, it was.

'So when can I expect to get an appointment, Mr Danelli?' She spied Hen. 'Oh, look, it's lovely Hen, the star stitcher himself.' She waved shyly and giggled.

'Hello, Mrs Crab.' Hen smiled back.

Uncle Bertie stepped protectively in front of Hen and Connie and said gently, but firmly, 'Mrs Crab, I will call you first thing tomorrow to arrange a fitting, Hestia as my witness. You may quickly pop inside and leave your details with our very capable senior fitter, Lottie.'

Mrs Crab hurried gratefully inside.

'Mr Danelli? Max Fairfax from the *Hampston Courant*, have you got time for a quick interview?' A man stepped out of the crowd with an expectant look on his face, holding a small notebook and pencil in his hand.

'I'd be delighted to, Mr Fairfax. The *Courant* is my newspaper of choice,' Uncle Bertie smiled. 'But, as I have already explained, it will have to be tomorrow. We are just about to close for the day. My family and I are taking a picnic out of town to enjoy the summer weather.'

Picnic! Connie mouthed at Hen.

'Very good, Mr Danelli. You must be very proud of your daughter and nephew,' Mr Fairfax said.

Uncle Bertie took a deep breath, his chest puffing with pride like a rooster clucking over his brood. 'I, and indeed our whole family, are incredibly, exceedingly proud of them both, but most especially dear Hen, who saved us all really,' Uncle Bertie said, smiling down at Hen.

Mrs Crab emerged from having given her details to Lottie, and Uncle Bertie hurried Hen and Connie inside. They waved goodbye to Simon as Uncle Bertie closed the shop door, twisting the key in the lock and chuckling to himself.

'What a morning!' He turned to Hen and Connie. 'Now, you two, hurry on and get changed.

We're off out to Seaborough for the afternoon to relax and spend some time together. I'll bring the motorcar around to the front. Oh, Henryton, there's a letter from your parents by the looks of things, here. And can you quickly run this parcel down to your grandmother please.'

Uncle Bertie handed Hen a hefty brown-paper parcel.

Hen hurried down to the basement workroom. Nana was just packing away whatever it was she had been working on as Hen put the package on the workbench. 'Parcel for you, Nana,' he said.

'Oh, it's probably just some fabric samples or button catalogues,' Nana said, waving him away.

'It's addressed to you, though,' Hen said, sliding the parcel to her.

'Oh?' Nana lifted a pair of scissors and quickly cut the string away, and then unwrapped the package.

Hen saw a soft fold of dark navy linen and Nana gave a gasp and stepped back quickly.

'What is it, Nana?' Hen asked, hurrying to her side.

And then he saw that the package was a collection of garments: jackets, dresses, trousers, blouses and shirts. Quite old-fashioned styles, though beautifully crafted.

Not just that – Hen realized that the topmost garment had a memory stitch in it.

Nana lifted it to reveal the second, which also had a memory stitch, as did the next and the next. 'But . . . where have they come from?' Hen asked, confused.

Nana picked up the note that had been enclosed in the parcel, and as she read it she lifted a hand to her mouth. She slid the piece of paper across the workbench to Hen.

It was Pepper's Affordable Fashions headed notepaper, but there was very little written on it.

I'm sorry.

These belong to you now and always should have.

Aldo

'He kept them safe. All this time . . .' She lifted the clothes up and smiled as though greeting old friends. 'I thought he'd sold them.'

'Whose are they?' Hen asked.

'These are our family's memories, Hen – look.' She lifted a simple plain white shirt that Hen recognized from her memory. It was her grandpa's wedding shirt.

'He sent them back to me,' Nana said, her voice edged with wonder and sadness.

Uncle Bertie's bell suddenly started clanging furiously from somewhere upstairs.

'What's that all about?' Nana asked, gazing up at the ceiling and wiping away tears.

'I dread to think,' Hen said. 'I thought Aunt Lucia had hidden the bell.'

They hurried upstairs and found Uncle Bertie, Aunt Lucia and Lottie waiting in the back hall. Connie was hurrying down the stairs, straightening a straw hat as she ran.

'What's going on?' Hen asked. 'Not spell-brats surely?'

'Well, actually,' Aunt Lucia said, 'your uncle has a surprise for you both.' Her eyes twinkled with mischief.

Hen and Connie stepped towards Uncle Bertie, who placed a gentle hand on each of their shoulders and then turned them to face the staircase. At the bottom, the latest addition to the family gallery was a photo of Hen and Connie with the memory coat, taken on the day of the guild competition.

'It was only right that you two should join the family gallery for all you did,' Uncle Bertie said.

Hen was quiet, emotion making him mute as he tried to work it all out. He smiled up at the portraits and they smiled back at him.

'Now then, shall we get on with this trip to the beach?' Uncle Bertie said brightly. 'Motor's out the front all waiting to go.'

Hen and Nana lingered for a moment looking at the gallery. Hen took Nana's hand and said carefully, 'Perhaps he was trying to repair things, fix things.'

'What? Who?' Nana asked, turning to look at him.

'Tiberius . . . ah, I mean, Aldo. You know, sending the memory garments back. Maybe that was his first step in mending things.' Hen smiled at Nana. 'I think you can mend anything, if you really want to.'

'Perhaps.' Nana leant forward and kissed him on the top of the head. 'My Hen. Let's go make some more memories, shall we?'

They walked through the shop, Nana grabbing her knitting basket and hat from the stool near the counter.

Outside the crowd had thinned out and the family was climbing into the car. Uncle Bertie was strapping a large picnic hamper to the back.

'Pull the door shut behind you, my boy,' Uncle Bertie called.

And as he did, Hen got a proper look at the new sign.